"Dead Air"

by Brendan Quinlan

Dedication:

For those who believed in me when I didn't.

"The world is in greater peril from those who tolerate or encourage evil than from those who actually commit it." - Albert Einstein

Chapter One

The studio felt alive, humming with the pulse of a thousand possibilities. Across the polished table, Julian Hayes smiled, adjusting his headset as the cameras clicked on. Today was a special day. A huge moment for DisruptTech, the show he'd worked tirelessly on for the past three years. And today, he was interviewing the one person he'd always admired: Trent Lawson, the visionary behind Eclipse: Reborn—a game that promised to change everything.

"Are we good to go?" Julian asked, glancing at the producer through the glass. A familiar buzz thrummed in his chest—a quiet thrill he recognized as anticipation.

Beyond the glass, his producers sat in their usual spots. Emma, sharp-eyed and headstrong, gave a small nod. Her white-silver hair, betraying its natural red at the roots, framed her intense green eyes. She wore a tailored sports jacket over a sleek, form-fitting top, her dark jeans completing the polished yet practical look. Beside her, Max exuded his usual laid-back confidence, cropped dark hair blending into a sharp fade. His hazel eyes were tired but alert, dressed in his signature green military jacket and oddly professionally tailored shorts.

Julian, in contrast, had neatly kept dark hair and a light five o'clock shadow. His style leaned toward smart casual—jeans and a well-fitted, effortless but put-together T-shirt. The producer gave him a nod, signaling to begin.

Julian leaned into the mic, his voice smooth and confident, excitement bubbling beneath the surface. "Welcome back to the DisruptTech Podcast, where we talk all things tech and gaming. Today, we have someone very special in the studio—Trent Lawson, the creative force behind Eclipse: Reborn, the game that will redefine our digital experience. Trent, welcome to the show."

"Thanks for having me," Trent said, his voice relaxed, confident—every inch the game developer who had once been the underdog and now stood on the cusp of something monumental.

"So, Trent," Julian began, shifting in his seat, "you've been talking a lot about how Eclipse is more than just a game—it's a whole new reality. How does that work exactly?"

Trent leaned forward, his eyes alight with passion. "It's simple, really," he said. "We're building a world, not just a game. Eclipse isn't about completing levels or beating bosses—it's about interacting with a fully immersive universe where your choices matter. We're not just creating entertainment; we're creating a space where players live and breathe the game, where every action has a consequence."

Julian nodded, a grin tugging at his lips. He couldn't help but admire the ambition in Trent's voice. Eclipse wasn't just a product—it was a statement. The future of gaming was here, changing how people would experience reality.

"That's incredible," Julian said, the words slipping out before realizing how profound they were. "You've essentially built a digital world where people can create their own lives. This isn't just about playing anymore—it's about living in the game."

"Exactly," Trent said, his eyes lighting up. "It's about creating a new kind of connection. Technology is evolving, and we're evolving with it. The future isn't about what we consume—it's about what we create. And Eclipse lets the player not just

"I think we have to be ready," he said softly, "because the world's changing whether we want it to or not. The question is, will we be the ones who control that change, or will it control us?"

Before Julian could respond, the producer's voice crackled in his earpiece, sharp and urgent.

"Julian, we need to wrap this up. Something's happening. We've just got an alert—don't know what it is. We had a surge here before. The internet's going down. I think the Grid is having issues."

Julian blinked, trying to process the words. He glanced at Trent, who had suddenly stiffened in his seat, his expression darkening.

"Wait, what do you mean, the Grid's been compromised?" Julian asked, trying to keep his voice steady though the tightness in his chest was hard to ignore.

"The whole damn thing," the producer continued, the panic creeping into his voice.

play, but build, shape, and live their own adventure."

There was a long pause as Julian processed this. He could almost see the future unfolding before him—Eclipse wasn't just a game; it was a new way of thinking, of experiencing life itself. A digital renaissance, with Trent Lawson at the helm.

But as he watched Trent talk, something gnawed at the edges of his mind. A faint feeling of unease. The world was spinning just a little too fast, and the momentum couldn't stop.

"Do you ever worry," Julian asked, his voice quieter now, "that all this change might be too much? That people aren't ready for a reality like this?"

Trent's grin faltered for a second, a flicker of something unreadable in his eyes. He looked at Julian as though weighing the question carefully before answering.

"Communications, transportation, everything. We're getting reports that major systems are going dark. We don't know what's happening, but it's bad."

The studio, which had been buzzing with excitement moments ago, now felt stifling, suffocating. Julian's pulse quickened as he looked around the room. The lights overhead flickered. It felt like the world was holding its breath for a brief moment.

"Julian," the producer urged, "we need to go live. Now."

Julian stood abruptly, his legs unsteady. The studio was eerily silent; the only sound was the rapid beeping of machines and the frantic chatter coming from the control room. He turned to Trent, who had gone pale, his hand gripping the table's edge. For the first time, Julian saw the vulnerability in his eyes.

"Is this… is this really happening?" Julian asked, his voice barely a whisper.

Trent didn't answer at first. He just shook his head as though still trying to process the weight of the words that had just been spoken. Then, with a deep breath, he met Julian's gaze.

"Yeah. It's happening."

Then, just like that, the decision was made. The producers called it. Early mark. The show was over for the day. But why? Why did it feel like the end of something much, much bigger?

Chapter 2:

The walk from George Street to Mountain Street wasn't far—maybe thirty minutes—the Map app "Elen" listed it as 2.4 km, but it felt longer than usual. Julian had always opted for the tram when the weather was right, but tonight, with the flickering signs and the occasional darkened tram, he figured walking was just as fast. Besides, the trams were jam-packed. He enjoyed the solitude of the city after hours, the way the streetlights cast long, eerie shadows over the pavement, and how the neon signs glowed against the quiet. It was as if the city itself had chosen to remain silent. People were probably still stressing— just not out loud.

His phone buzzed in his pocket.

"Helios would like to welcome you back, Julian," a soft, automated voice said.

It was Hera, his virtual assistant, always polite, always present. He didn't mind it most of the time. By 2099, people had long gotten used to technology, feeling almost human. With its neon-lit, corporate-dominated skyline, the city thrived on that blend of efficiency and familiarity.

"Thanks, Hera," he muttered, pushing open the door to his apartment.

The place was small but comfortable—starkly contrasting the sprawling glass towers downtown. It smelled of old sneakers and something faintly metallic—probably the air purifier working overtime. The room was dim, the low hum of appliances filling the silence. It was still too early to crash, but exhaustion clung to him. He figured he'd relax for a bit.

Julian tossed his bag onto the couch. He hesitated by the door. Most people relied on their phone's authentication app to unlock their apartment complex, but for some reason, he had a strange feeling—an itch at the back of his mind—that he might have to use his keys for the first time in a while. He grabbed them from the counter and pocketed them before heading out again.

Hunger gnawed at him. A late-night bite was in order.

A glance at his bank app showed his balance was running low, but it was enough for a cheap takeaway. He decided on the local Asian joint at the corner—the best Singapore noodles in the city.

The walk was short, but an unsettling buzz filled the air as Julian neared the shop. The neon sign flickered erratically, casting jittery shadows on the pavement. The usual warmth radiating from the open kitchen window was absent—just cold metal and the faint hum of an aging generator.

He stepped inside.

"Cash only," the woman behind the counter said flatly.

Julian blinked. "Cash? But you've always—"

"Cash only," she repeated, her voice laced with fatigue as if she'd had this conversation too many times today.

A strange tension settled over the place. The kitchen, usually bustling, felt subdued, the few other patrons eating quietly, avoiding eye contact. Julian hesitated before fishing out a few bills from his wallet. His dad's advice echoed in his mind: Always carry cash. You never know when the system might fail. Thank God Australia hadn't gone fully digital fifty years ago.

The woman took his money without a word, handed him the food, and turned away. There was no casual banter, no forced politeness—just a transaction.

Outside, the streets felt emptier than before. The city was in an unshakable stillness as though it were holding its breath.

When Julian returned to his apartment, he kicked off his shoes and collapsed onto the couch with his noodles. He flicked on the TV, half-hoping for news, but instead, a glossy ad for the latest luxury car filled the screen—smooth, polished, artificial. The words blended into meaningless white noise.

Click.

He turned it off.

"Hera," he called.

"Yes, Julian?" Hera's voice was smooth and efficient, as always.

"Any updates on the power situation? The lamps were flickering. Everything feels... off."

A brief pause. Then: "I'm sorry, Julian. There are no current local news reports available at this time. Would you like to hear more about the rumoured OmegaDeck 2?"

Julian frowned. The latest tech buzzword. The OmegaDeck 2 was the only gaming console left on the market, an all-in-one system that had replaced everything else. Everyone used it. But right now, he didn't care about virtual distractions.

"No, Hera. I need something real. Anything about the power? The outages?"

Another pause. Hera's voice crackled slightly, an unfamiliar distortion creeping into her usual cadence.

"I'm sorry, Julian. There is no new information regarding the power grid. Would you like to hear more about OmegaDeck 2?"

A chill ran down his spine. Something was wrong. Was it a cyber attack? A protest? Was this a corporate shutdown? But this felt different. Too quiet. Too sudden. It felt as though the world had ceased to exist.

The lights flickered. For a moment, everything dimmed before buzzing back to life, their hum now unnaturally loud. Julian's chest tightened. His instincts screamed at him. Was this a nuke? No. There'd be alarms. There'd be—

"Hera?" he asked cautiously.

There was a long silence. Then:

"...Power grid reserves... depleting... estimated... hours... backup systems... failing... in progress... please prepare... for longer outages..."

Julian's pulse spiked. This wasn't a simple outage. This was something catastrophic.

His eyes darted around the apartment. It wasn't just the lights. The fridge and his phone charger were among the numerous electronic devices struggling to survive. Screens flickered as though fighting to maintain their existence. The city outside, still glowing in the distance, felt like an illusion—like something was siphoning its very life from it.

He swiped his wrist device, shutting Hera off with a sharp motion.

Silence.

But the eerie hum remained. It was in the walls and the floor—like the entire city was part of a failing machine.

Julian set the noodles aside, his appetite gone. He needed to think. This wasn't just about the outages. The glitching AI, the strange urgency at the restaurant, the suffocating stillness in the streets— something bigger was happening.

Needing to clear his head, he turned to the bathroom. A shower. That might help.

Warm water rushed over him, grounding him for a moment. He closed his eyes, letting the rhythm of the stream calm him, but the unease refused to fade.

When he emerged, towel-drying his hair, he grabbed his phone. No signal. No bars. There were no interruptions to the service. Just nothing.

He glanced at the wall clock. The time didn't matter anymore.

Julian sat by the window, staring at the city skyline. On the surface, nothing had changed. The lights still flickered, the buildings still stood tall—but the air was different. The city wasn't just quiet—it was waiting.

Waiting for something to break the silence.

Julian took a deep breath and forced himself to eat.

Tomorrow would come.

And maybe—just maybe—it would all be fixed by then.

But deep down, he knew.

This wasn't a glitch.

This was the beginning of something much, much worse.

Chapter 3:

Julian didn't dream that night. Instead, he tossed and turned, never settling, until exhaustion finally pulled him under. Sometime around 3:35 a.m., the bathroom light flickered and died. The hum of the apartment stilled. A blackout. But Julian slept on.

When he woke, he experienced a dull headache and an unnatural silence. He groaned, rubbing his temples. "Hera, why didn't my alarm wake me?" There was no response. The curtains remained drawn, and the room was steeped in shadows, with only the faintest sliver of light seeping through.

His phone screen lit up, and dozens of notifications flooded in—every alert, every update, more dire than the last. Global systems were down, power grids were collapsing, and a national emergency had been declared.

For a brief moment, he just stared at the screen, heart pounding.

The phone signal must've come through.

The world, as he had known it, was gone.

He pushed himself up and stepped out onto the balcony. Below, the street was littered with stalled vehicles—electric cars, converted diesel models, even a Voltum Extreme Skyline, the kind only the ultra-rich could afford. He had always dreamed of owning one. Now, it sat abandoned like all the rest.

His phone rang, the screen flashing Producer.

He answered. "What's happening?"

"Julian," the voice on the other end crackled, barely cutting through the static. "It's over. Everything's gone dark. The grid's completely wiped. We're on our own now. The broadcast... we can't do it anymore. No one's coming to help."

The words hit like a hammer.

The future he had been so certain of had unraveled overnight.

And now, only one question remained: What do you do when the future you've built is suddenly erased?

Julian stepped into the streets a few hours later, and the world felt wrong.

The usual hum of city life—the constant flow of people and the rhythmic pulse of traffic—was gone. Instead, a heavy silence settled over everything. Cars sat abandoned, some with open doors as if their drivers had vanished mid-action.

Something was off.

A strange static charge clung to the air, sending a faint buzzing through his ears. He rubbed them, trying to shake the sensation. This wasn't just the eerie quiet of a blackout; it was deeper than that. Something had changed.

Movement caught his eye. Down an alley, a group of figures crouched around crates, rifling through supplies. Looters.

Julian's pulse spiked. He had never seen anything like this outside of news reports, and even then, it had always felt distant. Not anymore.

One of them looked up, his gaze sharp and predatory. He sized Julian up.

"You got a problem?" The man's voice was low, edged with warning.

Julian swallowed hard, his fingers twitching toward his phone. He pulled it out, only to see the screen—cracked, glitching. No signal. He swiped. Nothing. No service, no internet, just dead pixels staring back at him.

The looter took a step closer. "I said, get lost."

Julian raised his hands in a silent apology and backed away, turning swiftly onto another street. His heart pounded as he forced himself to walk, not run. Running would only make him a target.

The city felt teetering, like a held breath waiting to exhale. The edge of something irreversible.

His destination was clear—the studio. Maybe Emma was there. Maybe someone had answers.

A few blocks later, he turned onto a familiar street. The studio was just ahead, standing as it always had. Yet everything about the world around it had changed.

Just as he reached the door, his phone buzzed. Finally.

A message.

It was from Emma's number.

But it wasn't from her.

Where are you?

He reads it again, but before he can respond, another message pops up: "Julian, we've been trying to reach you. Call us. Right now."

Panic starts creeping in. The air feels heavier now as if something invisible is pressing in from all sides.

But then his phone buzzes again. This time, it's a new message from his producer, Max.

"We're coming for you."

Julian's throat tightens as he stares at the words. They're trying to find him. But the world outside is changing so fast, and he doesn't know what's happening.

Chapter 4

He turns to look down the street, his breath shallow, unsure of what's next.

Julian walked, but now it was slower. Each step felt heavier, like the world itself was waiting to see what he would do next. The silence was unbearable—no hum of machines, no rush of cars, no distant murmur of life. The city wasn't just quiet; it was hollow. He knew people had to be somewhere, but where?

The question gnawed at him.

His phone felt useless in his hand, yet he tried again—Emma, Max, anyone. Each call met with the same lifeless silence. His fingers trembled as he scrolled through his contacts, pressing name after name, but nothing changed. No connection. Just dead air. The chill in the morning air bit at his skin as he quickened his pace, searching for any sign of life.

Then, he saw it.

A convenience store, its glass doors shattered. The shelves were ransacked, goods scattered across the floor in reckless disarray. He stepped cautiously over broken bottles and torn packaging, his pulse quickening. Panic could do this. But was it only panic? Or was there something worse lurking beneath the surface?

In the dim light, he noticed them—people huddled in the back corner of the store. Their faces were drawn, their clothes dirtied. They barely moved, only lifting their heads to watch him as he entered. Their eyes, wide and hollow, made his stomach turn.

"Is it happening everywhere?" Julian asked, his own voice sounding foreign to him.

A woman, wrapped in a thin jacket, nodded. "We don't know. It just… stopped."

Julian swallowed hard. That was it. That was the feeling that had been twisting inside him since he woke up. It wasn't just a power outage. It wasn't just a glitch. Everything had simply stopped.

"Where is everyone?" he asked, though he wasn't sure if he wanted the answer.

The woman just gestured toward the door.

Julian stepped back outside, the weight of the emptiness pressing in on him. He had always been surrounded by noise, by movement, by the hum of an ever-running world. Now, it was suffocating in its absence.

Then, his phone buzzed. A vibration that felt unreal against his palm. Max's name lit up the screen.

He answered immediately. "Max?"

"Julian, where the hell are you?" Max's voice was frantic, cracking through static. "We've been trying to reach you. We can't get through to anyone else. What's happening?"

Julian turned in place, scanning the empty streets, the abandoned cars, the hollowed-out buildings. "I don't know," he said. "Something's wrong. It's not just a blackout. It's like… like everything's dead. Or trapped."

"We're coming for you," Max said. "You need to get to the studio. Now."

Julian stopped walking. The studio? He looked around again at the wrecked shops, at the people who weren't running or fighting but simply drifting. Like ghosts. As if they didn't know what to do now that the world had stopped moving.

"Max," Julian said, his throat tightening. "I don't think that matters anymore. I don't think anything does."

Another voice cut through the static. Emma.

"Julian! Are you okay? Where are you?"

Relief hit him like a wave, but it was quickly drowned by the weight of everything else. "I—I don't know," he admitted. "Everything's gone. No one knows what happened, but it's not normal. This isn't just the grid failing. This is something else. We have to figure out what's going on."

There was silence on the other end. Then Max's voice, firm and urgent.

"Stay put. We're coming to get you."

Julian hesitated, staring down the empty street. The city felt wrong, like a machine that had been running forever and had suddenly stopped without warning. He didn't know if staying in one place was the right call.

But he also didn't know if there was anywhere left to go.

The line crackled, then cut out.

Julian lowered the phone, staring at the dead screen.

The words Max had spoken still hung in the air, but Julian wasn't sure they meant anything anymore.

Stay safe.

How do you stay safe in a world that's already gone?

Chapter 5:

Julian's steps are more purposeful now. He heads towards the studio, the familiar route taking on a strange, surreal quality as he walks past streets that should be bustling but are instead eerily silent. It's like the city is holding its breath, waiting for something to break the stillness. But nothing does. The world is static.

His phone buzzes again, but he ignores it this time. The screen's dead reflection matches the emptiness around him. What's happening to the world? He can't wrap his head around it. An EMP? A global collapse? Everything's uncertain, and the weight of that uncertainty is crushing.

He reaches the DisruptTech Studio building—an old but reliable building, standing tall against the chaos. A flicker of comfort surges within him. At least this place feels familiar, like something hasn't completely broken down. But when he steps inside, the hum of the air conditioning, the usual sound of computers whirring in the background, is gone. It's quieter than it's ever been.

Julian walks into the main office area, the dark silence pressing down on him as he looks around. Empty desks, overturned chairs, papers scattered across the floor like they've been hastily abandoned. But then, from the back of the room, he hears footsteps.

The producers—Max and Emma—step into view, their faces drawn, eyes wide with worry. They've been looking for him. They exchange a quick glance, then rush toward him, pulling him into the security of the back room, away from the street and the noise.

"Julian," Max says, his voice tight with frustration. "What the hell is going on out there? What did you see?"

Julian collapses into the nearest chair, his mind still reeling. He tries to find the words, but they don't come easily. "I don't know... I don't think anyone does."

Emma's eyes search him, sharp as always. "Did you see the news? Anything?"

"There's no news," Julian says, shaking his head. "The whole city's just... shut down. No one's working. I tried to call everyone—nothing. It's all gone. The power's out, but this isn't just a blackout."

Max furrows his brow, leaning against the table as if the weight of the conversation is too much to bear. "You think it was... an EMP? I've been hearing rumors. A massive pulse, maybe even worldwide. People are just... lost."

"They're looting," Julian says, his voice low, like it still doesn't make sense. "Just taking whatever they can, acting like it's the end of the world. I saw it outside. People going crazy over nothing—empty shelves, stores already trashed."

Emma steps closer, her expression hardening as she absorbs the information. "It doesn't make sense. It's not just the power, right? There's something else... it's like the air is different, static, almost like something's still charging."

Max nods, his gaze turning inward as he processes the enormity of the situation. "I've been hearing reports from different areas. All signs point to it— no power, no signals, no communication. But we're still here, right? Still alive?"

"Barely," Julian mutters.

"Not barely," Emma says sharply, a glimmer of resolve flickering in her eyes. "We're still here, which means we can still do something about it. We need to figure out what happened, how it happened, and—most importantly—what's next."

Julian looks out the window at the streets below, at the empty spaces where people used to gather, work, laugh. It all seems like a distant memory now. He turns back to Max and Emma, his expression firming up as a sense of responsibility begins to settle in his gut.

"So what's the plan?" Julian asks, his voice clear.

"We try to find out who else is out there," Max says. "We've got the resources here. We have the means to communicate. We're not completely out of it yet."

Julian nods slowly, then looks back at his phone, still dead. "If we're going to make a difference, we need more than just our office here. We need a way to connect, to reach people who might still be out there, surviving."

"We'll find them," Emma says, her voice steady, though her eyes betray the worry beneath. "We'll rebuild. But first, we need answers. We need to know what we're really up against."

A moment of silence falls between them. Julian looks back to the streets, knowing this is just the beginning. They've all lost something today—the tech, the comforts of their old lives. But he knows there's no going back now.

It's time to adapt, to survive.

Chapter 6:

The studio feels eerily unfamiliar now. What used to be a lively, chaotic space buzzing with energy is now hollow, the hum of servers and chatter replaced by suffocating silence. The air seems heavier, the walls thinner. Max, Emma, and Julian shuffle around, aimlessly tidying up the wreckage of their old world. The power's out, and the oppressive stillness makes everything feel... wrong.

"So, we're really just... stuck here, huh?" Julian's voice cuts through the quiet like a tentative probe, testing the atmosphere.

"Feels that way," Max replies absently, flicking through old papers. "Kind of like 28 Weeks Later. You know, the part where everything's just... gone."

Emma glances over her shoulder with a smirk. "You mean 28 Days Later. Weeks was the sequel."

"Whatever." Max waves her off, rolling his eyes. "It's that vibe. Everyone disappears overnight, and we're just left to clean up the mess."

"I Am Legend comes to mind," Julian offers, leaning on the back of a chair. "Though, hopefully minus the zombie-vampire hybrids."

Emma laughs softly. "Yeah, I'd rather not have to go full Will Smith. My survival skills cap out at boiling water and keeping houseplants alive."

"Let's not forget Fallout," Max adds with a grin, though it fades quickly. "But this... this isn't even post-nuclear. It's like a quieter apocalypse. No sirens, no explosions, just... unplugged."

Emma frowns, crossing her arms. "It's unnerving, isn't it? We all grew up on these stories, movies, games—like we were training for something. But none of it prepared us for this. No clear enemy, no giant monster to fight. Just..." She gestures vaguely around the room. "Nothing."

"EMP, maybe?" Max suggests.

"What's that?" Julian asks, frowning.

"Electromagnetic pulse," Emma explains. "Knocks out electronics. Happens in wars sometimes—at least in theory."

"Wars?" Julian paces now, the tension in his voice rising. "Was it the resource war? That thing we kept hearing about? But how bad could it have been to... I don't know, pull the plug on everything?"

Max shakes his head. "We wouldn't even know. We were too busy bingeing Hideo Kojima games and chasing the next shiny tech gadget. All the headlines were background noise."

"That's just it," Emma says, her tone sharper now. "We were so distracted—by trends, launches, viral campaigns. We didn't see the writing on the wall."

Julian stops pacing, rubbing his temples. "But look around. This place—it's fine. The building's intact. Windows aren't shattered. If there was a war, shouldn't there be... something? Smoke? Damage? Anything?"

Max exchanges a glance with Emma. The same thought flickers between them, unspoken.

"This building," Emma says slowly, "it's almost like it was... built to last. Reinforced. Like a bunker."

Julian stares at her. "You think the studio was meant to survive something like this?"

"I don't know," Emma admits, scanning the room again. "But it feels like whoever designed this place knew more than they let on."

"Then where the hell is everyone else?" Julian's voice rises slightly, his frustration cracking through. "The designers, the editors, the execs—where are they? Why's it just us?"

Max exhales, setting down a stack of papers. "That's the question, isn't it? Did we get left behind? Or... did they know something we didn't?"

"That's insane," Julian mutters, resuming his pacing. "If they knew something, why wouldn't they tell us? We were in the same meetings. We saw the same projections. What did we miss?"

The silence that follows is deafening.

Max finally breaks it. "It doesn't matter now, does it? We're here. No one's coming to save us. If this place really is a safe haven, then it's on us to figure out why. And what comes next."

Julian glances between them, unease simmering beneath the surface. He knows Max is right. But the questions won't stop clawing at him, louder than the silence around them.

This isn't the world they were promised. It's something darker, quieter, and infinitely more dangerous.

And they're the only ones left to figure it out.

Chapter 7:

An hour later, the oppressive quiet of the studio has settled into an uneasy rhythm. The trio has spent the time organizing supplies, trying to ignore the elephant in the room: What happens next?

It's Julian who breaks the silence first, dropping into one of the chairs and rubbing his stomach. "Okay, I'm calling it. I'm starving."

Emma, still fiddling with the contents of a random desk drawer, doesn't even look up. "Same. I feel like I could eat an entire pizza by myself right now. And I'm not even ashamed to admit it."

"You're always craving pizza," Max says with a smirk as he leans against the doorway to the kitchenette. "Anyway, we've got protein bars in here. Couple of packs of instant noodles, too, if you're feeling fancy. It's not gourmet, but it'll keep us alive."

"Alive, sure," Emma replies, standing up and dusting her hands off. "But alive and miserable. You're telling me we're going to sit here eating protein bars while the world's falling apart? No thanks. I want real food—like an actual meal."

Julian perks up. "What about that burger place on the corner? They had those massive double cheeseburgers, and their fries? Amazing. Remember those truffle fries they did for a while?"

Emma grins. "Oh, yeah. And their milkshakes. That'd hit the spot right now."

Max raises an eyebrow. "You think they're open? In case you haven't noticed, the city isn't exactly buzzing with activity."

"Well, what about that soup place in the square?" Julian continues. "They're probably low-tech enough to keep going, right? Soup, bread… something warm."

"Or," Emma adds, her voice taking on a wistful tone, "we could try that bakery. You know, the fancy one with the sourdough loaves that weigh as much as a small child. And the sausage rolls? God-tier."

Julian groans. "Even a plain loaf of bread or a meat pie would be better than protein bars."

Max rolls his eyes but can't hide the small smile creeping onto his face. "You two are ridiculous. It's like the apocalypse hits, and your first thought is about carbs."

"Listen," Emma retorts, pointing a finger at him, "if this is the end of the world, I'm not spending my last days eating cardboard. I want real food."

Julian chuckles, but then his expression sobers as the reality of the situation sets in. "But seriously… is anything even open? And if it is, will they take cash? Or cards? What's the point if we can't pay for it?"

The group falls quiet for a moment, the weight of Julian's question pressing down on them.

Emma shrugs. "We won't know unless we check, right? Maybe someone's still out there trying to keep things running. If we don't look, we'll never know."

Max looks skeptical but nods slowly. "Fine. We'll go check. But we need to be smart about this. Stick together, don't do anything stupid, and if it looks sketchy, we come straight back here. Got it?"

"Got it," Julian and Emma reply in unison, already grabbing their jackets.

As they head for the door, Emma pauses, looking back at Max. "Hey, worst case, we don't find food, but we get a chance to scope out what's really going on out there. Could be useful."

Max nods. "Let's hope it's just a quick trip for bread and not something worse."

The three of them step outside, the air crisp and eerily still. The streets are empty, the shops dark. But somewhere in the distance, there's the faintest sound—a generator humming, maybe? Or a door creaking open?

The possibilities tug at their nerves and their curiosity. Hunger might have driven them out of the studio, but something tells them this trip is going to give them more than just food.

Chapter 8:

Max stands by the door, arms crossed, watching Emma and Julian gear up. "You sure about this?" he asks, the concern evident in his tone. "It's not like the old days when you just pop out for coffee and return in ten minutes."

Emma shrugs on her jacket. "We'll be fine. Someone's got to figure out what's going on out there, and sitting around here waiting for an answer isn't going to help."

"I still don't like it," Max mutters. "If something goes wrong—"

"It won't," Emma interrupts, flashing a reassuring grin. "Besides, you're here to hold down the fort. You can start worrying if we're not back in a couple of hours."

Julian adjusts his backpack and smirks. "Relax, Max. What's the worst that could happen?"

Max raises an eyebrow, unimpressed. "You want a list?"

Emma laughs and nudges Julian toward the door. "Come on, tough guy. Let's go find some food."

As Emma and Julian walk, the streets feel unnervingly empty, their footsteps echoing faintly against the surrounding buildings. The city, once so alive with chatter, car horns, and the hum of daily life, now feels like a hollow shell.

Emma glances at Julian. "You're quiet. Thinking about something?"

Julian shrugs, keeping his eyes scanning the buildings around them. "Just… how weird all this is. Feels like we're in a game or a movie, you know? Like this isn't supposed to be real."

Emma smirks. "Let me guess—Fallout again?"

Julian chuckles. "Nah. This feels more like The Last of Us to me. Like, any second now, we're gonna see some infected crawling out of the shadows."

"Well, let's hope they don't," Emma says, though her voice conveys unease. She changes the subject. "So… you mentioned something about your family the other day. You're close with them?"

"Yeah, I guess," Julian says, his tone softening. "My grandfather, especially. He was a designer and concept artist. First guy in our family to go to uni, back in the day. He used to tell me stories about how hard it was, trying to make a name for himself when no one even knew what concept art was."

Emma's eyebrows lift. "That's awesome. So, he's the reason you got into design?"

"Pretty much," Julian says, a small smile forming. "He'd show me these old sketches he did—dragons, spaceships, all this wild stuff. I thought it was the coolest thing ever. My dad, though… he went a totally different route. He's an engineer. Took after his grandfather, who was a diesel mechanic. Guess I'm the odd one out, sticking with the arts."

Emma bumps his shoulder lightly. "Odd one out? Sounds like you're keeping the creative legacy alive."

Julian grins at that, but the moment is interrupted by a faint noise in the distance—a clatter of metal, maybe. Both of them freeze, eyes scanning the shadows.

"Did you hear that?" Emma whispers.

"Yeah," Julian says, his voice tight. "Could be nothing. Could be something."

They exchange a glance, both silently agreeing to move faster. They round the corner and spot what looks like a small bakery. The sign is dark, but the faint smell of bread lingers.

"Think it's open?" Emma asks, trying to keep her voice light.

"Only one way to find out," Julian says, pushing the door open cautiously.

Inside, the bakery is dimly lit, but to their relief, a few workers are bustling around, seemingly unaware—or uncaring—about the chaos outside. The sight of fresh loaves and pies makes Julian's stomach growl audibly.

Emma smirks. "Guess we're in luck."

But as they approach the counter, the door behind them creaks open, and a shadow falls across the floor. Julian glances back and sees two figures standing there—hulking shapes that don't look like they're here for a friendly chat.

"Uh, Emma?" Julian whispers, nudging her.

She turns, her face falling as she takes in the newcomers. "Oh, great. Trouble."

The larger of the two men steps forward, his eyes scanning the bakery. "Nice place you found," he says, his voice gravelly. "Mind sharing?"

"We don't want any trouble," Julian says, raising his hands slightly.

The man smirks. "That's good. But trouble has a way of finding people."

Emma steps forward, her voice steady but sharp. "We're just here to grab some food and go. There's no need to make this a thing."

The man eyes her, his smirk growing wider. "Feisty. I like that."

Julian tenses, but Emma glances at him, silently telling him to stay calm. "Look," she says, her tone firm, "you can have your pick after we're done. Deal?"

The man chuckles. "I don't think you're in a position to make deals, sweetheart."

Before Julian can think, Emma takes a step closer, her voice dropping to a dangerous level. "Listen, sweetheart, we've had a long day. So unless you're looking to end yours early, I suggest you back off and let us do what we came here to do."

The tension is thick enough to cut, but the man hesitates, clearly debating whether the fight is worth it. Finally, he snorts and waves them off. "Fine. Take your damn bread."

Emma doesn't wait for him to change his mind, grabbing a loaf and a few meat pies before nudging Julian toward the door.

Once outside, they pick up the pace, not stopping until they're a few blocks away.

"Okay," Julian says, panting slightly. "That was… intense."

Emma laughs, though there's a slight edge to it. "What, you didn't enjoy the little chat?"

"Not as much as you seemed to," Julian says, raising an eyebrow.

Emma shrugs. "Hey, someone's got to keep things interesting."

As they walk back to the studio, the weight of the encounter settles over them. The city might be quiet, but it's far from safe. And with every step, they can't help but wonder: What's waiting for them next?

Chapter 9:

Back at the studio, the faint hum of a generator fills the quiet space as Max works on some equipment, his back to the door. He looks up when Emma and Julian step inside, arms laden with their haul.

"See?" Emma announces with a grin. "Told you we'd be fine."

Max raises an eyebrow but says nothing, watching as they place the bread and pies on the counter. "You're lucky. The streets aren't as empty as they look."

"We noticed," Julian mutters, pulling off his jacket. His eyes meet Emma's for a brief moment, and there's an unspoken agreement, not to mention the encounter in the bakery.

As Max begins sorting through their supplies, Emma grabs one of the pies and heads to the far side of the room. She motions for Julian to follow.

"Come on," she says. "Let's eat."

The rooftop of the studio offers a surprisingly peaceful view of the city. Emma and Julian sit on an old blanket, sharing the slightly warm meat pie and a loaf of bread. The sky is streaked with the fading light of the day, the last traces of sunlight casting long shadows across the empty streets below.

Julian leans back on his hands, exhaling deeply. "You'd almost think things were normal from up here."

Emma snorts. "Normal's overrated." She takes a bite of bread, chewing thoughtfully before glancing at him. "So… earlier, you mentioned your family. Your grandfather sounds like an interesting guy."

Julian shrugs, a small smile tugging at his lips. "Yeah, he was. Tough, but creative. He'd stay up all night working on projects, sketching ideas on scraps of paper. My grandmother used to joke that he'd forget to eat if she didn't shove a plate under his nose."

Emma chuckles softly. "Sounds like someone I know."

Julian looks at her, curious. "What about you? What's your family like?"

Emma hesitates, her gaze drifting to the horizon. "Complicated," she says after a moment. "My dad left when I was little. My mom… she did her best, but it was just the two of us. She worked a lot, so I kinda had to grow up fast."

Julian watches her carefully, sensing there's more she isn't saying. "That must've been tough."

Emma shrugs, her tone lighter than her expression. "It was what it was. She always said I was strong, though. Said I didn't need anyone to hold my hand."

"And do you believe that?" Julian asks, his voice gentle.

Emma meets his gaze, her usual confidence slipping just a little. "Sometimes. Other times… I don't know. I think I got so used to doing things on my own that I don't know how to let anyone in."

There's a pause as her words hang in the air, vulnerable and raw. Julian doesn't break the silence, letting her set the pace.

"I guess I've always been curious about you," she admits, her voice quieter now. "You seem… different. Like you're not trying to prove anything to anyone."

Julian tilts his head, a faint smile playing on his lips. "Maybe that's because I've got nothing to prove. Or maybe I'm just really good at hiding it."

Emma smirks, though there's warmth in her expression. "You're full of surprises, you know that?"

"So are you," Julian counters, his gaze lingering on her momentarily before looking away. "Guess we're both a little hard to figure out."

They sit in comfortable silence for a while, the day's tension giving way to a rare moment of calm. Emma picks at the edge of the blanket, her mind elsewhere, before speaking again.

"Thanks for coming with me today," she says softly. "I don't think I would've made it alone."

Julian glances at her, surprised. "You'd have been fine. You're tough, remember?"

"Maybe," Emma says with a small smile. "But it was nice having someone there. Just in case."

Julian leans back, his eyes on the first stars beginning to peek through the twilight. "Anytime."

As the night settles over the city, a faint spark seems to linger between them, unspoken but undeniable. In a world that feels more uncertain by the day, the connection between Emma and Julian offers a small, quiet reassurance—something neither of them had realized they needed until now.

Chapter 10:

———————>※<———————

The next morning, the sky is a muted gray, heavy with clouds threatening rain. Emma is perched on the studio's worn couch, flipping through a dog-eared notebook, while Julian tinkers with an old set of speakers he found in the storage room. The static hums faintly, filling the space with a low, restless energy.

"You know," Emma starts, glancing up from the notebook, "I never really took you for the techy type."

Julian smirks without looking up. "I wouldn't call myself techy. Just resourceful."

Emma tilts her head. "Was that your thing growing up? Fixing stuff?"

Julian sets the screwdriver down, his expression softening as he leans back. "Not really. That was more my grandfather's thing. He loved that kind of stuff. Always had some kind of project going—fixing radios, building models, sketching designs. He could never sit still."

Emma raises an eyebrow. "Sounds like an interesting guy."

Julian nods, a faint smile tugging at his lips. "He was. Big history nerd, too. Loved Assassin's Creed and Fallout. I swear, half my childhood was spent listening to him ramble about some historical figure or telling me stories about our family—how his dad was a diesel mechanic, how he was the first one to go to uni. He was always learning, always curious. Loved podcasts, music, all kinds of stuff."

Emma leans forward, intrigued. "What kind of music?"

"Everything. Country, rock, even old-timey stuff from the 30s and 40s. He used to say music was like a time machine—you could feel the soul of an era in a song."

Emma chuckles. "That's... kinda poetic."

Julian shrugs, a flicker of pride in his expression. "He had his moments. But the thing he loved most was radios. Said they were magic. Thought it was incredible that voices and music could just travel through the air, like ghosts."

Emma looks thoughtful, her gaze drifting to the speakers. "Radios…" she murmurs, almost to herself.

Julian notices the shift in her tone. "What about them?"

Emma's eyes narrow as an idea takes root. "Radios don't rely on WiFi or cell towers. They just… work, don't they? If you have the right frequency."

Julian sits up straighter, the static from the speakers seeming to buzz with new energy. "You're saying we could use them?"

Emma nods slowly. "Think about it. The old networks, like the ones people used decades ago—shortwave, longwave. They were independent of all the stuff we rely on now. If we could find a transmitter and a receiver, we could communicate with people, maybe even find others out there."

Julian's brow furrows in concentration. "It's not a bad idea. But those kinds of radios aren't exactly lying around anymore. Most people moved on to digital a long time ago."

"Maybe," Emma says, her voice steady, "but if anyone could make it work, it's us. Your grandfather didn't pass all that tinkering knowledge down for nothing, did he?"

Julian chuckles, though there's a spark of determination in his eyes. "Guess I'll have to channel my inner history nerd. You think Max would know where to start?"

Emma shrugs. "If he doesn't, we'll figure it out. We always do."

For a moment, they sit in silence, the idea of reviving a forgotten technology filling the room with a quiet, hopeful tension. The hum of the static feels less like noise and more like a whisper of potential.

Emma glances at Julian, a small smile playing on her lips. "You know, your grandfather sounds like the kind of guy who'd thrive in a situation like this. Bet he'd have a solution already."

Julian laughs softly, his gaze distant. "Yeah. He'd probably have us building our own radio tower by now."

Emma's smile widens. "Well, maybe we'll get there. One step at a time."

As the rain begins to patter against the windows, the two of them sit quietly, their minds turning over the possibilities. The world outside might have fallen silent, but deep down, they both know that somewhere, the airwaves are still alive, waiting for someone to listen.

Chapter 11:

The room hums with a new kind of energy. The idea of using a radio to broadcast has taken hold, but as Julian and Emma sit across from Max, the uncertainty is clear in the air.

"I still think it's worth a shot," Julian says, breaking the silence. "If we can find a way to get power to the equipment, we could start sending out a signal. Maybe there's someone out there listening."

Max rubs his temples, a skeptical look in his eyes. "We don't even know how to do that. We lost all the analog towers years ago. We were using digital until… what? The 2050s? And now? Now everything's on Wi-Fi, and even that's unreliable." He looks at the equipment in front of them—old recording gear, a few microphones, and a busted power supply. "This isn't gonna work."

"But we can at least try," Emma adds, trying to sound more convincing. She leans forward, eyes bright with determination. "Look, we've got the gear for recording. We just need power, and we need a proper transmitter. There has to be something out there we can use."

Max shakes his head, rubbing the back of his neck. "We don't even have a proper antenna, let alone the infrastructure to make it work."

Julian furrows his brow, considering it. "What if we just… find one? There's gotta be something out there."

Emma suddenly brightens. "Wasn't there a bookstore just around the corner? I remember passing it before. Books? Old books, maybe something that could help us. I'm pretty sure no one's going to loot that place. Who needs books in a world like this, right? But people would protect them. People still love books."

Max looks at her incredulously. "What do you need a book for? You can't just go picking up any random survival guide and expect it to have what we need."

Emma shrugs nonchalantly. "We need something to read, right? Besides, we could find a book on transmitters, or old-school radio frequencies. Maybe something from the pandemic era, when people were learning to survive in the most basic ways. Maybe there's something in there about old equipment."

Julian's face lights up at the thought. "Yeah, the pandemic days. I remember hearing about people using radios back then. It was like this whole underground network of broadcasts. Maybe some of those guides are still in circulation."

Max sighs but relents. "Alright, fine. I'll go with you. But don't expect to find much. I still think we're wasting time on this."

Emma smiles at him, a spark of hope flickering in her eyes. "Wasting time or not, it's worth a shot."

Chapter 12:

The street outside the bookstore is quieter than Emma and Julian expected, though the occasional rumble of distant vehicles reminds them that the world is still moving. The bookstore sits between two decaying buildings, its faded sign almost blending into the grime-covered walls. It looks as though no one's bothered to clean up in decades.

Max steps outside first, squinting into the midday sun. "You guys ever been here before?" he asks, sounding more incredulous than curious. "What the hell is this place?"

Emma glances over at Julian, her lips twitching in a smirk. "No, but I've been hearing about it for a while. It's got something we need."

"Books?" Max scoffs. "You sure? This place looks like it's been forgotten by everyone."

Julian steps up beside them. "They've got old manuals—maybe even something on analog radio. We need a transmitter, and this might be the only place left that could have any useful info."

Max looks around again, skeptical. "I don't know. You think anyone's even touched this place in years?"

Emma smiles knowingly. "People still care about books, Max. And not just for kindling. Trust me, if there's anything left in this city, it's here."

They approach the door, which is noticeably sturdier than anything else. The frame's been reinforced with iron bars, and the windows nearly blacked out. A single faded bell above the door lets out a soft chime as they enter.

Inside, the atmosphere is thick with the smell of old paper and wood. Shelves upon shelves line the walls, filled with volumes of every size and shape. Most are worn, the pages yellowed and brittle, but some still look pristine. There's a strange, almost sacred quiet in the air as if the books are being protected by something invisible.

Emma steps forward, looking around. "This place is... impressive."

Max frowns, his hands in his pockets. "Yeah, if you're into dead things."

Before Julian can respond, a voice calls from behind a row of shelves, cutting through the silence.

"Password?"

The three of them freeze.

"Password?" Julian repeats, a little thrown off.

The voice comes again, this time more insistent. "Password, or you don't get to come in."

Max rolls his eyes. "This is a joke, right? We're not even in a bunker. It's a bookstore."

Emma, however, looks intrigued. "It's part of the charm," she mutters, then turns to Julian. "Maybe something old? Like, something from the past."

After a brief moment of hesitation, Julian steps forward. "History," he says.

There's a pause. Then, the door creaks open slowly, revealing a woman standing on the other side. She looks at them suspiciously, her arms crossed over her chest. "You said the magic word," she says dryly before stepping aside to let them enter.

The atmosphere is warmer than expected despite the lack of windows. The bookshelves are packed with every genre imaginable—fiction, non-fiction, reference material—but Emma immediately notices how certain books are stacked with care as if someone's gone to great lengths to preserve them.

"I wasn't expecting company," the woman says, eying them. "You come for kindling?"

"No," Emma says quickly, "We're looking for something specific. Something on old radio transmitters, manuals—anything that could help us send a signal."

The woman's gaze softens a little. "Well, you're in luck. No one's asked for something like that in years. Everyone just wants paper for firewood." She gestures for them to follow her. "Come on, I'll show you where we keep the older stuff."

As they walk, the shelves seem to narrow, guiding them to a back corner where books are stacked higher and further apart. Emma can't help but glance at romance novels, thrillers, and fantasy series titles. But there's also an undeniable beauty in seeing them preserved despite the world falling apart.

The woman pulls a dusty, leather-bound book off the shelf. "This one might do," she says, handing it over. The cover is old, the title faded, but the text is still legible: Radio Communication in the Early 20th Century.

Emma flips through the pages, eyes scanning the diagrams of radio equipment, transmission towers, and early wireless communication methods. It's exactly what they need.

Lucille, as she introduces herself, hands them another book. "This one's a little different, but it talks about the history of communication. How things evolved from analog to digital."

Max, who had been silent up until now, finally cracks a grin. "You really are into history."

Lucille smirks back. "Guess I am. It's all we have left, right?"

As they head back toward the front, Emma stops suddenly, glancing at the rows of fiction. "Actually," she says, turning back to Lucille, "do you have any stories? You know, for... sanity. Something to escape into or even something about surviving this kind of thing?"

Lucille's eyes light up. "Now that I can help with." She starts pulling books off the shelves, moving with practiced ease. "For escapism, you can't go wrong with fantasy. Maybe Tolkien or something a little lighter, like Pratchett." She pauses, grabbing another. "This one's for survival stories—Jack London, or if you want something grittier, The Road."

Finally, she pulls out a smaller, well-loved paperback and hands it to Emma. "And this one… Roadside Picnic. It's got survival, a little bit of mystery, and... well, let's just say it'll make you think."

Julian leans in, glancing at the book. "I've heard of that one. Something about stalkers and the Zone?"

Lucille nods. "It's more about the people than the world. You'd like it."

Emma tucks it under her arm with a small smile. "Thanks. For everything."

Lucille gestures toward the door. "Just don't lose the books. They're worth more than you think."

Chapter 13:

A dim lantern lighted the small room they'd holed up in for the night, its faint orange glow casting long shadows across the cracked walls. Outside, the wind howled through the city's empty streets, carrying the occasional distant noise that made them all pause to listen. But for now, it was quiet.

Julian sat cross-legged on the floor, the 20th Century Radio Communication book spread before him. His brow was furrowed, one hand propping up his chin while the other traced over the old diagrams of radio towers and transmitters.

"Did you know," he said suddenly, his voice breaking the silence, "that the first radio signals sent through the air weren't even voices? They were just dots and dashes. Morse code."

Emma, absorbed in Roadside Picnic, looked up, blinking as if coming out of a trance. "Morse code? Like the SOS thing?"

"Yeah," Julian nodded. "It was all they had at first. In the late 1800s, some guy—uh, Marconi, I think— figured out how to send electrical signals through the air. They started with Morse code because it was simple and didn't need a lot of bandwidth."

Emma leaned forward, intrigued. "So… they couldn't talk to each other at first? Just tap out messages?"

"Exactly," Julian replied, leaning forward to emphasize his point. "It wasn't until the early 20th century that they figured out how to transmit actual voice signals. AM radio—Amplitude Modulation—was the first big leap. They could send music, news, speeches. It changed everything. People didn't feel so isolated anymore because they could hear voices, real voices, coming from miles away."

Emma set her book down on her lap, looking at Julian with a small smile. "You really know your stuff," she said.

Julian shrugged, glancing up from his book. "I like to read... whenever I can," he said, his voice dropping slightly, a glint of something teasing in his eyes. "Got to pass the time somehow."

Emma raised an eyebrow. "Is that the only way you pass the time?" Her lips curled into a playful smile.

Julian paused, then leaned in just slightly. "I could think of a few other ways."

There was a moment of silence, both exchanging glances that lingered a little too long. Julian's smile was faint but present—like he wasn't sure if he should keep pushing but wasn't quite ready to pull back.

Emma, however, seemed unfazed. She leaned back against the wall, a light chuckle escaping her lips. "I'm not sure you'd keep up."

He smirked, clearly intrigued. "Oh, I think I could."

A warmth spread between them in the room's quiet, the flickering light from the lantern casting a golden glow over their faces. But just as quickly, Emma shifted in her seat and picked up Roadside Picnic again as if to break the moment, though the slight grin tugging at her lips betrayed her.

"Guess I'll keep reading then," she said softly, but her voice had a lilt to it that wasn't quite the same as before.

Julian laughed softly, returning his attention to his book, though his mind was still slightly off-kilter from their exchange. He glanced up again, noticing how Emma's eyes lingered on the pages of her book, but the silence between them was comfortable. The moment had passed for now, but there was no doubt it would stay with them for a while.

Max's loud snore broke the tension, and they both chuckled. The wind outside rattled the windows again, but the small glow of the lantern and the soft hum of their conversation made the room feel... safe.

For now, they had stories, old knowledge, and each other. It wasn't much, but it was a start.

Emma glanced up from Roadside Picnic, the pages now forgotten as she met Julian's gaze. There was a mischievous glint in her eyes.

"Do you think the EMP could be... aliens?" she asked, her tone light and teasing, though there was a hint of genuine curiosity behind the question.

Julian looked at her, eyebrows raised in surprise. "Aliens? Like... Roadside Picnic aliens?"

"Yeah," Emma said, her lips curling into a sly smile. "You know, mysterious forces that just shut everything down, leave you stranded with no answers. Maybe they're waiting for us to figure it out... or maybe they've just lost interest in us completely."

Julian let out a soft laugh, shaking his head. "Well, I guess that'd be one way to explain the sudden chaos. But if they're waiting for us to figure it out... I think we might be in trouble."

Emma's smile widened as she leaned back, clearly enjoying the banter. "Hey, I'm not saying it's definitely aliens. I just thought it was a funny thought. But you never know. Maybe we'll find some weird zone around here, full of strange artifacts and... I don't know, dangerous creatures."

Julian couldn't help but laugh, leaning back against the wall. "That would be just our luck, wouldn't it? Stumbling into an alien wasteland full of things that want to eat us."

They both shared a quiet laugh, the tension from earlier completely gone. But in the back of his mind, Julian couldn't shake the idea—maybe Roadside Picnic wasn't such a far-off idea after all.

However, Emma's eyes were still on him, a quiet curiosity hidden behind that teasing smile. The moment lingered longer than expected, as if the EMP and its mysteries weren't the only unspoken things between them.

Chapter 10: Broken Bread

When he woke up, Julian first noticed the cold, unfamiliar weight of a book pressing against his cheek. His neck ached from the odd angle, and the pages of the 20th-century communications book were crinkled under his head. He rubbed his eyes, groaning quietly as he sat up, blinking into the dim light.

Max was already awake, sitting on the floor, hunched over with a loaf of bread in his lap. His face was swollen and bruised, a fresh cut above his eyebrow, and his shirt was torn. Emma was next to him, kneeling, holding his arm gently. Her eyes darted up as Julian stirred.

"Max..." she whispered, but the concern in her voice was sharp.

Max barely looked up, chewing a mouthful of bread, which he seemed to savor despite everything. "What?" he grunted.

"Max..." Julian's voice was harder now, his concern breaking through the grogginess of sleep. "What the hell happened to you?"

Max shrugged, still chewing, before answering. "Got the bread... bakery's fine. People, not so much." He swallowed, then grimaced, "But I think they weren't too keen on the idea of me just taking bread without... a bit of a fight."

Emma moved aside to let Julian closer, looking at Max with disbelief and pity. "Max, you went to the bakery by yourself? In that state?"

Max shrugged again, his face pained but resolute. "Needed to get something. Something real... the bread would help."

Julian frowned, crouching down beside him. "I get it, but that was a stupid move."

Max's eyes flickered, a brief flash of frustration. "We're alive, aren't we? I'm fine." He shook his head, but there was a weariness in his voice. "I just... wanted to do something useful. Something worth getting out of bed for."

The silence lingered for a moment before Julian spoke, his voice quieter. "We need to stick together, Max. Going off on your own... that's how people get hurt."

Max didn't answer immediately, his gaze distant as he slowly reached for the bread again. He took another bite, chewing slowly, his eyes avoiding Julian's.

Emma stood up, her hand resting on her hip. "The bread's great, but next time, maybe think before you head out. You could've gotten worse than a few bruises." Her voice softened then, a little more gentle. "We'll be careful. We'll figure it out together."

Max didn't look up, but he gave a nonchalant shrug. "Fine. Next time, I'll bring company." He paused, looking at them both with a half-smile. "But I got the bread. So... we good?"

Emma let out a small laugh, the tension easing a little. "Yeah, we're good. But you owe us a story. I mean... who beat you up over bread?"

Max just shrugged again, not in the mood for further details. Julian shot him a look before glancing back at Emma, an unspoken agreement passing between them to let Max have his moment.

But inside, Julian knew this wasn't just about bread. Max was getting worn down. They all were.

Chapter 14:

The room was thick with tension, the kind that simmered quietly in the corners as they ate. Max had finished the bread, and Emma had offered him some water, though he barely acknowledged it. Julian had grabbed the book again, though his focus was clearly split. He was glancing at Max now and then, his brow furrowed as he tried to make sense of the situation.

Max wasn't looking at him, though. His attention was fixed on the window, watching the darkening skyline as though trying to avoid something. Or someone.

The silence grew heavy, and Emma finally broke it, her voice soft. "Max... You should clean up. You've still got some blood on your face."

Max gave a short grunt but didn't move. He wiped the cut above his brow with the back of his hand, smearing the blood into his shirt. "I'm fine. I don't need your pity."

Julian clenched his jaw, fighting the urge to snap at Max. The tension between them had been building since Max returned with that bread. It wasn't just the injuries—it was something deeper. Something unspoken.

"We all need to stick together," Julian said, his tone firmer now. He was starting to feel the weight of the strain in the room, making him impatient. "We're getting by because we help each other. Max, you can't just run off on your own like that."

Max's eyes flickered to Julian, then quickly away, as if he were refusing to meet his gaze directly. "I didn't ask for your advice, Julian," he muttered, his voice low.

Emma frowned, her brow furrowing. "Max, don't take it the wrong way. Julian's just—"

"I'm not taking anything the wrong way," Max cut her off, his voice suddenly sharp. His gaze flickered briefly toward Emma, and Julian noticed the subtle tension in his body when he glanced at her. But he said nothing, looking instead at the wall as if there were something more important there.

Julian's fingers tightened around the edge of the book, the edges of his knuckles white from the pressure. He could feel the subtle shift in Max's behavior, like a crack forming in a wall. Something was off, and he grew more frustrated every second.

"You didn't need to go by yourself," Julian repeated, the words clipped. "You could've waited until we were ready. But you're too damn stubborn to listen."

Max's eyes shot toward him this time, his face a mask of annoyance and something else— resentment, maybe? But there was a dark flicker behind his eyes that he didn't want to acknowledge. His jaw clenched, and the two of them locked eyes for a brief moment.

"Don't start," Max muttered under his breath. "I'm not a child."

The air between them crackled. Emma shifted uncomfortably on the couch, unsure how to intervene, but it was clear now that the tension wasn't just about the bread. Something deeper had been simmering between Julian and Max for a while.

Julian's patience was wearing thin. He had to hold himself back from saying something harsher, but the truth was starting to settle in.

Max was jealous. Not of Emma, exactly—he didn't want her—but of how Julian and Emma were starting to connect. The subtle tension was more than just the usual rivalry; it was something about how they were beginning to share moments. The way they talked and smiled at each other when the world felt like it was breaking around them.

Max wasn't interested in Emma, at least not in the way Julian might think. But he could feel the shift. He was losing his place in this fragile little group. And it irked him more than he cared to admit.

Julian could feel it, too, that quiet shift in the air between them. It wasn't the usual back-and-forth banter they shared. There was something more brittle about it now.

Emma, sensing the tension, hesitated. Her hand hovered awkwardly between them before she stood up. "I'm going to check on the rest of the supplies," she muttered, breaking the moment before they could say anything else.

The door clicked shut behind her, leaving Julian and Max alone.

Max sat there, eyes still locked on the wall, avoiding the long overdue conversation. Julian could feel his pulse quicken, annoyance and confusion clawing at him. He opened his mouth to speak, but nothing came out. He knew Max was hurt, knew that Max wasn't just angry about the bread or the fight—it was about something else.

Max stood abruptly, brushing past Julian as he headed for the door. "I'm going out for a walk. I need to clear my head."

Julian didn't stop him. He was too exhausted for that.

Max paused just before leaving, glancing at him one last time. His voice was low, almost like an afterthought. "You're really starting to enjoy her company, huh?"

It wasn't a question, but Julian felt the weight of it all the same. His throat tightened, but he said nothing.

Max's eyes narrowed slightly before he turned away, exiting the room.

The door clicked shut behind him, leaving Julian alone with his thoughts.

Chapter 15:

The room was quiet, except for the wind's low hum outside and the occasional creak of the old building. The night had fallen heavy, and Emma had taken a moment to gather her thoughts. She was trying to ignore the tension between Julian and Max, but it seemed like it was lurking, ready to snap.

She walked down the hallway, her footsteps muffled on the worn wood floor, but something caught her attention as she passed Julian's room. The door was slightly ajar, and a muffled sound came from inside.

At first, she thought it was nothing. Maybe he was reading again or sorting through his thoughts. But then the sound came again—a quiet, stifled sob.

Her heart dropped into her stomach, and she pushed the door open without thinking. Julian was sitting on the floor, his back against the bed, shoulders shaking. He had his hands pressed to his face, his body trembling with silent sobs.

"Julian?" Emma's voice was soft and tentative, as if afraid to disturb a delicate moment.

Julian looked up, his eyes wide with surprise, though the tears hadn't stopped falling. His face was tear-streaked, his eyes red, and his hair a mess from running his hands through it in frustration.

"Emma... I'm sorry," he choked out, his voice thick with emotion. "I didn't mean... I just can't... I don't know how to..."

Emma didn't wait for him to finish. She knelt beside him, her hand gently resting on his shoulder, offering what little comfort she could.

"Hey, it's okay," she said, voice low and soothing. "You don't have to apologize. It's a lot. Everything's a lot right now. I'm here. You don't have to be strong all the time."

Julian wiped his eyes roughly, trying to stop the tears, but they kept coming, his shoulders still trembling. "I just... I'm tired, Emma. I'm so damn tired. Every day, it's just... one thing after another. And I don't know how much longer I can keep pretending it's okay."

Emma's heart broke for him. She didn't have all the answers, but she knew one thing—he didn't need to be alone.

She moved closer, wrapping her arms around him in a gentle hug. Julian stiffened for a moment, unsure of how to react, but then he melted into her embrace, letting out a shaky breath.

"It's okay," she whispered again. "You don't have to carry all of this by yourself."

For a long moment, they stayed like that, Emma holding him, letting him cry without saying a word.

Meanwhile, Max was far from the safe space of their little hideout. The streets outside were quiet, but the tension in the air was palpable. His feet took him further from their makeshift home, through alleys he had learned to avoid and backstreets he had never dared to explore.

He was looking for something. What, exactly, he wasn't sure. But he needed to find anything that would give him an edge.

The city had changed since the blackout. Everything felt wrong and twisted. As Max wandered through the quieter parts of town, he found himself in an area he'd never noticed before. It was a dilapidated old building hidden behind collapsed market stalls.

He hesitated at the entrance, the door creaking slightly as it swayed in the wind. Something about it felt off, but his curiosity was stronger than his caution. He stepped inside cautiously.

The place was dusty and dark, with shelves half-fallen and papers scattered on the floor. But then he saw it. Something gleaming in the corner of the room, half-hidden beneath a pile of broken crates.

His pulse quickened as he stepped closer, his eyes narrowing in disbelief.

It was a gun.

A real one. An old-fashioned revolver, its barrel shiny and clean despite the dust around it. It practically glowed in the dim light, almost like it was waiting for him.

Max's heart pounded in his chest. This was bad and dangerous, but he couldn't stop himself. His hand moved on its own accord, reaching out for the weapon, fingers trembling as he wrapped them around the cold metal.

He pulled it free and inspected it carefully. It was heavier than he expected, and the grip felt solid in his hands.

The weight of it felt strange, unsettling. He didn't want to use it. Hell, he didn't even know how. But the power it represented, the control—it was a stark reminder of how far things had gone.

Max stood there for a moment, the gun in his hands, staring at it with a mix of fear and fascination. He knew he shouldn't take it. He should put it back. But... part of him wanted to keep it.

For protection. Or it could be the sheer power of holding something like that. Something that could make him feel invincible.

He glanced around the room, unsure of what to do next. This wasn't his world. He didn't belong in places like this. But the longer he stood there, the more he realized that the world they had once known was gone. And in this new world, survival was everything.

Max shoved the gun into the back of his jacket, the weight of it pressing against his spine as he turned to leave.

But the unease in his gut wouldn't go away. He was heading down a dangerous path now. He could feel it. And once you start walking down that road, there's no telling how far you'll go.

Chapter 16:

Max's mind buzzed as he walked back through the streets, the gun's weight in his jacket a constant reminder of the decision he'd just made. His steps were slow and deliberate like he was trying to push away the nagging thoughts in his head. But something was pulling at him, something he couldn't quite shake.

The streets were empty for the most part, but the occasional flicker of movement in the distance kept him alert. He rounded a corner, the fading light of the day casting long shadows across the cracked pavement. Then he saw him.

A figure, hooded, moving cautiously down the street. Someone who looked like they didn't belong. Max's instincts kicked in before his brain could even process it. The stranger wasn't one of the usual survivors—no, this guy looked like trouble.

Max didn't think. His hand shot out, pulling the gun from his jacket. His finger hovered on the trigger briefly, but it was enough. In a blink, the figure's eyes widened, and there was a flash of panic before the sound of the shot rang out through the still air.

The stranger crumpled to the ground, his body lifeless before it hit the pavement.

Max stood frozen, staring at the body before him, his chest heaving with each ragged breath. His mind was scrambling, a whirlwind of shock and fear.

What had he just done?

The gun's weight felt heavier in his hand like it was seeping into his bones. He was shaken, his body trembling as the adrenaline flooded his system. But then, something else started to creep in.

The power.

It was like a spark in the pit of his stomach. The sensation of control—the way the gun had made him feel. At that moment, he hadn't been powerless. He hadn't been a victim. He had been the one deciding what happened and holding all the cards.

Max swallowed hard, his heart pounding, but the dark feeling lingered. He could feel it now, like an itch in his veins, an urge to keep going, to keep controlling, to keep having that power.

His mind raced, his thoughts snapping back to the gun, to what he had just done. The violence, the finality of it, still echoed in his ears.

But then—just as quickly as it had started—his thoughts snapped back to Julian.

Julian wouldn't have done this. He wouldn't have pulled the trigger without hesitation or a second thought about the consequences. Julian would have found another way that didn't involve killing.

Max's grip on the gun tightened, his knuckles white as the weight of the situation bore down on him.

What had he become?

He wanted to drop the gun. Throw it away, forget about it. But the pull of that power was like a drug, and it was only growing stronger. He could feel it gnawing at him, tempting him to keep the gun, to keep using it. It was dangerous, he knew that. But it was also the only thing that made him feel... alive in this broken world.

Max took a shaky breath, forcing himself to step away from the body, his legs unsteady beneath him. He needed to get back. He needed to see Julian to remind himself of what was right.

But even as he walked back toward the hideout, the temptation lingered. The power. The control. It whispered to him, coaxing him to embrace it, to stop caring about the things he had once valued.

And the more he thought about it, the more he realized—he wasn't sure if he could stop anymore.

Chapter 17:

The night had settled into an uneasy silence, only broken by the occasional creak of the building settling. The faint glow of the dying fire flickered against the small room's walls, casting long shadows across the floor.

Julian had managed to drift off, the weight of his mental exhaustion pulling him into a restless sleep. Emma curled up beside him, had also fallen asleep, her breath soft and steady. The exhaustion was clear on both faces, the toll of the past few days weighing on them.

Max stood at the room's entrance, watching them for a moment. His eyes flickered between Emma and Julian, an odd mix of frustration and something darker lurking beneath the surface. He didn't feel guilty about what had happened earlier—he couldn't afford to—but something gnawed at him, something he couldn't quite place.

The gun in his hand felt heavier now, almost alive like it had its pulse. He stared at it for a long time, tracing the cold metal with his fingers, lost in his thoughts. The noise of the world outside seemed muffled as if the weight of everything—his actions, his choices—was drowning out everything else.

Max's fingers tightened around the grip of the gun, and a dark thought flashed through his mind.

What if?

What if it was Julian? What if Julian was the problem? What if he could end it all right here, right now, and solve everything? There would be no more doubts, no more hesitation. Julian was the one who kept questioning him, kept looking at him with that judgmental gaze. He didn't understand the need for power, for control.

The gun felt right in his hand. He could feel the rush, the pull to act. He had done it once already. What was stopping him now?

Would it solve things?

Max's eyes flickered between the gun and Julian. His thoughts spun out of control, like a broken record stuck on the same line. Violence had always solved things in the past, hadn't it? Back when the world still made sense, when everything was simpler. Max could take what he wanted when he could dominate when he didn't have to ask questions.

His mind wandered back to the streets—the fear, the desperation, the chaos. It had always been there, and Max had learned early that you had to be strong. You had to fight to survive. That was the only rule that mattered.

Violence had always solved things before.

But would it now? Would it solve the tension between him and Julian, this growing rift that had only been made worse by their differences? Max's mind raced, but the more he thought, the more he realized that what he wanted, what he craved, wasn't something as simple as taking Julian's life.

It was power, control, and the certainty that he could bend the world to his will. He could kill Julian, anyone, but it wouldn't fix what was inside him. It wouldn't give him what he wanted.

Max let out a slow, steady breath, his fingers loosening their grip on the gun. The thought of taking a life, of taking Julian's life, unsettled him more than he cared to admit. He wasn't sure why, but something inside him recoiled.

Not Julian.

Max swallowed hard and pushed the thought to the back of his mind. He didn't want to think about it anymore.

He turned, leaving the room, his eyes dark with frustration. He made his way to the small lounge in the foyer, the gun still in his hand like an anchor. The weight of it seemed to pull him further down, and he slumped into the seat, staring at the cold metal in his grip.

He wanted to forget. He wanted to sleep, but the thoughts wouldn't stop. They kept racing through his mind, urging him to do something—to do anything to make the noise inside his head go away.

But as he sat there, the tension thick in the air, the reality of his actions hit him.

He wasn't sure what he was anymore, what he wanted, or what he needed. The world felt too heavy and too broken, and he was just a piece of it, caught in the middle.

As his eyes closed, he tried to push everything out of his mind. But the gun was still in his hand, cold and unforgiving. And no matter how much he tried to avoid it, he knew that soon, his choice would come back to haunt him.

Chapter 18:

The morning sun filtered weakly through the cracks in the building's boarded-up windows. The air was cold, but Emma and Julian had been planning their next move since the night before. They needed components for the transmitter—a long shot, but the only shot they had.

Max was still asleep on the couch in the foyer, his arm thrown over his face as if he were trying to shut out the world. Julian couldn't help but glance at him briefly, the tension from the previous night still lingering in the air. He wondered what was going through Max's mind but couldn't afford to dwell on it now. They had a task to focus on.

Emma pulled her jacket tighter around her shoulders, gathering what little gear they had left. "Are you ready?" she asked, her voice soft and almost distant.

Julian nodded, gathering his things. They'd be gone for most of the day. They could check for the necessary equipment in a few places: a camera shop, an old electronics store, and, if they were lucky, a scrappy or junkyard on the outskirts of town.

They stepped out into the street, the world still eerily quiet. The city around them felt like a ghost town—empty, abandoned, as if everything had been frozen in time. They had learned to move swiftly, keeping to the shadows and avoiding the occasional roving group of desperate scavengers. Emma was alert, her eyes darting from side to side, while Julian kept his head down, focusing on the task ahead.

The first stop was a small camera shop. The glass in the windows was cracked, but the door was still intact. The shelves were mostly bare, except for a few old tech remnants. The dust in the air seemed thick like the building had been untouched for years. The counter was empty, and there was no sign of the owner or anyone else around.

"This place is a bust," Emma muttered, her fingers brushing over the shelves. "Most of the good stuff's probably long gone."

Julian nodded. "We'll check the electronics store next. Maybe we'll get lucky."

The electronics store was in slightly better shape. Some wires hung from the walls, and a few machines had been left behind. It looked like the looters had come and gone but not completely cleaned it out. Julian immediately started going through the shelves, picking up components and wires, trying to identify what they might be able to use for the transmitter.

Emma searched through a pile of old tech, muttering to herself. "We need something with a decent circuit board... And a receiver. No one's had the resources to make this work for years."

"You think Max knows how to do this?" Julian asked, pausing to look over at her.

"Not sure," Emma replied, tucking a few loose wires into her bag. "But it's worth a shot. If we can get a transmitter working, we can find out what's left out there. Maybe there's someone listening."

"Or we can listen to them," Julian added quietly.

Emma shot him a glance, raising an eyebrow. "You mean like a distress signal?"

"Something like that," Julian said, his voice tight. "We need to know if there are others."

By mid-afternoon, they had gathered what they needed from the camera shop, the electronics store, and a scrappy junkyard they stumbled upon on the outskirts of town. The streets were empty, save for the occasional stray dog or scavenger, and the sun hung low in the sky, casting an orange glow over everything.

As they walked back toward the building, Julian's hand wrapped tightly around the components they'd scavenged, his heart pounding a little faster. They had what they needed, and now they had to figure out how to make it work.

But as they approached the building, they saw something that stopped them dead in their tracks.

Max was standing outside, leaning against the wall, his hand gripping something shiny and cold. Julian's stomach dropped as he saw the gun in Max's hand.

Emma froze beside him, her eyes widening. "What the hell is he doing?"

Max didn't notice them at first, lost in his thoughts as he ran his fingers over the gun. His face was unreadable, but the tension in the air was palpable. Julian could feel his pulse quicken, a mix of confusion and anger rising inside him.

They both moved cautiously toward Max, their footsteps almost silent on the cracked pavement. Julian wasn't sure what to say, but it didn't matter. The sight of Max holding the gun like a weapon for power sent a shiver down his spine.

"What the hell, Max?" Emma's voice was a sharp whisper, but it was enough to catch Max's attention.

Max looked up, startled, his eyes darting between them. He looked like he had been caught, though his face quickly shifted into something more guarded. "I... I found it. It's just... just a precaution," he muttered, lowering the gun slightly but not letting go of it.

Emma didn't seem convinced. "A precaution for what?"

Max's lips tightened, and he didn't answer immediately. Instead, his eyes flickered to the gun in his hand again, his grip tightening. The moment felt charged like there was a weight in the air that none of them wanted to acknowledge.

Julian stepped forward cautiously, trying to keep his voice steady. "Max... you don't need this. Not now."

Max stared at him, his eyes cold. "I think I do."

The silence stretched out between them, thick and uncomfortable. Finally, Max shoved the gun into his jacket, though the tension in his posture remained. "I'll be fine. You two do whatever you need to do. I'm staying out here."

Julian glanced at Emma. Neither wanted to push the issue further, not with the components they needed to get back inside and start working.

But as they walked past Max, Julian couldn't shake the feeling that something had shifted between them. Max was becoming someone different, and Julian wasn't sure whether it was for the better or worse.

Chapter 16: Escape to the Unknown

The weight of the decision sat heavily on Julian's chest. Every time he looked at Max, his mind swirled with doubt with unease. There was a creeping tension that had only grown since their last conversation. The gun had changed everything. Max had changed. And now, the place they had called their home for the past few weeks, the studio—once a shelter, once a haven—felt safe.

Emma hadn't said much after their encounter with Max, but Julian could see it in her eyes. She knew. She understood. They couldn't stay here, not with Max becoming unpredictable and not with the constant gnawing fear that had begun to take hold of their lives.

They sat quietly in the small, dim-lit room where they had spent the night. Max had finally passed out on the couch in the foyer, his breathing deep and even, the gun still tucked in his jacket. They knew it was their chance.

"Julian," Emma whispered, her voice barely above a murmur. "We can't stay here anymore. Not with him like that."

Julian nodded, running a hand through his disheveled hair. "I know. I've been thinking about it since we found him with the gun." He sighed, his eyes distant as he stared at the wall. "We need to go. I have a place. It's not far. My old apartment."

"Is it safe?" Emma asked, her voice tinged with caution.

"It should be," Julian replied, though his words had an edge. His apartment had been locked up, untouched since before the chaos hit. If everything had gone as he remembered, it would still be standing, still locked, his. But even then, the thought of returning to a place once a sanctuary now felt foreign. The world had changed too much. The streets had changed. People had changed.

And even if the apartment was still intact, was it enough? Would it be enough for them?

"Max won't be awake for a while," Julian said, trying to shake off the unease. "We can gather everything we need while he's out. Get in, get out. We leave before he wakes up."

Emma's gaze flickered over to the sleeping form of Max in the foyer, a frown creasing her forehead. "He's dangerous now, Julian. We don't know what he's capable of."

"I know," Julian whispered, his voice a mere breath. "But we can't keep living like this. Not in fear. Not anymore."

The hours passed quickly as they silently moved, gathering what little they could. Their few belongings were packed hastily, nothing too valuable. The transmitter parts they had scavenged earlier were wrapped carefully in cloth and tucked into Emma's bag. The rest—anything they might need to survive in the days to come—was thrown together without much thought.

As they moved through the building, Julian felt the weight of their decision settle in. Every step they took felt like they were leaving a piece of themselves behind. The studio had once been a home, a place where they had found some semblance of normalcy. But now, it felt like a cage—a trap.

They moved quickly but cautiously, glancing at Max every few seconds to ensure he was still asleep. His slow, steady breathing was the only sign that he hadn't woken, and they both held their breaths whenever he shifted, praying he would stay unconscious for just a little longer.

Finally, with everything packed and ready, they stood by the door, Emma's hand on the handle, Julian's gaze lingering on Max one last time. The silence in the room was suffocating.

"Are you sure about this?" Emma asked, her voice a whisper as she looked up at him.

"I am," Julian said, his voice firm now despite the doubt gnawed at him. "We can't stay here. We need to find somewhere safe. Somewhere we can breathe again."

Emma hesitated but then nodded. "Let's go."

They opened the door slowly, trying not to make a sound. The hallway was quiet, the dim light from the streetlamp casting long shadows across the floor. It felt like the entire world was holding its breath, waiting for them to make their move.

They slipped out of the building, careful not to disturb the silence. The streets outside were empty, as they had been for days, save for the occasional echo of distant footsteps or wind rustling through abandoned streets. The city felt deserted—silent as if it, too, had given up.

They made their way toward the apartment building, their footsteps light and quick. Julian kept glancing over his shoulder, but no one followed them. The streets were empty, as they had been for weeks.

The apartment building came into view, an old, rundown structure that had seen better days. Julian hadn't returned since before the collapse, but he hoped it was still intact.

As they reached the entrance, Julian fumbled for his keys. The moment felt surreal like they were returning to a life that no longer existed. He unlocked the door, his fingers trembling slightly as he pushed it open.

The apartment was dark, the only light coming from the narrow windows on the far wall. It was as he remembered it—sparse, a little worn, but still his. The furniture was still in place, and there were no signs of damage.

They stepped inside, the door clicking shut behind them. For a moment, Julian felt a wave of relief wash over him. It was safe. The apartment was safe.

But then, as Emma set down her bag and began to look around, Julian's gaze turned to the window. The world outside seemed so far away, but everything seemed to be closing in on them.

They had found a haven, but it didn't feel safe anymore. Not really.

Max's image flashed in Julian's mind, the way he had held that gun. The uncertainty that had settled between them was only growing. No matter where they went or how far they ran, it was clear now— nothing could truly protect them from what was coming.

And in that moment, Julian realized something even more unsettling: the danger wasn't just out there.

It was inside them, too.

Chapter 19:

The apartment was quiet, too quiet. Julian and Emma stood in the small, dim-lit living room, surrounded by boxes and discarded bags. Though familiar in a distant way, the room felt strange now. Each piece of furniture that had once belonged to Julian's old life seemed foreign after everything.

Emma stood by the window, peering out at the darkened cityscape. The streetlights flickered faintly in the distance, but otherwise, the city felt like a ghost town.

Julian was on the couch, his hands running over the transmitter components they'd managed to gather. It was a task that should have been a welcome distraction, but nothing could distract his mind from what had just happened.

Max. The gun. The tension. The escape.

"Do you think we did the right thing?" Emma's voice broke the silence. Standing by the window, her eyes trained on the empty streets outside. "Leaving like that? It feels... wrong."

Julian set the components down on the coffee table with a soft thud, his gaze lingering on them before he met her eyes. "We didn't have much choice," he said quietly. "Max was... changing. And this place, this... it wasn't safe anymore."

She nodded, but there was a small frown on her face. Something unspoken was hanging between them. Julian could feel it but didn't have the words to address it.

"And now?" she asked, her voice tentative. "What do we do now?"

Julian leaned back on the couch, crossing his arms over his chest. "Now? We finish what we started." He motioned to the components, his face set in determination. "We get that transmitter up and running. Then we see what happens."

"Right," Emma murmured, but her eyes drifted to the window. "And after that?"

"After that," Julian repeated, leaning forward. His voice was low but sure. "We figure out what happens next."

Emma let out a small, ironic laugh, staring into the darkness. "I don't think I ever expected us to be in this position. I mean, if you just wanted me to move in with you, you could've just asked."

Julian blinked at her, taken aback by the bluntness of her words. He felt his chest tighten in response, a mixture of surprise, unease, and—was that embarrassment?

"I..." He ran a hand through his hair, laughing awkwardly. "It's not like that, Emma. You know that."

Emma turned around slowly, her lips curling into a teasing smile. "I mean, you know... If I had to pick a roommate in the middle of a crisis, I suppose you wouldn't be the worst choice."

Julian raised an eyebrow, but his expression showed a hint of warmth. "You're a funny one, you know that?"

She shrugged nonchalantly, her tone softening. "We're all a little funny now, I think." She glanced around at the sparse surroundings, the once cozy apartment now feeling odd... hollow. "Just trying to keep it together."

Julian nodded, his gaze turning inward. "Yeah."

There was a quiet moment between them, one that felt strangely comfortable despite the weight of everything else pressing down on them. Emma wandered over to the couch and sat beside him, her leg brushing against his. It felt like a silent reassurance, a connection they hadn't lost even through everything that had happened.

"So," Julian started, his voice low as he turned to face her. "What does this make us?"

Emma looked at him, raising an eyebrow. "What do you mean?"

"Are you still my producer?" Julian asked, hinting at something deeper, something unspoken. He wasn't sure what he meant by it—whether it was just a simple question or if it was more, but in that moment, he needed the reassurance.

She paused, her gaze flickering between him and the window as if weighing the question's implications. For a moment, her expression was unreadable. Then, she shrugged again, this time with a slight smile.

"Well," she said lightly, "I suppose I still have a job to do. You're gonna need all the help you can get if we're going to get this thing working."

Julian couldn't help but laugh at that, the sound of it feeling strange after all the tension they'd lived through. "I'd be lost without you."

Emma gave him a sidelong glance, a glimmer of something in her eyes. "Good thing you don't have to be," she said, her voice a little too soft to be entirely casual.

Julian felt his heart skip a beat at the implication, but he said nothing, unsure how to respond. The tension was still there, hanging between them like a thin thread, but they didn't need to address it for now. Not yet.

"Well," Julian said, clearing his throat, trying to push the moment away. "I think we've got work to do." He motioned toward the components on the table. "Let's get this thing done."

Emma nodded, but her eyes lingered on him for a moment before returning her attention to the task.

They knew things had shifted—between them, within themselves, and in the world around them. But for now, they couldn't afford to dwell on it. There were bigger things to focus on. Bigger things to survive.

But deep down, they both knew that the question lingered, unspoken: What would they do when the world they knew finally settled into the chaos they were trying to escape?

And was there a place for them—together—in whatever came next?

Chapter 20:

It had been a week of sleepless nights, scattered moments of quiet conversation, and a constant buzz of focus in the apartment. Julian had barely left the makeshift workspace he'd set up on the small table, surrounded by wires, components, and the relics of his past—old computer parts, half-dismantled studio mics, and a wealth of salvaged tech from the abandoned shops they'd visited. Each day blurred into the next as he tinkered with the transmitter, his mind consumed with the task.

Emma, ever patient and supportive, had been by his side—offering encouragement, help when needed, and even a few distractions when it seemed like Julian was about to crack under the pressure.

But today was different. Today, something clicked.

Julian stared at the monitor, his fingers hovering over the keyboard. His old computer, which had seemed like a relic of a bygone era, flickered to life after a week of coaxing. He'd scavenged parts from every electronic store and repair shop they could find, piecing together something barely functional yet perfect. The transmitter was finally coming together, its final connections making sense. The stolen mics—his precious studio mics—were now rigged up, ready for use.

His heart raced with anticipation, the moment's weight settling into his bones.

"Emma, I think... I think it's working," Julian muttered, his voice a mix of disbelief and excitement.

Sitting on the couch, half-heartedly flipping through a book, Emma immediately looked up. Her eyes widened, a smile spreading across her face.

"No way," she whispered, standing and walking toward him. "You did it?"

Julian nodded, his fingers hovering over the keys as he prepared to test the transmitter. The screen flashed briefly, showing the familiar interface he had once used, and then the transmitter's hum started to fill the room.

It wasn't perfect, but it was enough.

"We're live," Julian said, his voice filled with wonder.

Emma stepped closer, her eyes not leaving the screen. For a moment, neither of them said anything. It was as though the world had stopped for just a second, caught in the stillness of their success.

Then, Emma's gaze shifted to Julian, her eyes softening as though seeing him in a new light—someone who had carried them this far, who had somehow managed to pull the impossible off. She didn't speak. There was no need for words.

Feeling the weight of her gaze, Julian finally looked up from the screen. For a long moment, neither moved as though something unsaid was hanging between them. The hum of the transmitter was the only sound, filling the silence that had settled.

And then, without thinking, Emma leaned in. The kiss was gentle at first—tentative, almost hesitant—but it quickly deepened, a rush of unspoken emotions flooding to the surface. Julian's hands moved instinctively, pulling her closer, his body responding to the closeness, the warmth.

It was everything—the culmination of weeks of tension, fear, exhaustion, and a quiet hope that they could, against all odds, survive this. They could feel the world around them fall away, the chaos outside seeming miles away as they lost themselves in the moment.

When they finally pulled apart, both were breathless, their faces flushed. The room seemed to hold its breath with them.

Emma bit her lip, a slight smile tugging at the corner of her mouth. "I've been meaning to do that for a while," she said softly, her voice almost playful.

Julian chuckled, still trying to catch his breath. "You have, huh?" His eyes were warm, full of something he hadn't realized he'd been holding onto.

But there was no time to linger on words. The reality of their situation—their world—suddenly rushed back to Julian. He sighed, running a hand through his hair, but his smile didn't fade. "We should probably figure out what's next."

Emma nodded, stepping back to give him space. But the connection between them was undeniable now, and the lingering tension felt less like a weight and more like something that would carry them forward.

The transmitter was up and running, and the computer worked. They had everything they needed to broadcast their message and reach anyone who might still be out there.

But for now, Julian couldn't shake the feeling that this moment of connection and success was what they needed the most. Everything else would come in time.

As Julian turned back to the screen, Emma's hand brushed his arm, a silent promise that they weren't in this alone. The world might be collapsing, but they could face whatever came next together.

"We'll figure it out," she said softly, her voice a quiet resolve.

Julian gave her a small smile and returned to the screen, but this time, he had new energy and purpose. For the first time in a long while, the future seemed a little brighter.

Chapter 21:

The apartment was bathed in the soft glow of evening light, the hum of the transmitter filling the silence. Julian sat before the monitor, adjusting the frequencies as Emma watched him closely. She had been quiet for a while, lost in her thoughts, until she finally spoke up, her voice gentle but firm.

"Julian," she said, her tone encouraging, "maybe it's time you try sending something. I mean, what's the point of all this work if we don't actually broadcast?"

Julian hesitated, fingers hovering over the dial. He'd focused on getting the transmitter functioning, ensuring everything was right. But now that it was, he didn't know where to begin.

Emma stepped closer, giving him a soft nudge. "It's not just about the tech, you know. It's about connecting. You've built this thing for a reason. You've got a voice to share."

He met her eyes, and for a moment, he almost saw doubt in her gaze. Was he ready to send something into the unknown? To put himself out there, to reach for something in the vast emptiness of the world outside?

But then Emma smiled, which made the uncertainty feel a little smaller. "Besides," she added, her voice playful, "you've got a captive audience now. Who knows who's out there."

Julian nodded, his fingers slowly turning the dial to different frequencies. He was about to speak into the mic when something caught his eye—a small, dusty guitar leaning against the wall in the corner of the room.

Without thinking, he stood up and walked over to the guitar. Emma watched him, her curiosity piqued. The guitar was old but still in decent shape. He strummed a few chords, his fingers awkward and unsure, then sighed.

"You play?" Emma asked a hint of amusement in her voice.

Julian glanced at her, a sheepish smile tugging at his lips. "I can barely play anything. I only know a couple of songs… Hot Cross Buns, and… Johnny Cash."

Emma raised an eyebrow. "Hot Cross Buns, huh? You're full of surprises, Julian."

He gave her a half-laugh, strumming the guitar again, but his fingers seemed to find the rhythm this time. "Alright," he said, his voice more hesitant now, "I'll give it a shot."

And with that, Julian began to play, the familiar chords of "Walk the Line" filling the room. His voice was shaky at first, the uncertainty clear in every note, but as he sang, there was something raw and real about it. Something that wasn't about perfection but about the moment. About the connection.

Emma watched him closely, her eyes softening as she listened to him utter the words. His voice was not quite steady but undeniably genuine. She had never heard him sing before, and though it was rough around the edges, she found herself in awe of him. The world outside seemed to disappear for a moment as his music filled the apartment, and for just a brief second, things felt normal again.

When he finished, he looked at her, slightly embarrassed, his fingers still on the strings. "That was probably the worst version of 'Walk the Line' you've ever heard."

Emma shook her head, a smile breaking across her face. "No," she said softly, "it was perfect."

She didn't elaborate, but how she looked at him said everything.

Julian chuckled, setting the guitar down, and returned to the transmitter. "Well, that was probably the most I'll ever play in front of anyone."

Emma raised her eyebrows. "If you can play, play. Who knows, maybe someone out there will appreciate it."

He gave her a small smile, though he felt the pressure of the moment weighing on him again. He couldn't help but feel like everything was building to this moment—the moment they reached out and made their presence known in the world.

Taking a deep breath, Julian adjusted the transmitter again, and this time, he didn't hesitate. He spoke clearly into the mic, his voice steady and firm despite the growing tension in the air.

"This is Julian, calling anyone who can hear. Unknown Sydney signal, we're broadcasting. If you can hear this, please respond."

He let out a breath he didn't realize he'd been holding, and for a moment, nothing happened. The transmitter hummed, the silence almost deafening. Emma stood beside him, her expression unreadable, but there was a quiet hope in her eyes.

And then, suddenly, the static on the radio crackled, breaking the silence.

"This is RAAF control," a voice crackled through the speaker, sharp and clear despite the static. "We've found a signal. Unknown Sydney signal, come in."

Julian's heart skipped a beat. He looked at Emma, disbelief written across his face. She met his gaze, her expression a mix of shock and hope.

"We're not alone," she whispered, almost to herself.

Julian's hand shook slightly as he adjusted the dial to get a clearer connection. His mind raced—RAAF control? The Royal Australian Air Force? What did that mean? Who else was out there?

"RAAF control, this is Julian," he said, his voice steady despite his heart racing. "We're in Sydney, broadcasting from an undisclosed location. Can you hear us?"

The static on the line grew louder, and for a moment, Julian thought they might lose the connection. Then, the voice crackled back to life, clearer now.

"Julian, this is RAAF. We've received your signal. Please stand by for further instructions. We need to verify your location and status. Over."

Julian sat back in his chair, stunned, the weight of what had just happened sinking in. Emma was silent, her eyes wide with disbelief, as she processed the reality of their situation. They had made contact. After all this time and everything they had been through, they finally reached someone.

The room felt still, as if the air held its breath.

And then, slowly, Julian spoke, his voice quieter now. "We've got a chance, Emma. We've got a chance to rebuild. To connect."

Emma nodded, a smile playing on her lips as she met his eyes.

"It's only the beginning," she said softly.

And together, they waited, not knowing what the next moment would bring but knowing for the first time in a long while that they weren't alone.

Chapter 22:

The radio crackled with static as Julian leaned closer to the transmitter, his pulse racing. Emma sat nearby, the guitar resting against the wall, her arms wrapped around her knees. The connection to the RAAF was thin, but it was there—a fragile thread tying them to the outside world.

"This is Julian," he repeated, adjusting the dials precisely. "We're broadcasting from an apartment building in Ultimo. Can you hear me clearly?"

The static buzzed for a moment, followed by the sharp, clipped voice of the RAAF operator.

"Ultimo? Confirm your position, over. Is this near the CBD? Over."

Julian exchanged a glance with Emma, who nodded in silent encouragement. He leaned into the mic. "Yes, just west of the city. Apartment complex, high enough to get a signal out. Over."

The line went quiet momentarily, and Julian could feel his nerves mounting. Then, the voice returned, slightly clearer now.

"Understood. This is Glenbrook RAAF Base, west of Penrith. Repeat: Glenbrook. Not Richmond. We're receiving your signal loud and clear. How in the world did you manage this? Over."

Julian blinked, momentarily thrown by the curiosity in the operator's voice. "Honestly?" he began, his voice tinged with nervous laughter. "Scavenging. I had an old analog transmitter in storage. Found some spare components from a camera shop and electronic stores. Managed to piece it together. Took a week of trial and error. Over."

The response came quickly, the tone almost disbelieving. "That's impressive. Analog's not exactly common anymore. Most folks wouldn't even know where to start. Over."

Julian felt a small swell of pride but kept his focus. "Had some old manuals. Picked up bits and pieces over the years. Desperate times, you know. Over."

Another pause, and then the operator's voice softened slightly, shifting from formality to curiosity. "Understood. What's your status? How many are with you? Any injuries or urgent needs? Over."

Emma leaned forward, whispering, "Tell them everything."

Julian nodded. "There are three of us. Myself, Emma, and Max. We're uninjured, but supplies are running low. We're stable for now, but... we could use support. Over."

The operator's voice turned sharper, more focused. "Noted. Can you confirm any threats in your immediate area? Hostiles? Groups of interest? Over."

Julian hesitated, his thoughts immediately flashing to Max's recent behavior—the tension, the gun. He decided against mentioning it. "Nothing organized. Just the occasional scavengers and troublemakers. We've managed to avoid major conflict. Over."

"Copy that," the operator said, the tone turning brisk. "We're currently assessing your location. There's been significant activity near the CBD— might explain your troubles. You mentioned a working analog setup. Are you capable of sustaining it for extended communications? Over."

Julian glanced at the transmitter, then back to Emma. "As long as we don't burn through what little power we have, yes. But it's not exactly stable. Over."

The static wavered momentarily before the operator's voice returned, tinged with admiration. "Understood. You've done an incredible job, given the circumstances. We'll do what we can to assist. Tell us—what do you need most? Over."

Emma leaned closer to the mic, her voice firm but measured. "Food. Water. Maybe tools to help stabilize the setup? We don't have much in the way of defenses, either. Over."

The line went quiet again, and Julian could feel the weight of the silence. Then, the operator's voice returned with a hint of reassurance. "Copy that. We're logging your request. It might take time, but we'll work on sending assistance. In the meantime, maintain this frequency. We'll check in regularly. If anything changes—threats, supplies, health—reach out immediately. Understood? Over."

"Understood," Julian replied, his voice steady despite his emotions. "Thank you, Glenbrook. This means a lot. Over."

The static hummed again before the operator's final words came through. "Stay safe out there. You're not alone anymore. Glenbrook out."

The radio fell silent, leaving only the faint hum of the transmitter in the room. Julian leaned back in his chair, the weight of the conversation settling over him. Emma watched him closely, her expression a mix of relief and something deeper.

"We're not alone," she said softly, her voice almost breaking.

Julian nodded, his hands still gripping the edge of the desk. "We've got a chance," he murmured, repeating his words from earlier. "A real chance."

Emma smiled, her gaze lingering on him momentarily before she reached out, resting a hand on his arm. "You did it," she said.

For a moment, the world outside seemed just a little less threatening. The connection to Glenbrook had brought more than hope—a sense of purpose, a reason to keep moving forward. But beneath the relief, Julian couldn't shake the nagging feeling that their challenges were far from over.

Chapter 23:

The static on the transmitter settled, leaving Julian and Emma alone in the apartment with an almost surreal silence. Julian stared at the makeshift setup, the weight of the conversation with the RAAF sinking in. He had done it—reached someone. Yet the sense of accomplishment didn't bring him the relief he'd hoped for.

Emma broke the quiet, leaning against the window and gazing at the dim cityscape. "So, they're sending someone," she said, her voice cautious.

"Yeah," Julian replied, running a hand through his hair. "A convoy. They said it'd take a day or two to organize, but they'll be here soon."

Emma turned, her arms crossed, her gaze sharp. "Julian, why did you mention Max?"

Julian blinked, caught off guard. "What do you mean? They asked about who's with us. I didn't want to lie."

Emma shook her head, her expression a mix of frustration and concern. "Max isn't the same, Julian. You've seen it. He's unpredictable. Dangerous, even. Why bring him into this? He doesn't need to be part of their plans—or ours."

Julian looked away, his jaw tightening. "I know he's changed, Emma. But he's still... Max. I can't just leave him out. We've all been through too much together."

Emma stepped closer, her tone softening but still firm. "That's not the same as trusting him. You saw how he looked at us—at you. He's not just angry anymore, Julian. He's something else."

Julian met her gaze, his own conflicted. "I know," he admitted quietly. "But I can't write him off. Not yet. I keep thinking... maybe there's still a way back for him."

Emma sighed, leaning against the edge of the table. "You always want to fix things. But this might not be something you can fix, Julian. You need to be ready for that."

The room fell silent again momentarily, the weight of her words settling heavily between them. Julian shifted uncomfortably, glancing at the transmitter. "When the convoy gets here, I'll handle it. I'll make sure Max doesn't... doesn't cause any problems."

Emma didn't look convinced, but she nodded, letting the subject drop. "Just be careful," she said, her voice soft. "We can't afford any more surprises."

Julian nodded, his thoughts racing. The knot in his stomach tightened at the idea of facing Max, knowing how fragile their balance had become.

Emma moved to the window again, her silhouette framed against the faint light of the city. "You did good tonight, though," she said after a moment. "Getting through to Glenbrook? That's huge. It's a step forward."

Julian allowed himself a small smile. "Yeah," he said quietly. "A step forward."

But as he stared at the transmitter, the hum of its static faint in the background, he couldn't shake the feeling that every step forward brought new risks, new shadows creeping ever closer.

And Max, somewhere in the city, was one of those shadows.

Chapter 24:

Max wandered through the deserted streets of Sydney, his steps aimless but purposeful in their madness. The world outside the studio no longer held any fear for him. The things that had once seemed insurmountable—loneliness, hunger, death—had become familiar companions. Now, he moved with a singular, chaotic intent, driven by a thirst for control, for release, for something he couldn't name.

He didn't know where Emma and Julian had gone. It didn't matter. He would find them eventually. For now, the world was his to roam.

The Quay stretched out before him, eerily quiet. The once-bustling waterfront, with its ferries, tourists and street performers, was now a graveyard of forgotten echoes. Max took it all in with a detached gaze, his fingers trailing over the cold metal of the gun tucked into his waistband.

He passed a toppled police cruiser, its windows shattered. The vehicle was a grim reminder of how quickly the order had dissolved. Something caught his eye—a faint glint of metal beneath the driver's seat. Max smashed the remaining glass with the butt of his gun and reached inside, pulling out a shotgun.

"Lucky day," he muttered, a twisted grin creeping across his face.

The weight of the weapon felt satisfying in his hands. He rummaged through the car, finding a box of shells in the glove compartment. He loaded the shotgun, slinging it over his shoulder as he continued his aimless journey.

The streets around Circular Quay were a patchwork of ruin and silence. Max's footsteps echoed as he walked, his eyes scanning for movement. He wasn't looking for food or shelter or safety. He was looking for something to break.

The first shot was almost instinctual. A crow perched on a lamppost, its beady eyes watching him with idle curiosity. The blast of the shotgun sent it tumbling to the ground, its wings flailing for a brief, pitiful moment before going still.

Max laughed—a sharp, humorless sound rang out into the emptiness.

"Guess you didn't see that coming," he said to no one, stepping over the bird's lifeless body without a second thought.

As he wandered further, he began to notice signs of life. Scavenged cars pulled into makeshift barricades. Empty cans and bottles strung up on wires to create alarms. Someone had been here recently, maybe even still was.

The thought sent a thrill through him. He gripped the shotgun tighter, his breath quickening.

Max found another police car, this one overturned on its side. The trunk had been pried open, but whoever had done it had been in a hurry. Max found more ammunition, a service pistol, and a bulletproof vest inside. He took it all, arming himself like a one-person army.

By the time he reached the edge of the Quay, the sun was dipping below the horizon, casting the city in shades of orange and red. Max stood there for a moment, staring out at the water. The waves lapped against the shore, indifferent to the chaos on the land.

"I'll find you," he said softly, his voice carrying on the breeze. "Emma. Julian. I'll find you, and we'll see who's really in charge."

His mind spiraled, his thoughts fractured and incomplete. The lines between right and wrong, friend and foe, had long since blurred.

Max turned away from the water, his eyes glinting with something dark and unhinged. He moved back toward the city, his steps no longer aimless. He didn't know where Emma and Julian were.

But he would keep looking.

And when he found them, he would show them what he had become.

Chapter 25:

The apartment was quieter than the studio, the faint hum of life outside barely audible through the thick walls. Julian had managed to salvage enough from the studio to make the space functional: a few blankets on the worn-out couch, an old lamp that flickered faintly when connected to a makeshift battery, and the stolen studio mics now rigged to a cobbled-together transmitter.

It wasn't much, but it was home—for now.

Emma sat cross-legged on the floor, flipping through a battered magazine she'd found in one of the apartment's drawers. The glossy pages, faded and curled at the edges, were a relic of a world that felt impossibly distant. A world of bright advertisements and smiling faces that seemed to mock their current reality.

Julian was hunched over the transmitter setup, his fingers deftly adjusting the dials. His brow furrowed in concentration as he double-checked the connections and scribbled notes on a scrap of paper. Two days of relative calm had given them time to regroup and strategize, but the tension lingered like a storm cloud on the horizon.

"You've got the frequency steady this time," Emma said, glancing up from the magazine.

Julian nodded without looking at her. "Yeah, it's holding. Should make it easier to reach out again when the RAAF calls back."

Emma set the magazine aside and leaned back against the couch. The apartment, though modest, felt cozier than the studio ever had. Maybe it was the smaller space, the absence of Max's brooding presence, or just the sense of being in a place untouched by their shared history.

"Feels almost normal here," she said softly, her voice carrying a wistful edge.

Julian finally turned to look at her, his expression a mix of exhaustion and faint amusement. "Normal? In what universe?"

Emma shrugged. "I don't know. This one, maybe. It's not like we have much to compare it to."

Julian chuckled dryly and turned back to the transmitter. His laughter faded quickly, replaced by a more somber tone. "We need to figure out what to say if they press us about Max."

Emma tensed slightly but nodded. "We've been honest so far. Maybe that's enough."

"They'll want details," Julian said, his voice tinged with unease. "How we ended up together. What happened to him. Why we left."

Emma hesitated, then sat up straighter. "We tell them the truth—most of it, at least. Max was an old friend. He's... changed. He's dangerous now. We had to get away before he turned on us."

Julian sighed, running a hand through his hair. "It's not like we can explain everything. They'll think we're incompetent or lying if we tell them how unhinged he's become."

"Then we focus on the facts," Emma said firmly. "He's armed. He's unstable. And we're scared of what he might do if he finds us."

Julian nodded, though his jaw tightened. "I hate selling him out like this."

"He sold himself out," Emma said, her tone sharper than she intended. She softened it quickly. "Look, I know it's hard. But this isn't the same Max you knew. You said it yourself—he's not the same."

Julian leaned back in his chair, his gaze distant. "Yeah. I know."

The silence followed was heavy, filled with the unspoken weight of their shared guilt and uncertainty. After a moment, Emma moved to sit beside him, her shoulder brushing against his.

"Hey," she said gently. "We're doing what we can. That's all anyone can ask."

Julian glanced at her, his expression softening. "Thanks, Emma."

They sat there momentarily, the flickering lamp casting long shadows across the room.

"Do you think they'll help us?" Emma asked quietly.

"The RAAF?" Julian shrugged. "They seem interested enough. But whether they can do anything about Max... I don't know."

Emma sighed, resting her head against his shoulder. "I guess we'll find out."

As the hours ticked by, they continued to work, their conversations weaving between logistics and fleeting moments of levity. The apartment, with its mismatched furniture and amateur setup, felt like a fragile sanctuary—a place where, for a little while, they could catch their breath.

But even here, the shadows of the past lingered, and the knowledge that Max was out there, somewhere, weighed heavily on them both.

Chapter 26:

The knock at the apartment door came just after sunrise. It was sharp and deliberate, like someone accustomed to having their authority recognized. Julian and Emma exchanged a glance before Julian stood, his heart pounding.

The man standing in the doorway looked like a relic from a history book—or a fever dream. He was tall and broad-shouldered, his tan uniform worn under a black bulletproof vest emblazoned with a faded "RAAF" logo. On his head, tilted at a rakish angle, was an old Anzac slouch hat, which Julian remembered from black-and-white photos of World War I diggers. The look was completed by a leather holster on his hip and a rifle slung across his back.

"Morning," the man said, tipping the brim of his hat. His voice carried a relaxed drawl, almost at odds with the sharpness in his eyes. "You must be Julian and Emma."

Julian nodded, stepping aside to let the man in. "And you must be the RAAF official."

"That's one way to put it," the man said with a chuckle, striding into the room with the confidence of someone who'd seen worse than this apartment's ramshackle state. He extended a hand. "Captain Flynn. Good to meet you."

Emma stood awkwardly by the makeshift transmitter, her arms crossed. "Captain Flynn. Didn't know the Air Force was in the habit of dressing like cowboys."

Flynn grinned, the kind of grin that came with a story. "Well, ma'am, when the world goes to hell, you make do with what you've got. Found the hat in a storeroom. Figured it'd suit the new world order."

Emma raised an eyebrow but didn't press the point.

Flynn surveyed the apartment, his gaze lingering on the transmitter setup. "I'll give it to you—this is impressive. Analog's a dying art these days. Or it was."

Julian leaned against the table's edge, trying to suppress the nervous energy coursing through him. "You said you'd answer our questions. We've been trying to piece together what happened since the EMP, but we're working blind."

Flynn nodded, his expression turning serious. "Fair enough. Here's the short version. That blast? EMP, alright. Wiped out anything digital across most of the continent. Whole world, for all we know. Satellites, grids, communications—all fried. Australia's been thrown back a good century and a half."

"Back to the 1850s," Emma murmured, half in disbelief.

"More or less," Flynn agreed. "No phones, no internet, no power grids. Bushrangers are popping up again—robbery gangs and loners. Desperate people doing desperate things. Police and military are about all that's left keeping some semblance of order. We're stretched thin, but we're holding."

Julian frowned. "But why analog? Why did the RAAF keep using it?"

Flynn tilted his head as if surprised by the question. "Always been a contingency. Digital's great, but it's vulnerable. Analog's harder to kill. Not flashy, but it works." He gestured at their setup. "Like this. Smart thinking, by the way. Shows you've got the kind of grit we're looking for."

Emma narrowed her eyes. "Looking for?"

Flynn leaned against the wall, his posture casual but tone heavy with intent. "We're rebuilding. Slowly. People like you, resourceful, able to think on their feet—you're exactly the kind of folks we need. You managed to get this thing running and signal us. That's no small feat."

Emma crossed her arms. "And what exactly are you offering in return?"

Flynn gave her a steady look. "Safety. Supplies. A chance to be part of something bigger than surviving day to day. We're working on reconnecting settlements, finding out who's left and what we've got to rebuild with."

Julian exchanged a glance with Emma, uncertainty etched on both their faces.

"And Max?" Emma asked, her voice firm.

Flynn sighed, adjusting the brim of his hat. "That's another thing we'll have to deal with. If he's armed and dangerous, we'll find him. We've seen his type before. The world's full of people who couldn't handle the shift. Some adapt, some don't."

Emma stiffened. "He's not a type. He's our friend. Or he was."

Flynn's expression softened just slightly. "I get it. But if he's a threat, we'll do what we have to. For everyone's sake."

The room fell into a heavy silence, the weight of Flynn's words settling over them.

Finally, Julian cleared his throat. "What happens now?"

Flynn pushed off the wall, straightening his hat. "Now? You keep this thing running. Stay in touch. And when you're ready, we'll talk about next steps." He paused, glancing back at the transmitter. "This thing... it's more than just a signal. You've got the potential to reach people, give them something to hold onto. You ever thought about broadcasting more than just a call for help?"

Julian blinked. "Like what?"

"Music," Flynn suggested. "Stories. News. People need more than food and safety. They need hope. If you've got the means to provide that, you should."

Emma perked up. "You think we could pull that off?"

Flynn shrugged. "With the right equipment, maybe. We'll see what we can scrounge up. Analog's not exactly lying around in bulk, but we might have something at the base."

Julian nodded slowly, the gears turning in his mind. "It's worth trying. If I can help people keep sane, keep connected..." He hesitated. "But what do we call you? Your operation, I mean."

Flynn smiled faintly. "The peaceful folks around here call us the Diggers. Seemed fitting, given the hat and all. We're not the army we used to be, but we're digging through the rubble, trying to build something new."

Julian smirked at the name, then extended a hand. "Alright, Digger. Let's see what we can do together."

Flynn clasped Julian's hand firmly. "You've got yourself a deal."

As Flynn stepped out, his boots echoing in the hallway, Julian and Emma were left with the quiet hum of their transmitter and a fragile sense of purpose.

Chapter 26: Did That Happen?

The apartment felt strangely quiet after Flynn left, the silence heavier than the hum of the transmitter and the soft buzz of city air filtering through the cracked windows. Julian and Emma sat on the worn-out couch, staring at the transmitter as if it might speak first.

Emma broke the silence. "Did that just happen?"

Julian laughed nervously, running a hand through his messy hair. "Apparently. I guess we're… part of some military-cowboy operation now?"

Emma smirked, hugging her knees. "And they want us to broadcast... what exactly? Hope? Music? Like we're the new age public radio?"

Julian leaned forward, resting his elbows on his knees. "Honestly? I don't even know. I mean, when I set this thing up, it wasn't supposed to be a full-blown operation. Just a beacon, something to find other people. Now it's... bigger."

Emma studied his face. "You don't sound totally against it."

He hesitated, then turned to look at her. "I'm not. It's just... a lot. Flynn showing up, the Diggers, the idea of us being some kind of station for people to tune into." He shook his head, smiling faintly. "Never thought I'd be on the other side of the mic."

Emma grinned. "Living the dream, huh? Julian Hayes, radio star. Just had to wait for the apocalypse to make it happen."

Julian chuckled, but his smile faded. "It's not just a joke, though, is it? People need something. Music, news, even just a voice telling them they're not alone. We could be that."

Emma leaned back, her gaze drifting to the ceiling. "It's a lot of pressure. What if we screw it up?"

Julian gave a dry laugh. "Emma, I don't think there's a guidebook for this. We're already making it up as we go. Besides, you've always been the one to keep me from screwing up."

Emma glanced at him, her expression softening. "So, what? We just keep doing what we're doing? Except now we've got the military listening in?"

"Apparently." Julian sighed. "But if we're going to do this, we'll need to step it up. Better gear, more power. Maybe even... I don't know, an actual show plan?"

Emma laughed, the sound light and genuine for the first time in days. "You? A planner? That's a good one."

Julian grinned, nudging her. "Hey, I'm serious. If we're going to help people, we've got to do it right. And we can't just play Johnny Cash on repeat."

Emma tilted her head, mock thoughtful. "I don't know. 'Ring of Fire' on loop might not be the worst thing."

They both laughed, the tension easing for a moment. After the laughter died down, Emma spoke again, her tone more serious. "Do you think we're ready for this? If Flynn comes through, people will actually be relying on us."

Julian met her gaze. "I don't know if we're ready. But I do know one thing."

"What's that?"

He smiled faintly. "We're not doing this alone. And if there's anyone I'd want by my side trying to pull off an apocalypse radio station, it's you."

Emma rolled her eyes to deflect the warmth rising to her cheeks. "Flattery will get you nowhere, Hayes."

Julian smirked. "Worth a shot."

The hum of the transmitter filled the room as they sat together, their shared determination sparking something new—something steady, something hopeful.

Chapter 27:

A week had passed, and the hum of the transmitter now felt like an old friend. Julian and Emma sat at the small table in the corner of the apartment, slurping down two-minute noodles with all the enthusiasm one could muster when eating the same thing every day for breakfast. Like the noodles, their conversation was quick and comforting—another part of their new routine.

Julian paused between bites, looking down at his bowl, deep in thought. "You know," he said, his voice laced with nostalgia, "remember Fallout 3? With Three Dog and the whole radio thing?"

Emma looked up, raising an eyebrow. "You mean the guy who always had something to say about the Wasteland? Yeah, I remember him. Always got on my nerves, but at least it was something to listen to while scavenging."

Julian grinned. "Right? And then there was Mr. New Vegas in Fallout: New Vegas. That guy had style. Smooth voice, a little quirky, but he made the whole desert feel a little more... alive." He paused, tapping his fingers on the table as he furrowed his brow. "But what was that other one in Fallout 5? Or was it 6? Maybe 7? You know, the one with the guy who just played music all day long, and no one knew who he really was?"

Emma took a slow slurp of her noodles before shaking her head. "I dunno, I can't remember. But I get what you mean—those characters, their voices...

made it feel like the world wasn't completely gone. It was like they were still holding on to the past, trying to make something of it."

Julian nodded, lost in thought. "Exactly. I mean, this is us now. We're the ones broadcasting into the void. Just... no crazy post-apocalyptic music stars to back us up."

Emma chuckled. "Right. We're pretty much just a couple of weirdos with a transmitter and a stockpile of noodles."

Just then, a crackle over the radio interrupted their conversation. Julian leaned over, adjusting the dials on their makeshift receiver. A familiar voice came through, clear and steady.

"Julian, Emma, you out there? This is Flynn."

Julian's face lit up as he recognized the voice. "Flynn? Is that you?"

"Yeah, it's me," Flynn responded, his voice sounding surprisingly upbeat. "I hope you two are still kicking. Got some news for you."

Emma leaned closer, intrigued. "What's up, Flynn?"

"We've been monitoring your broadcast," Flynn said, a hint of amusement in his voice, "and we've got something that might help. We know where you're at, and we're sending a truck your way in a day or so. Along with a couple of fresh supplies, and—get this—some music gear."

Julian's eyebrows shot up. "Music gear? You're kidding."

Flynn chuckled. "Nope. A full music player setup, and we've got a stash of CDs, records, and hard drives packed with tracks. All compatible with your equipment, so you'll be able to play anything you want. We're bringing it all, plus a new solar generator to help with that makeshift battery you've been running on."

"Flynn, you're a lifesaver," Julian said, his voice filled with excitement. "We've been starving for new content, something to break the silence. Music... real music... That's going to be a game-changer."

"You're welcome," Flynn replied. "It's not much, but it'll make things easier. Plus, having a truck will help with the supplies. We'll be there soon, just hang tight."

"Got it," Julian said, already feeling the weight of the past week lift off his shoulders. "We'll be waiting. Thanks again, Flynn. We won't let you down."

"You won't need to," Flynn responded with a laugh. "Just keep that signal strong. We're all listening."

With that, the transmission ended, leaving only the soft crackling of static in the room. Julian looked at Emma, his smile wide.

"They're really coming," he said, almost in disbelief.

Emma laughed, shaking her head. "This is almost too good to be true."

Julian leaned back in his chair, looking at the transmitter. "This could be it. This could be the thing that finally gets us on the map. With real music, new supplies, and a truck... we might actually make this station work. Maybe we can even connect with more people out there."

Emma grinned. "All this from noodles and a nostalgia trip."

Julian shrugged. "Sometimes the universe gives you what you need when you least expect it."

They sat there, the quiet settling in again, but the air felt different this time. There was something to look forward to now. Something real.

"One day at a time, right?" Emma said, her eyes gleaming.

"One day at a time," Julian agreed, already thinking ahead to what was coming next.

Chapter 28:

The days stretched on, each one bringing them closer to the arrival of the truck and the supplies Flynn promised. In the meantime, Julian had decided it was time to get serious about their station's voice. He hadn't spoken on a podcast in what felt like an eternity, and though he still had the rhythm of it in his head, it was different now—rawer, less polished. The weight of the world had a way of altering even the most familiar skills.

One morning, Julian stood in front of the makeshift transmitter, the soft hum of the equipment filling the air. He cleared his throat, his voice tentative as it filled the room.

"This is Julian Hayes, and you're listening to the only broadcast that's still going strong in the wasteland... or at least, we're trying to be. It's been a while, folks, and we've all had our share of... well, let's just call it 'time apart' from the airwaves, huh?"

He chuckled, but it sounded forced. He paused, running a hand through his hair, trying to shake off the awkwardness.

"Anyway, here we are, still here, talking to no one and everyone at the same time, trying to connect with what's left of the world. If you're out there, really out there, you know what it's like. We're all a little broken, a little scraped up, but maybe—just maybe—there's still a little bit of hope in the air."

He took a breath, then tried again, this time with more confidence.

"Okay, okay. Let's try that again, but with a little more flair." Julian grinned to himself, already laughing at the thought of trying to sound like the iconic voices he admired in the Fallout broadcasts.

He tried again, a bit more exaggerated this time. "Alright, folks, buckle in! This is Julian Hayes, coming to you live from the wasteland with the only station that's still fighting to keep the music alive! If you're stuck in the middle of nowhere with nothing but dust, ruins, and... well, maybe a bushranger or two trying to make life harder—don't worry. You're not alone. This station is all you've got."

Emma, who had been quietly watching from the kitchen counter, leaned against the doorframe with a mischievous grin on her face. "I think you're ready, but you know what would make it better?" she said, stepping into the room.

Julian raised an eyebrow. "What's that?"

"You need a sponsor announcement. A little touch of that post-apocalyptic charm."

Julian laughed, shaking his head. "You think so? Alright, hit me with your best shot. Let's see what you've got."

Emma smirked and walked up to the mic, adjusting it with exaggerated care. She paused for dramatic effect, then leaned in, her voice smooth and a little playful as she spoke into the transmitter.

"If there's an issue, a bushranger getting you down, or maybe you've just had one too many run-ins with the local wildlife, don't stress. The local digger is here to help! That's right, folks. You've got a problem, and the diggers have a solution. Whether it's a busted vehicle, a broken-down shelter, or just a wild pack of scorpions that need a little... recalibration—the diggers are your go-to crew for getting things back on track. Find your nearest digger, and remember: they're here to help. No task too big, no bushranger too stubborn."

Julian burst out laughing. "I think you've got a future in radio, Emma."

She shrugged, smiling smugly. "What can I say? I've got a knack for selling things." She gave a mock bow, then stepped back from the mic. "Your turn, Julian. Let's see if you can top that."

Julian grinned, adjusting his posture and trying to sound more professional as he leaned into the microphone. "This is Julian Hayes, coming to you live from... wherever we are, still holding onto whatever fragments of civilization remain. If you've been surviving long enough to hear this broadcast, you're already doing better than most. But don't worry—we're here to help keep you going, one song and story at a time. Stay tuned, folks. We've got more coming your way."

Emma nodded approvingly. "Better. Much better."

Julian laughed. "I'll get there. It's just... you know, it's different when you're talking into a void, but I think I've still got it."

Emma grabbed a cup of water from the counter, raising it in a mock toast. "To the voice of the wasteland. May it carry farther than we can see."

"To the voice of the wasteland," Julian echoed, clinking his own cup with hers.

The room settled into a comfortable silence as they continued to practice and tweak their broadcasts. Julian was starting to feel it—there was something about speaking into the airwaves that felt right, even if the world outside was still dark and silent. Maybe the voice would help bridge the gap, maybe it wouldn't. But it was worth trying. And, if nothing else, it kept them both feeling connected to something larger than their small, makeshift world.

Chapter 29:

The sound of an approaching truck broke the quiet monotony of their days. Julian and Emma had been busy organizing their makeshift station when the rumble of a vehicle drew their attention. They both jumped to their feet, excitement flickering in their eyes as they rushed toward the apartment's entrance.

Through the window, they could just make out a familiar figure—Flynn, accompanied by another digger. The truck pulled into the parking lot, its engine coughing and sputtering as it came to a stop. The two men jumped out, and Julian and Emma quickly made their way down the stairs to meet them.

"Hey there, Julian! Emma!" Flynn called out, waving with a broad grin. "Sorry it took a bit longer than expected, but we made it. Supplies are in the truck, and I've got a generator here to help you guys out. And this," he said, motioning to the music player strapped to the back of the truck, "should help you get the station sounding a lot better."

"Flynn!" Julian said, shaking his hand with enthusiasm. "It's good to see you, mate. You weren't kidding about the truck. This is a beauty."

The digger, a large, grizzled man with a weathered face, clapped Julian on the shoulder. "Got it in good shape. Should run just fine on the friction engine, no issues with fuel. You've got a good supply for now, but keep an eye on it. No one should get their hands on it. It's a solid ride."

"Thanks," Julian said, looking over the truck with a mix of awe and relief. "We'll take good care of it."

Flynn nodded. "Glad to hear it. Now, let's get these supplies unloaded." He gestured to the back of the truck, where boxes of canned goods, water, and other essentials were stacked high. The generator sat beside them, looking bulky but sturdy.

The digger set to work immediately, unpacking the generator and carefully setting it up in a corner of the room, where a small space had been cleared. The hum of the engine kicked in, and the lights flickered on, a welcomed sign of progress.

Flynn and Julian stepped aside, watching him work with efficiency. "Once it's up and running, you'll have no trouble charging whatever you need, and your transmitter should be stable now," Flynn said with a satisfied nod. "You're good to go on that front."

After a moment, the digger stepped back, wiping his brow. "All set. Should be good for a long while. If there's any issue, just let us know."

Julian couldn't help but feel a wave of gratitude. "Mate, you're a lifesaver."

"Yeah, thanks," Emma added with a smile. "We really appreciate it."

Flynn chuckled, grabbing a couple of cold cans from a cooler in the truck. He tossed one to Julian, then another to Emma. "No worries, folks. We're all in this together, right?"

They clinked their cans together in a silent toast, each of them feeling the weight of everything that had led to this moment. For a few seconds, the tension of the world outside faded into the background.

"Well, we'd better head out," Flynn said after a pause. "We've got a few more stops to make, and you two deserve some peace and quiet. Enjoy the truck, the supplies, and the tunes. Just don't go messing with the engine too much. It's a friction engine, so it should run without a hitch for the foreseeable future."

Julian laughed, his fingers already itching to explore the truck. "Don't worry, we'll keep our hands off it. Thanks again, Flynn."

Flynn smiled and turned to leave, his footsteps echoing in the hall as the digger followed suit. "Take care, you two. We'll check in soon. Don't let anything get too crazy while we're gone."

As they left, Julian and Emma made their way back upstairs. The apartment felt a little more like home now—there was power, the promise of comfort, and, for the first time in days, a bit of normalcy creeping back in.

Inside, Julian eagerly tore into the boxes, pulling out stacks of CDs, records, and even a few well-worn cassettes. The sight of them brought a wave of nostalgia, even though most of the bands inside were from an era past theirs. It didn't matter.

"Look at this," Julian said, pulling out a classic Cold Chisel album. "These guys... they've got soul."

Emma leaned over, scanning the titles. "I think my dad used to listen to these guys," she said, grinning. "And Icehouse... that's a name I haven't heard in a while."

Julian held up a Johnny Cash album, raising an eyebrow in mock surprise. "I didn't expect to find the Man in Black in here. But hell, if we're doing this, we might as well do it right."

They sat down on the floor, flipping through the collection. As the music player hummed to life, the opening strains of "Working Class Man" by Jimmy Barnes filled the apartment. They both paused, letting the familiar rhythms take over.

"Bit past our generation, but…" Emma shrugged, her smile softening. "It's got charm."

Julian nodded. "Yeah. It's good music. Real music."

The tunes rolled on—old Aussie rock, soulful ballads, and even some Johnny Cash to boot. They laughed, reminisced, and let the sound of the past fill their space, at least for a little while.

It wasn't the world they once knew, but it was something. And that was enough for now.

Chapter 30:

———————⋙❧⋘———————

Max stumbled through the desolate streets; his eyes glazed over as he tried to focus on the dim shapes moving in the periphery. He could hear the crackling of distant fires, the clink of bottles from his bag, and the familiar sound of his last escape. The air smelled like ash and decay, a constant reminder of everything he had lost.

Once, he had been a soldier in the Australian Army before being a producer on the podcast at DisruptTech! —a protector. A man with a purpose. Now, he was nothing more than a shadow, a wreck of what he used to be. The thrill of battle had dulled, replaced by a gnawing emptiness that no drink could fill.

He hadn't set out to become a raider. It wasn't some grand plan—just survival. But somewhere along the way, the violence had become part of him. It was easier, he told himself. Easier than facing the reality of what the world had become. Easier than the constant memories of comrades lost, of a world that had slipped through his fingers like sand.

Max's footsteps slowed as he passed the remnants of a burnt-out building. The flicker of a fire in the distance caught his attention, and he knew it was only a matter of time before he reached the others. The raider camp was nearby, their territory marked by makeshift barricades and the smell of cheap liquor. It was where he belonged now, where his mind had twisted him into a beast that prowled the outskirts of the crumbling city.

He hadn't thought about Emma and Julian in weeks. They had been a part of his past—something distant, a life he barely remembered. They were survivors, clinging to a thread of hope in the ruins. He was something different now. A predator. A man who had traded his humanity for a bottle, for fleeting moments of numbness.

The sound of laughter echoed from the camp, low and cruel. The raiders were already drunk, or perhaps high—he didn't care anymore. He was no different than them now. Just another lost soul walking a path he didn't know how to leave.

Max entered the camp, greeted by the usual insults and jeers. The leader, a grizzled man named Moody, was sitting on an overturned crate, taking swigs from a large bottle of something that reeked of cheap rum. He looked up as Max approached, squinting through bloodshot eyes.

"Max, you alive?" Moody sneered, tossing him a bottle. "Come join the party. You look like shit, but I'm sure you've got room for more."

Max didn't answer. He just took the bottle, cracked it open, and drank deeply, the burn in his throat momentarily drowning out the voices in his head. The rest of the raiders gathered around, their faces a mixture of boredom and cruelty. They didn't care about him, not really. Not like they used to.

They passed the bottle around, laughing as they shared their brief escape from the desolation surrounding them. But Max couldn't shake the feeling that something was missing. He had no idea when it had started—this void, this emptiness. It used to be filled with purpose, with comradeship. Now, it was just the alcohol, the violence, and the endless cycle of survival.

"Max," one of the younger raiders said, his voice slurred. " Have you ever thought about what happened to the others? The ones who used to fight with us?"

Max's eyes flickered toward him, the question hitting a nerve. He thought about the old crew—the ones who had kept their heads above water and made it out when the rest fell apart. Emma. Julian. He hadn't heard their names in so long.

But there was nothing left for him in that world. Not anymore.

"Forget them," Max muttered, tossing the bottle back to Digger. "It's too late for that now. All that matters is what we do next."

The words felt hollow even as they left his mouth. He could barely recognize himself or remember the man he used to be. The raider's life was all he knew now. The thrill of the kill, the moments of drunken oblivion—it was all that kept him from facing the reality of his decay.

He turned away from the group and stumbled toward the outskirts of the camp. The others didn't notice. They were too lost in their indulgence, too consumed by their self-destruction to care.

Max collapsed on the edge of the camp, his back against a pile of wreckage. The sky above was dark, the stars barely visible through the smoke and haze that filled the air. He cracked open another bottle and stared at the city's distant lights, wondering if anyone else was out there, still holding on to something.

It didn't matter. Nothing mattered anymore. Not the people he had left behind, not the world that had crumbled. All that was left was the alcohol, the numbness, the endless spiral downward.

He closed his eyes, letting the darkness take over.

Max sat in the darkness, the bottle pressed to his lips, trying to escape the thoughts gnawing at him. The distant sounds of the raiders faded, but the emptiness inside him only grew. It was a familiar ache he didn't know how to fix. It had been so long since he'd felt anything like purpose.

His thoughts were interrupted by the sound of boots crunching on gravel. He jerked his head up, trying to focus through the haze of alcohol. The shadowy figures moved closer, their steps deliberate and slow.

Flynn.

Max's pulse quickened as he recognized the man's distinctive gait, the very same person who had crossed paths with him weeks ago. Alongside Flynn was another figure—someone bigger, familiar but not quite.

The figure's posture was rigid, military. A digger.

Max's heart dropped into his stomach as Flynn's voice called out in the night, his tone sharp but carrying no fear. "Max, right? Thought that was you."

Max's hand gripped the bottle tighter, but he didn't respond. He didn't want to and wasn't sure if he could, not in his state.

Flynn stopped a few paces away, taking in Max's disheveled appearance. "What the hell happened to you?" His words weren't harsh, but there was a note of disappointment in them. The kind of disappointment that made Max feel like a failure. It cut deeper than any of the jeers from the raiders.

Max stood up slowly, swaying slightly. "What do you want, Flynn? Thought you'd be busy saving the world."

Flynn's eyes narrowed, and the digger beside him crossed his arms, scanning the surroundings. They weren't just here for a chat. Max could feel it.

"I'm not here to lecture you, Max," Flynn said, his voice softer now but firm. "But we've got orders. We've been tracking you for a while. You've crossed a line. You're a bushranger now, and that's not something we can ignore. You've been causing trouble, hurting people."

Max's gaze dropped to the ground, and he clenched his jaw. "I didn't hurt anyone," he muttered, but even he could hear the lie in his voice.

Flynn wasn't fooled. "That's not how it works. You're part of the problem now, Max. You've become a danger to everyone around you."

Max looked up at Flynn, a fire of anger in his eyes. He hated being lectured and reminded of everything he had lost. "What? Do you think you're some kind of savior now? You're just another one of them— pretending to be better than the rest of us."

The digger stepped forward, his hand on his weapon, but Flynn held him back. Flynn's face softened, almost regretful, but it didn't change the reality of the situation.

"You don't have to keep doing this, Max. You can come with us. We'll get you help. It's not too late."

Max felt a cold sweat forming on his brow. The alcohol buzz was wearing off, and the clarity was creeping in. He was trapped, but the idea of returning to being someone else—someone who wasn't broken—made his skin crawl. He wasn't that man anymore. The man who fought for something. The man who had a cause.

The man who cared.

"You can't stop me, Flynn," Max spat. "You don't know what it's like out here. You think you can just walk in and save me? Well, you're too late."

Flynn didn't say anything for a long moment. He just looked at Max, his expression pained. "I'm not trying to save you, Max. I'm trying to stop you from destroying yourself. And right now, you're the only one who can choose what happens next."

Max's chest tightened, but before he could respond, the digger quickly grabbed Max by the arm with a force that stunned him. The raider's instinct kicked in, but he was too drunk, too slow.

He tried to pull away, but Flynn's hand was on his shoulder, holding him steady, grounding him. "Max," Flynn said again, his voice low and firm. "You're coming with us."

Max fought the urge to scream, to lash out, but something in Flynn's eyes stopped him. Maybe it was the pity. It could be the finality. Whatever it was, Max knew. This was the end of his road. This was when the world that had swallowed him whole finally spat him back out.

They marched him out of the raider camp, past the people who didn't care, past the fires that had burned everything good inside him. As they walked through the night, the only sound was the crunch of boots on gravel.

"Don't make it worse, Max," Flynn said, his voice rough but resolute. "Come quietly. We're not your enemy."

Max didn't respond. His head hung low as they approached the truck. It was over. The fight, the anger, the hopelessness. Everything he'd become.

As they loaded him into the back of the truck, Max's gaze lifted momentarily, catching the flicker of light in the distance. He thought he saw something—a small flicker of hope. But it was too far away..

Chapter 31:

The transmitter hum filled the air, a comforting, familiar sound after days of practice. Julian sat at the desk, his fingers hovering over the buttons, ready to hit "Go" on their first official broadcast. Emma sat beside him, her notebook open, scribbling down last-minute thoughts for breaks and announcements.

"Ready?" Julian asked, looking over at her with excitement and nerves.

Emma nodded, her expression steady but with a spark of anticipation. "Let's do this."

Julian took a deep breath and switched the microphone on.

"Good morning, or whatever time it is where you are," he said, his voice tentative initially but growing more confident. "This is Julian Hayes, and welcome to the first official broadcast from the Wasteland Station. A station for the survivors, the dreamers, and everyone still out there who needs to hear a voice from the old world."

He paused momentarily, glancing at Emma, who gave him an encouraging nod.

"We're here to keep you company, to play music, to talk about the things that matter, and, well, to remind you that even in the ruins of the world, there's still life left in us."

Emma took over for a moment, her voice warm and grounded. "Today, we've got a mix of old favorites and hidden gems—songs that remind us of the world that was. It might be a bit of a trip down memory lane, but we're all in this together, and we've got plenty of tunes to help us remember the good times. We'll also be sharing updates, stories, and hopefully some laughs. But for now, let's get into it."

Julian leaned forward, hitting the button to play the first track of the day—a song that resonated with both of them. A classic that had once echoed through city streets, now a symbol of a time long gone, they let the music fill the airwaves, a bridge between the past and the present.

Throughout the day, they alternated between songs and announcements. Emma would chime in with breaks, chatting about the current state of the world, reminding listeners of the supplies they had available, and even mentioning a sponsor here and there. It was surreal to have a semblance of normalcy again, even if only through a makeshift radio station.

As the evening approached, they neared the end of their first full day on the air. Julian sat back, adjusting the mic as he spoke into it, feeling more comfortable now, like he was reconnecting with something he'd almost forgotten.

"And that's a wrap for today," Julian said, his voice carrying the moment's weight. "Before we sign off, I want to play one last song. This one, I found while going through some old music files. It's from a game that was in development before all of this happened. A game called Eclipse Reborn. The man behind it—well, his name was Trent Lawson."

He paused, a flicker of something crossing his face—perhaps the weight of lost dreams or simply the echo of the old world.

"Trent had this ambition to create something new. A world, a future—like something out of fiction. I remember reading about it, and back then, it seemed like a crazy dream. A game, a new world. But now? Now it feels like it was closer to the truth than any of us realized."

Julian took a breath, looking down at the turntable where the vinyl spun. "I don't know if Trent's out there listening—if he's still fighting for that future he imagined—but if you are, Trent, I hope you remember this: You matter. Like everyone else. We're all still here, fighting to build something new from the ashes."

He nodded to Emma, who gave him a quiet, understanding smile. The song began to play, its opening notes familiar, nostalgic, and bittersweet. It was a tribute to the dreams of those who had tried to rebuild what was lost.

As the last notes faded away, Julian leaned back in his chair, the sound of silence settling between them.

"Tomorrow, we'll be back," he said softly, slightly smiling. "One day at a time, right?"

Emma nodded. "One day at a time."

The transmitter hummed on; their voices no longer echoed in the air but as a lifeline. As they sat there in the fading light of the day, it felt like they weren't just surviving anymore. They were living. And maybe—just maybe—they were part of something bigger than themselves.

Chapter 32:

The final track faded into the station's quiet hum, the last note lingering in the air before it dissipated. Julian sat still, his hand resting on the console. He reached over and switched off the recording, the screen blinking once before the soft glow of the radio station's equipment became the only light in the room.

For a moment, neither of them spoke. The weight of the day hung between them—there had been so much that happened, so much they'd shared. Music, memories, their voices reaching out into the unknown, hoping to find anyone listening. But it was more than just a broadcast; it was something deeper, something real.

A single tear rolled down Julian's cheek, unnoticed at first by him, but Emma saw it. She reached out, her fingers gently brushing the tear away before it could fall any further.

Julian's chest tightened and felt like he couldn't breathe momentarily. It was as if the emotions of the day, of everything that had led them to this point, all hit him at once. He had fought hard to hold onto hope, keep going, and push through everything. But in that quiet moment, he allowed himself to feel it all—the exhaustion, the loss, the fear, and, most of all, the love.

Emma moved closer, wrapping her arms around him and pulling him into her embrace. Julian leaned into her, his forehead resting against hers. The weight of the world and everything they'd endured seemed a little lighter in her arms.

For a long time, they sat like that, not speaking, just holding each other. For a while, the world outside seemed distant and irrelevant. At that moment, they were the only two people who mattered, the only two who knew what it felt like to keep going when everything else was falling apart.

Finally, Emma whispered, her voice soft but steady, "I love you, Julian."

The words hung between them, a confession that felt like a promise, a truth waiting to be spoken. Julian's heart swelled with emotion, and he pulled her even closer as if afraid the moment would slip away.

"I love you too," he said, his voice thick with the weight of it all. "More than anything."

Emma smiled, her hand gently caressing his back. "We're going to make it, Julian. Together."

Julian closed his eyes, the warmth of her touch grounding him, and for the first time in a long while, he felt like maybe—just maybe—they could make it. They had each other. And that was enough.

A sense of peace washed over them as they stayed there, wrapped in the room's quiet. The world outside was still broken, still uncertain. But in that small, makeshift station, in their little corner of the world, they had everything they needed to keep going.

And for the first time in a long time, Julian felt like the future, whatever it might hold, was worth facing—because he wasn't facing it alone.

Chapter 33:

The weight of the world outside felt miles away as Julian and Emma sat at the small table in the corner of the room. A single lamp cast a soft glow over the space, giving the apartment a warmth it hadn't had in what felt like forever. The radio station, the transmitter, and everything outside this moment seemed distant, almost irrelevant. Here, it was just them, the flickering candle between them and the two beers they were savoring in the quiet of their small sanctuary.

It had been a long day—full of work, anticipation, and the highs of their first official broadcast. But now, the tension had dissolved. The laughter, the nervous glances, and the shared feeling of accomplishment and hope all mingled in the air around them.

"Here's to us," Julian said, raising his beer. The clink of the bottles was almost symbolic, a quiet declaration of everything they had just been through and everything they were still going to face together.

"To us," Emma echoed, her eyes meeting his over the rim of her bottle.

They sat back, sipping slowly. The simple pleasure of the moment felt like a luxury they hadn't known in a long time. But it wasn't just the beer or the fact that they were drinking without the looming shadow of survival that made it special. It was the connection, sharing something, and having this moment together. For once, the world felt... right.

And then, as if they were both thinking the same thing, Julian stood up. He moved to the makeshift stove, and Emma raised an eyebrow.

"Are you serious?" she asked, laughing softly.

He turned with a grin. "I think it's time for a real meal."

Emma couldn't help but laugh, but the thought of something other than instant noodles, beans on toast, or whatever scraps they had scavenged felt like a dream. She watched in fascination as Julian opened a small tin and began working his magic. He had found a small stash of canned goods earlier, and the thought of something resembling a real meal—just the idea—made her stomach flutter.

Moments later, the smell of freshly cooked food filled the air, and Julian brought over two plates. On them were what looked like the most luxurious baked beans on toast either of them had ever seen. The beans were rich and creamy, the toast just the right kind of crispy, and even a few herbs had been sprinkled on top.

They just stared at the plates for a moment, wide-eyed in disbelief.

Emma couldn't stop herself from laughing. "This is... this is heaven," she whispered, taking a tentative bite.

Julian sat across from her, savoring his first bite like a rare delicacy. "I never thought I'd say this, but baked beans on toast has never tasted this good."

They both chuckled at the simplicity of it all, but neither of them had felt the taste—the warmth, comfort—in a long time. They ate slowly, savoring every bite, their laughter echoing softly in the apartment.

It wasn't just the food that felt luxurious. It was the moment—the quiet, shared experience. It felt like a first date, something they had never truly had. They had been so focused on survival, on pushing through, that they hadn't taken the time to slow down and enjoy each other's company. But now, they were here, in this space, and it felt like the most natural thing in the world.

Once the meal was finished, Julian moved the plates to the side and returned to his seat. Emma leaned back in her chair, her eyes meeting his. There was something unspoken between them now—a deeper understanding, a connection that had always been there but was only beginning to bloom fully.

Without another word, Julian stood, extending his hand to Emma. She hesitated for only a moment before taking it. He pulled her gently into his arms, his touch soft but firm, as if he had waited a lifetime for this moment.

And then, it happened. A kiss. Slow at first, tentative, as if testing the waters. But it didn't take long for the passion for rising, for the kiss to deepen, to become something more. Their hands moved instinctively as if they couldn't get close enough, as if they had been waiting for this for so long.

Their kisses became more urgent and desperate, as if the world around them no longer mattered. The weight of the past, the pain of the present, and the uncertainty of the future seemed to fade away in the warmth of their embrace.

They stumbled toward Julian's bed, their bodies tangled together. Neither cared about the chaos outside, the world that had fallen apart. For now, this was all that mattered. They fell onto the bed, their movements slow at first, then quickening as if they both couldn't hold back anymore.

The world outside was gone, and it was just them. No radio broadcast, no worries about survival. Just two people, lost in each other's arms, finally allowing themselves the moment they had both been craving.

When it was over, they lay together, still tangled in each other's embrace. Their breathing slowed, the weight of the day finally lifting, leaving behind a peaceful stillness. Julian held Emma close; his arm draped protectively over her as they drifted asleep.

It wasn't just the meal, the kiss, or even the making of love that made this moment special. It was the fact that they had found something to hold on to—a small piece of normalcy in a world that had lost so much.

And as they slept, wrapped in each other's arms, they knew that whatever the world had in store for them, they would face it together.

Chapter 34:

The sunlight streamed softly through the curtains, casting a warm glow across the room. Julian's eyes fluttered open, the light a gentle wake-up call that felt like a calm after the storm. He shifted slightly, noticing how the cool morning air contrasted with the warmth of the bed. Then, as his mind cleared, he became aware of Emma's chest's gentle rise and fall beside him.

He froze momentarily, the night's events before rushing back in waves. The intimacy, the quiet connection they'd shared—it all felt like a dream.

His eyes traced the outline of Emma's face, soft in sleep; her lips parted in peaceful slumber.

Then, slowly, he realized something else. They were both naked, their bodies intertwined under the covers. A small grin tugged at the corner of his lips. He couldn't help but feel a mix of tenderness and awe, the night having unfolded into something beyond anything he could've imagined.

Emma stirred beside him as if on cue, a soft sound escaping her lips before she blinked her eyes open. She stretched slightly, then turned toward him with a smile that reached her eyes.

"Good morning," she murmured, her voice soft but full of warmth, before pressing a gentle kiss to his lips.

Julian chuckled softly and returned the kiss with a smile. "Good morning, indeed," he said, his voice thick with affection.

However, the peaceful moment didn't last long as a familiar crackling sound filled the air. The radio transmitter that had become a constant part of their daily routine buzzed. Julian's heart skipped a beat, knowing they were about to shift back into reality.

Emma raised an eyebrow, a mischievous glint in her eyes as she sat up slightly, her body warm next to his.

"Guess we're back to work," she said, grinning as Julian reached for the transmitter. He turned the dial, and then Flynn's voice came through clearly, cutting through the quiet morning like a beacon.

"Julian, Emma, you two there? Come in, over," Flynn's voice crackled through the speaker, a slight pause before he continued. "Got a couple updates for you before you go on air. We had someone come by the RAAF base, a guy named Trent. Says he's heard your broadcast and wants to meet the people behind the radio. Don't know if that's something you want to do, but thought you should know."

Julian raised an eyebrow at the mention of Trent. He didn't recognize the name immediately, but something about it sounded familiar. The brief mention of a meeting piqued his curiosity. They rarely got such requests, especially from someone close enough to the military to visit the base.

Before he could respond, Flynn's voice became more serious this time.

"And, uh, we found your friend, Max," Flynn said. "Or, as the locals are calling him now… 'Mad Max.' Apparently, he's been causing some trouble, but we've got him under control. Thought you'd want to know."

Julian's heart skipped a beat at the mention of Max. He had hoped that Max might be alright, but hearing his name now—especially with the "Mad Max" moniker attached—sent a chill down his spine.

Emma's expression shifted, concern flashing across her face. Julian could feel the tension in the air, both from the news and the weight of everything that had happened over the past few days.

"We'll be on air in about an hour," Flynn added, breaking the silence. "I'll keep the truck parked near the usual spot. Let me know if you want to meet up, over."

"Roger that, Flynn," Julian replied, his voice steady but his mind racing. "We'll be ready. And thanks for the updates."

The transmission ended with a soft click, and the room fell into an almost unnerving silence. Julian sat back, staring at the radio transmitter for a moment longer. The mention of Trent and Max had both thrown him for a loop. What was it about Trent that was so familiar? And Max—what had happened to him to earn that name, "Mad Max"?

Emma gently placed a hand on his shoulder, her touch a grounding presence. "We've got this, Jules," she said, her voice reassuring. We'll figure it all out."

Julian turned to her, taking in the soft understanding in her eyes. She was right. Whatever came next, they'd face it together.

He smiled faintly, leaning in to kiss her once more before the rush of reality set in again. They had a broadcast to prepare for, and things were about to get even more interesting.

Chapter 35:

The day began with a new sense of energy that both Julian and Emma could feel coursing through their veins. After a quick breakfast of some of their last stash of two-minute noodles, they dressed, preparing for the day's broadcast. The excitement in the air was undeniable. They weren't just surviving anymore—they were making something real, something lasting.

As they set up the equipment in their makeshift studio, the familiar hum of the transmitter filled the room. They exchanged a glance, both knowing that today felt different. This wasn't just about playing music anymore. It was about sharing their story, world, and journey with whoever listened.

Julian cleared his throat and adjusted the microphone. Emma gave him a thumbs-up from across the room, settling into her seat, ready to chip in when needed. Julian turned the dial, and the soft buzz of the transmitter clicked before his voice rang out clearly.

"Good morning, world!" Julian's voice was bright and full of energy, and the excitement was contagious. "Welcome back to the airwaves, where we're still playing the hits, sharing the stories, and—"

Emma leaned in, grinning at the mic. "And having a laugh, of course. It's another day in paradise, folks."

Julian laughed, his heart light as he continued. "You might notice a little more energy today. That's because, believe it or not, we might have a guest joining us soon—someone who's been off the radar for a while. Stay tuned for that update in the next few days. You don't want to miss it."

They played a song to transition into the next segment, and the upbeat melody filled the airwaves. Julian and Emma exchanged a quick smile before Julian continued speaking into the mic, his tone shifting to something more reflective.

"Now, onto some news that's closer to home. We've got an update on the bushranger we've been hearing rumors about, a name that's been causing some stir lately: Mad Max."

Emma nodded as she took a breath. "Yeah, believe it or not, we used to know him. Max was a producer on the podcast we used to host back before... well, before everything changed." She paused, glancing at Julian for a brief second. "We actually saw the decline, you know? Max was part of something bigger, and to see him end up this way—it's… it's hard."

There was a moment of silence, a deep understanding passing between them. Julian's hand hovered near the transmitter as his voice softened.

"It's surreal, really. Back then, we all worked together. We were a team, creating something we thought could change the world. But somewhere along the way, Max lost his way. The world broke in ways we couldn't predict, and it broke him, too. Now, he's a bushranger, causing chaos, living on the edge. But the Max we knew... I don't think he ever intended for things to get this far."

Emma picked up where he left off, her voice steady though it carried a trace of sadness. "It's easy to see how someone could fall through the cracks in a world like this. But we all knew Max and know he's not just 'Mad Max.' He's still that guy we used to know, lost in the madness. I don't know what happens next, but we'll keep an eye on the story."

They both paused momentarily, letting the weight of their words sink in. It was strange to talk about someone they once worked with, now so far removed from their old lives.

"Anyway," Julian continued, pushing the melancholy aside for now. "We'll keep you all updated on that one. For now, let's lift the mood a bit."

With that, they switched back to a more upbeat track, the music spilling into the airwaves, light and energetic. It was a transition back to what they did best: sharing music, laughter, and stories with whoever was listening.

As the day wore on, Julian and Emma kept the broadcast going, taking breaks to joke around, share a few memories, and talk about their favorite music. They played various songs, from old classics to some of the newer tunes they'd been finding in the music boxes Flynn had delivered.

The energy in the room was contagious, and it was impossible not to get caught up in the joy of it all. Despite the chaos outside their little sanctuary, they created something that felt right and made them feel alive again.

As the afternoon wore on, Emma broke in with her sponsor announcement, her voice playful but clear: "If you've got a bushranger on your tail, or you're just in need of a good tune, remember—your local diggers are here to help. And hey, if you're listening in from anywhere, don't forget, we're all in this together."

Julian chuckled, shaking his head in amusement at the sponsor plug, but it didn't stop him from chiming in. "And speaking of tunes, here's a classic for you folks. If you don't know it, you will now."

They played a song, and Julian and Emma sang along by the end, their voices harmonizing imperfectly but happily.

The day passed in a whirlwind of music, laughter, and brief moments of reflection. There were no more calls from the outside world, no more chaos. The steady rhythm of their voices fills the air, offering a small sense of normalcy in an otherwise fractured world.

As the broadcast ended, Julian leaned back in his chair, satisfied but exhausted. Emma grinned at him from across the room, her eyes sparkling with the same energy that had carried them through the day.

"You know," she said, tapping a finger on the desk, "this isn't so bad. I think we could get used to this."

Julian nodded a tired but content smile on his face. "Yeah, me too."

And as the last song of the day played out, they sat in the silence that followed, knowing that despite everything, they were making a difference, even if it was just in their little corner of the world.

Chapter 36: A Poetic First Guest

As the final notes of the day's last song faded out over the airwaves, Julian leaned into the microphone, his voice warm and steady.

"Well, that wraps up today's broadcast, folks. Thanks for tuning in, wherever you are. Stay safe, be kind, and we'll see you tomorrow."

Emma smiled as she reached over to flip off the transmitter. "Another day in the books," she said, leaning back in her chair.

Julian stretched, feeling the pleasant ache of a full day's work. "Not bad for a couple of makeshift DJs."

Just as they started packing up for the night, the soft crackle of the radio broke through the room. A familiar voice came over the static.

"Julian, Emma—Captain Flynn here. You on the line?"

Emma darted to the radio, adjusting the frequency. "We're here, Flynn. What's up?"

Flynn's voice came through clearer now, calm but with a hint of excitement. "I've got something I think you two will be interested in. We've got Trent

Lawson here at Glenbrook Base. He's been asking about you ever since he heard the broadcast."

Julian's eyes widened, his heart skipping a beat. "Trent Lawson?" he repeated, incredulous. "Are you serious?"

"Dead serious," Flynn replied. "We figured you might want him as a guest on your show. If you're keen, we can drop him off tomorrow and pick him up later. Sound good?"

Julian shot Emma an eager look, and she grinned, clearly just as excited. "That sounds... amazing," Julian said, his voice practically trembling with enthusiasm. "Trent Lawson as our first guest? It's almost poetic."

"Thought you might feel that way," Flynn said with a chuckle. "We'll bring him by midday tomorrow. One more thing—just so you know, Max is locked up here at Glenbrook. No need to worry about him causing any more trouble."

Julian exhaled a breath he didn't realize he'd been holding. "That's good to hear. Thanks for the update, Flynn."

"No problem," Flynn replied. "We'll see you tomorrow. Over and out."

The room was quiet again, save for the faint hum of the equipment. Julian turned to Emma, his face a mixture of disbelief and excitement. "Trent Lawson. On our broadcast. Can you believe it?"

Emma laughed, shaking her head. "Not really, but it's happening. I guess the world's got a funny way of working sometimes."

Julian leaned back in his chair, his mind already racing with ideas. "This is huge, Emma. The guy's a visionary. Before everything went to hell, he was trying to create a new world through his game. And now..." He gestured around them, the weight of their reality unspoken but understood.

Emma placed a hand on his shoulder, grounding him. "And now he's stepping into our world," she said softly. "It's going to be a great show."

Julian nodded, a grin spreading across his face. "Yeah, it is. Let's make it one to remember."

Chapter 41: The Eclipse of Trent Lawson

A brisk knock on the door echoed through the quiet space. Julian and Emma exchanged a glance, both nervous and excited. Julian quickly crossed the room, pulling open the door to reveal Captain Flynn standing there, his imposing figure framed by the sunlight. Beside him stood a man Julian almost didn't recognize.

Trent Lawson.

But not the confident visionary he remembered. This Trent seemed smaller somehow, his shoulders hunched, his eyes darting nervously around the room. His hands were shoved deep into the pockets of a worn jacket, and he offered a small, uncertain nod as Flynn clapped him on the back.

"Here he is," Flynn said, his tone warm and encouraging. "Thought I'd make the handoff in person. You're in good hands, Trent. Julian, Emma, I'll be back in a few hours to pick him up."

"Thanks, Flynn," Emma said with a smile.

Flynn tipped his cap and stepped back, leaving Trent in the doorway. Julian stepped aside to let him in, extending a hand.

"Trent," Julian said, his voice steady. "It's been a while."

Trent hesitated before taking the offered hand. His grip was loose, almost hesitant. "Yeah," he murmured. "It has."

Emma offered a reassuring smile as she stepped forward. "Welcome, Trent. Come on in. Make yourself comfortable."

Trent shuffled inside, his movements uncertain, and sat at the edge of a chair as if ready to bolt. Julian closed the door, exchanging a concerned glance with Emma before sitting across from Trent.

"You doing okay?" Julian asked gently.

Trent gave a short laugh, though it lacked any real humor. "I don't know," he admitted. "I guess I'm still... adjusting. It's just... strange being here. With you. I didn't think I'd ever see you again."

Emma poured him a glass of water and handed it to him. "You're safe here, Trent. Take your time. There's no pressure."

Trent nodded, clutching the glass tightly as if it were an anchor. He looked up at Julian, his expression conflicted. "The last time I saw you... was during the interview. The one about Eclipse Reborn. The day the EMP hit."

Julian nodded slowly, memories flooding back. "That was a hell of a day."

"Yeah," Trent said softly. "One moment, we were talking about reshaping reality in a virtual world. The next... reality reshaped itself." He stared into the water, his voice growing quieter. "I thought I was ready for anything. I wasn't. Not for this."

Julian leaned forward, his tone calm and reassuring. "None of us were, Trent. But you're here now. That says a lot."

Trent glanced up, his eyes searching Julian's face. "I don't feel like the same person," he admitted. "Back then, I was so sure of myself. I had all these big ideas, all this ambition. And now..." He trailed off, shaking his head.

Emma sat beside him, her voice gentle. "It's okay to feel that way. The world's changed. We've all changed. But that doesn't mean you don't have something valuable to offer."

"You don't have to be the guy you were before," Julian added. "Just be you. Whatever that looks like now."

Trent's grip on the glass loosened slightly, and he took a slow breath. "Thanks," he said quietly. "I'm... I'm not sure how to do this. Talking. Being... normal."

Emma smiled. "You don't have to figure it all out at once. Just take it one step at a time. And if you're up for it, we'd love to hear what's on your mind when we go on air."

Trent hesitated, then nodded. "Okay," he said, his voice steadier now. "I'll try."

Julian clapped him on the shoulder, a small smile on his lips. "That's all we ask."

As they settled in, Emma and Julian began walking Trent through the setup, talking him through the process and easing his nerves. Slowly but surely, Trent started to relax, his words coming more easily, his confidence returning in small, tentative steps.

By the time they wrapped up their conversation, there was a flicker of the old Trent in his eyes—a glimmer of the man who once dreamed of changing the world.

Chapter 36:

The hum of the transmitter filled the apartment as Julian and Emma sat cross-legged on the floor, surrounded by scattered notes and diagrams. They'd been at it for hours, debating everything from signal ranges to what content might resonate with listeners in a shattered world.

Julian leaned back against the couch. "You know, the last interview I did before... all this was with Trent Lawson."

Emma looked up, tilting her head. "Trent Lawson... the game developer?"

Julian nodded, a faint smile tugging at his lips. "Yeah. He was working on Eclipse Reborn, the next big thing in gaming. I remember thinking at the time it was just another hype machine, but now?" He chuckled dryly. "Feels like he saw all of this coming."

Emma set her notebook down. "Do you think he's still out there? Or anyone else we used to work with?"

Julian shrugged, his expression darkening. "I've been trying not to think about it too much. It's easier that way. But... I don't know. Trent was resourceful. He might have made it. As for the others…" He trailed off, his gaze fixed on a distant point beyond the window.

Emma gave his arm a reassuring squeeze. "If we're here, others might be too. And maybe, if this radio thing works, we'll find them."

Julian glanced at her, his eyes softening. "You think so?"

"I know so," Emma said firmly. "You've got that stubborn kind of optimism. It's contagious."

Julian laughed lightly. "That's one way to put it." He looked back at the transmitter. "It just feels weird, you know? Thinking about everything we left behind. The station, the team... it was my whole world for so long."

Emma nodded. "It was mine too. But the world's changed, and we're still here. Maybe that means we've got a chance to build something new—something better."

Julian met her gaze, a flicker of hope sparking. "You really think we can do that?"

Emma smiled. "I wouldn't still be here if I didn't."

The weight on Julian's chest felt a little lighter for the first time in days. "If Trent's still out there, I'd like to play his game soundtrack on the station. It feels... right. Like a connection to the world we had before."

Emma nodded. "Then we'll do it. One day at a time, right?"

Julian nodded, his resolve hardening. "One day at a time."

The two of them sat together, the apartment's quiet filling the spaces between their thoughts. In that moment, they weren't just survivors—they were dreamers, clinging to the hope that there was still a reason to keep going even in the darkest times.

Chapter 37:

The air crackled with anticipation as Julian and Emma prepared for their first guest broadcast. The energy in the room was palpable, and as Julian adjusted the microphone, Emma gave him an encouraging nod. Trent sat quietly beside them, his hands fidgeting with his jacket and eyes darting nervously.

Julian leaned into the microphone, his voice steady and warm. "Good morning, everyone. This is Julian Hayes, and you're listening to Echoes of the Future. Today's a special day because we have our first-ever guest joining us. He's someone from my past—a man with big dreams and a bigger heart. Please welcome Trent Lawson."

Emma chimed in, her tone light and inviting. "Throughout the day, we'll be chatting with Trent, asking him a few questions, and letting him pick some of the music. No pressure, Trent. Just take it at your own pace."

Trent gave a small, shy smile, leaning into the microphone. "Thanks, Julian. Emma. It's... it's good to be here."

Julian leaned back, letting his tone turn conversational. "First off, let's catch up. Trent, how've you been holding up?"

Trent hesitated, his expression darkening. He cleared his throat, his voice quiet but steady. "I was living in Springwood with my Nan. We managed to hold out for a while. She... she passed a few weeks ago." His voice broke slightly, and he paused, collecting himself. "There wasn't any way to get her medication locally. The diggers hadn't found us yet. I... I was lost for a bit."

Emma reached over, placing a reassuring hand on Trent's shoulder as he continued. "One night, I heard your first broadcast over her old radio. I couldn't believe it—people managing to do this. Then... my name came up. You even played the song from my game." He wiped at his eyes, his voice trembling. "I... I can't tell you what that meant to me. It gave me hope."

Julian's voice softened. "We're glad you're here, Trent. Truly."

Sensing the emotion in the room, Emma smiled and gestured to the music console. "Why don't we take a little breather? Trent, pick the next song."

Trent nodded, his voice still shaky. "RIP by Bring Me the Horizon."

Julian raised an eyebrow, shooting Emma a mock expression of disbelief. "That's... uh, an intense choice for the moment, but alright. Here's RIP by Bring Me the Horizon."

The song played, filling the room with its raw energy. As the last chords faded, Julian leaned back in. "Alright, let's dive into the big one. Trent, back before everything changed, you were working on Eclipse Reborn. Can you tell us a little about it? What was the game going to be?"

Trent's eyes clouded as he thought, his voice quiet at first. "Making games was never easy. We had so many teams—art, design, programming, marketing, QA. It was a huge effort. Eclipse Reborn was supposed to redefine gaming, the way Rockstar did for open worlds, or George Lucas did for... those old Star Wars movies."

His voice grew stronger as he spoke, the passion from his old life bubbling to the surface. "It wasn't just about the gameplay. It was about creating a world people could lose themselves in, a story that stayed with them long after they put the controller down."

Emma leaned forward. "That sounds incredible. It's inspiring, Trent."

He nodded, a faint smile on his lips. "Yeah, but... it's hard knowing no one will ever experience it now. All that work, all those dreams... they're just gone." He paused, his voice softening. "But who knows. Maybe one day, someone will pick up the pieces."

Emma offered him a reassuring smile. "We never know what the future holds."

Trent nodded, and Julian gestured to the console again. "Your turn for another pick."

Trent glanced through the options. "Icehouse by Icehouse."

Emma gave a playful grin. "Another banger, but definitely eerie. You've got a vibe going here, Trent."

The song played, its haunting melody filling the air. As it ended, Julian leaned into the microphone, his tone lighter. "Alright, Trent, here's a fun one for you. Are you, by any chance, related to Henry Lawson?"

Trent blinked, caught off guard. "Uh, I don't really know. I'm not a history buff. My Nan and Pop knew more about our family tree, but..." He paused, thinking. "There was this story my Nan used to tell, about a poet or writer in the family way back. Maybe? I guess it's possible."

Julian grinned. "Well, that's something. We might have a descendant of one of Australia's greatest writers on air right now."

The conversation continued, alternating between lighthearted moments and deeper reflections. Trent even tried his hand at a sponsor announcement, stumbling through the script with a sheepish grin. "If there's an issue, a bushranger getting you down, locate your local digger—they're here to help," he read, laughing at his awkward delivery.

Julian chimed in. "Nailed it. You're a natural."

Trent chuckled. "Mind if I do one for a place in Springwood? There's this little shop that fixes up old Game Boys, makes them functional again. They deserve a shoutout."

The day rolled on, filled with music, stories, and laughter. As the sun began to set, Emma leaned into the microphone. "This has been an incredible day. Trent, thank you for sharing your story with us."

Julian nodded, his smile warm. "And to everyone listening, thanks for tuning in. We'll be back tomorrow with more music, more stories, and hopefully more hope."

It was a wild broadcast they'd all remember for a long time.

Chapter 38:

T

he broadcast wound down as Julian flipped the switch, letting the room fall into a quiet hum. Emma stretched her arms above her head, her smile soft but full of energy. Across from them, Trent sat motionless, his eyes glistening with an emotion that was hard to place.

"Trent?" Julian asked cautiously, leaning forward.

Trent blinked as if pulling himself out of a dream. His voice was thick with gratitude. "I... I needed that. More than you know." He stood abruptly, walked over to them, and, without warning, pulled them both into a tight hug.

Emma chuckled softly, patting his back. "You did great, Trent. Seriously. People out there will love hearing your story."

Julian, though not usually one for displays of affection, didn't pull away. Instead, he gave Trent a reassuring pat on the shoulder. "You okay? I mean... really okay? You don't have to go back alone if you don't want to."

Trent stepped back, smiling faintly. "I'll be alright now. This... this reminded me there's still good in the world. People still care. And that's enough to keep going." He hesitated for a moment. "I've been staying at Glenbrook Base the last few days. It's a refuge settlement now. They're doing a lot to make it livable again."

Julian nodded. "That's good. You'll be safe there."

Trent's expression darkened slightly. "Yeah... it's safer than it was. Glenbrook Cinemas used to be a big refuge spot, but bushrangers moved in and wrecked the place. The diggers are trying to sort it out, though. They're doing their best."

Before Julian could respond, a knock came at the door, followed by Flynn stepping inside. The captain looked worn but composed, his uniform streaked with dirt and the unmistakable smell of gunpowder clinging to him.

Flynn tipped his hat in greeting. "Time to head back, Trent."

Trent nodded, grabbing his coat. "Thanks again, both of you. For everything."

As Trent turned to leave, Julian called out. "Hey, Trent. Stay safe, alright?"

Trent smiled a little more confidently this time. "I will. Thanks, Julian. Emma."

Flynn motioned for Trent to follow, but as he turned to leave, he glanced back at Julian and Emma. "By the way... I'd avoid the Central Station area for a while. Got a guy calling himself 'Captain Moonlight' holed up there. Trouble brewing, and it's best you don't get caught in it."

Julian raised an eyebrow. "Captain Moonlight? Seriously?"

Flynn smirked, his hand resting on the brim of his hat. "People are getting creative with names these days. Anyway, stay out of trouble."

Flynn tipped his hat again and led Trent out the door.

The room fell silent, the weight of the day settling in. Emma leaned back in her chair, her expression thoughtful. "You think Trent will be okay?"

Julian nodded slowly. "I think so. He's tougher than he looks."

They sat in silence for a while, the hum of the equipment the only sound. Finally, Emma broke the quiet. "You know... since the diggers started coming by, we've been pretty lucky. Safe. But... what if something changes? What if we have to go out scavenging again?"

Julian frowned, the question hanging in the air like a heavy cloud. "We've been fine so far, but... yeah, you're right. Things could change."

Emma hesitated before speaking again. "Maybe we should think about getting a weapon. Just in case."

Julian didn't answer right away, his mind turning over the idea. He'd never liked the thought of carrying a weapon, but the world wasn't what it used to be. "It's... a thought," he finally said, his voice quiet.

Emma nodded, her gaze distant. "Just something to think about. You know... be prepared."

They lapsed into silence again, the world's weight pressing in on them. Outside, the sun began to set, casting long shadows across the room. For now, they were safe. But in a world as unpredictable as this one, they both knew safety was never guaranteed.

Chapter 39:

The night had settled into an almost sacred stillness. Julian and Emma lay tangled together in bed, the faint glow of moonlight sneaking through the gaps in the curtain. The world outside was a distant hum, but it was just the two of them at this moment.

Emma shifted, propping her head up on her hand. "It's funny how quiet we're trying to be," she whispered with a smile. "We could be talking full volume, and no one would even notice."

Julian chuckled softly, his arm draped over her waist. "Force of habit, I guess. Still feels like someone's gonna shush us if we get too loud."

Emma laughed, her voice still subdued despite her own words. "Probably because that's what you always did when we recorded the podcast."

"I had to! You were the worst for laughing too loud," Julian teased, grinning. "Your laugh practically blew out the mic."

Emma rolled her eyes but smiled. "You're not wrong. It was kind of a problem."

There was a comfortable pause, the kind only shared between two people who had nothing to prove to each other.

Julian tilted his head slightly, his expression softening. "Hey... did you ever finish Roadside Picnic? I haven't seen you reading it in a while."

Emma's eyes lit up. "Oh, I binged that. Couldn't put it down. That plot twist? Wild."

"I told you," Julian said with a satisfied grin. "It's a classic for a reason."

"Yeah, yeah," Emma said, nudging him playfully. "I should read The Hobbit next. It's been on my mind. You know... I still think about some of the books in that little bookshop we passed before we found this place. I'd love to go back someday."

Julian raised an eyebrow. "The one with the creaky floors and that bell over the door?"

"That's the one," Emma said, her smile growing wistful. "There were so many books I didn't get to look at. I bet we could find something amazing. Maybe even something we could read out on air— short stories, poems, little yarns for people to listen to."

Julian considered the idea. "That's... actually kind of brilliant. People would love that. It's different, something calming for everyone. Might even help us feel a bit more connected."

"Exactly!" Emma said, her enthusiasm bubbling over. "And, hey, maybe the clerk is still there. They could be an interesting guest, too. I bet they'd have some great stories about the books people used to buy."

Julian smiled, brushing a strand of hair away from her face. "We'll have to add that to our growing list of ideas."

Emma's expression shifted slightly, her tone becoming a little more serious. "Speaking of lists... maybe we should jot something down for Flynn in the morning. About... you know, a rifle. And ammo."

Julian frowned but nodded. "Yeah. Just in case. The diggers keep us safe, but... who knows how long that'll last."

"Exactly," Emma said softly. "It's not about wanting to use it. Just... being prepared."

Julian grabbed a scrap of paper and a pencil from the nightstand, quickly scribbling down the note. When he set it aside, Emma leaned into him, her head resting on his chest.

"Do you think things will ever... feel normal again?" she asked quietly.

Julian stared at the ceiling, his hand absentmindedly running through her hair. "I don't know. But... moments like this? They feel pretty close to normal."

Emma smiled against his chest. "Yeah. They do."

The quiet stretched out again, warm and comforting. Eventually, their breaths evened out, and the world outside faded away entire

Chapter 40:

The sunlight streaming through the cracks in the curtains didn't wake Julian—it was the sharp crackle of the radio, followed by Flynn's unmistakable voice, thick with early-morning energy.

"Morning, you two," Flynn drawled, the usual humor in his tone. "Rise and shine! Early bird catches the worm, or whatever the fuck it is."

Julian groaned, rubbing his face as Emma stirred beside him, her hair a messy halo around her face. "We slept in," Julian muttered, reaching for the radio.

Emma yawned, sitting up and pulling the blanket around her shoulders. "Flynn's got impeccable timing."

Julian clicked the radio. "We're here, Flynn. What's the update?"

"Well, I've got a few tidbits for you," Flynn began. "Bushrangers have taken control of the Bells Line of Road. Mitchell's Pass is a no-go zone for the moment. And, get this, a pub in Penrith—The Red Cow—has reopened for business. Can't say I recommend it, but hey, it's there if you're feeling brave. Oh, and as I said yesterday, Central Station's still a no-go. Captain Moonlight's dug in there pretty deep."

Julian shivered involuntarily, a flash of his nightmare creeping into his thoughts. "Anything else we need to know?"

"That's about it for the moment," Flynn replied. "Anything you two need before I do my rounds?"

Julian hesitated, the uneasy feeling from his nightmare gnawing at him. "Uh, Flynn... is there any chance you could find us a rifle and some ammo? Just in case."

The radio went silent for a beat before Flynn chuckled. "A rifle, huh? What's got you spooked, Jules? Did the missus see a spider?"

Julian smirked despite himself, though the unease hadn't left him. "Something like that."

"I'll see what I can scrounge up," Flynn said. "Diggers are good at taking things out, but I get it. Sometimes you gotta feel safe, especially in your line of work."

Emma leaned over the radio. "Also, Flynn, we think we've got a neighbor in the building. They left us a note saying they listen to our show. Could you check on them for us next time you're here? Just to make sure they're friendly."

"Neighbor, huh?" Flynn said, his tone curious. "Didn't think anyone else was still squatting in that place. But sure, I'll see what I can find out. You'll owe me a drink if they're a weirdo, though."

Emma laughed. "Deal."

"Well, that concludes the news for now," Flynn said. "You two have yourselves a happy broadcast today. I'll swing by later if I can."

"Thanks, Flynn," Julian said.

The radio crackled off, and the room fell into a soft silence.

Julian leaned back against the headboard, exhaling slowly. "Feels like things are getting a little more... complicated."

Emma nudged him playfully. "Welcome to the apocalypse, Jules.

Chapter 41:

The song faded out, and the quiet hum of the room filled the space again. Julian and Emma sat across from Ardi, who had introduced herself as an international student from Indonesia. She had been staying in the building for a while, but they'd never crossed paths until today.

"So, you're from Indonesia?" Emma asked gently, trying to ease Ardi into the conversation. "That's a long way from here."

Ardi nodded, her dark eyes glinting with nostalgia and uncertainty. "Yeah. I was studying at Torrens University, right before everything... changed. I came here for a better education, but now everything's... different. The world's different."

Julian leaned forward, his curiosity piqued. "What brought you to this building? I mean, how did you end up here?"

Ardi hesitated momentarily, her fingers nervously playing with the hem of her sleeve. "After things started falling apart, I stayed with some friends for a while. But as things got worse, I moved here. It's quieter. Safer, for now."

Emma nodded thoughtfully. "Yeah, we've been here for a bit. It's not much, but it's a place to lay low and keep working. We're still trying to figure out the whole surviving part, but we're getting by."

Ardi smiled faintly. "I heard you on the airwaves. It was the first time I felt like someone else might be out there, thinking the same things. I wanted to come talk, to see if maybe there was a chance for something else. Maybe some help."

Julian shared a glance with Emma. Something about Ardi's words hit close to home. They'd been surviving in isolation for so long, it felt good to know they weren't the only ones reaching out. There were others, even if they weren't sure where to turn next.

"Well, you've come to the right place," Julian said, his voice warmer now. "We're trying to make this work—keeping the broadcast going, sharing what we know. But there's a lot we don't know, too. If you need help, we can figure something out."

Ardi's face softened, her eyes reflecting gratitude. "Thank you. I'm not sure how much I can offer, but maybe together we can find a way to keep going. I've been surviving, but I feel like I'm just… waiting. Waiting for something to change."

Emma tilted her head, considering the words carefully. "I get that. I think we're all waiting for something. But maybe the change is up to us. You never know what's possible until you try, right?"

Ardi nodded slowly, the tension in her shoulders easing. She seemed to be absorbing the warmth of their words, and for the first time in a long while, she looked like she might believe things could get better.

Julian turned his attention to the conversation between the three of them, realizing there was so much more to ask. "So, what were you studying at Torrens?" he asked, genuinely curious.

"Business," Ardi replied, her voice quiet. "But honestly, it was more about the experience. I was looking for something more than just the degree. I wanted to learn, explore, and find a way to help others."

Emma smiled softly. "Sounds like you were already thinking about how to make a difference, even before all this happened."

Ardi's face brightened a little at that. "Yeah. I always wanted to do something meaningful. I just didn't expect it to be this. But I'm learning to adapt, I guess."

Julian leaned back in his chair, folding his arms, deep in thought. "It's been a struggle for all of us. Trying to keep the old world in mind while surviving the new one. But maybe there's a way we can all help each other. We're not alone in this, not anymore."

Ardi nodded again, a sense of determination now clear in her eyes. "I want to be part of that. I've been thinking a lot about what's next. And it's not just about survival—it's about finding a way to rebuild, to contribute."

Emma's face lit up at her words. "I think that's what we've all been searching for. A purpose, you know? Not just living day by day, but moving forward, finding new ways to create something."

Julian smiled at her. "Exactly. So, we're all in this together now. No more waiting. We're going to keep doing what we can."

Ardi's gaze softened. "I'm glad I found you two. It's good to know there are others who understand. Maybe we can do something meaningful with this."

The conversation continued, a feeling of camaraderie slowly settling in the room. There was something hopeful in the air now that hadn't been there before. Despite the uncertain world outside, inside this space, there was the beginning of something new. And that, for now, was enough.

"Chapter 48: The Broadcast and the Uncertainty

Julian and Emma set up for the day's broadcast, the radio equipment humming softly as they plugged in the final cables and adjusted the levels. Something was comforting in the routine now, even as the outside world spun in unpredictable ways.

"Alright, folks, you're tuning in to the most reliable station in the wasteland," Julian started, his voice steady and warm. "Today's broadcast is packed with some interesting updates, and we've got some special things in store for you. But first, let's get the news out of the way."

He glanced at Emma, who gave him a thumbs-up, signaling her readiness to take the lead.

"First up," Emma began, her voice clear and concise, "The Bells Line of Road is officially under bushranger control. Mitchell's Pass is a no-go zone for now. It's looking a little too dangerous to take that route, so be careful if you're traveling. I wouldn't recommend it."

Julian nodded in agreement. "Yeah, and as Emma mentioned, The Red Cow pub in Penrith has reopened. It might be a little too early for any of you to be thinking about a pint, but if you're out that way, just keep your eyes peeled. It might be risky, but you never know."

Emma chuckled lightly. "Sure, if you want to risk your life over a drink. No thanks."

Julian grinned. "Hey, some people need the comfort. Anyway, Flynn also confirmed that Central Station is still a no-go zone. Captain Moonlight is holed up there, and we don't want any part of that."

Emma raised an eyebrow. "Sounds like a whole lot of trouble just waiting to happen."

"Definitely," Julian agreed. "And here's a little tidbit we got from Flynn—he's keeping an eye out for a rifle and some ammo for us. Just in case, you know. Better to be prepared."

Emma gave him a sidelong glance, picking up on his tension. "Yeah, just in case." She then shifted to a more light-hearted tone. "And we think we've got a neighbor in the building! Someone's been listening to our show, five stories up, and they even left us a note. They're eager to meet us, so maybe we'll have a new friend—or, you know, another face to share the burden of the apocalypse with."

Julian laughed, trying to shake off the heaviness. "Here's hoping they're not a psycho, right?"

Emma smiled and turned to the mic. "We'll have to find out next time we see them. But for now, let's keep things moving and get some music in here. We've got plenty more to talk about today, so stick around."

The broadcast continued, music played, and they joked about the bizarre reality they found themselves in. But beneath their broadcast's laughter and rhythm, Julian couldn't shake the feeling of unease. The rifle, the neighbor, and the unknowns in the world outside felt like a dangerous game that he couldn't fully understand but couldn't ignore.

As the hour passed, their voices became a reassuring constant, a brief escape for whoever was listening. But for Julian, the thought of what was coming next lingered like a shadow, waiting for its moment to reveal itself.

Chapter 42:

The hum of the small apartment was calming as Julian and Emma finished setting up for the next broadcast. The usual routine settled in, though today Emma seemed particularly excited. Julian glanced over at her as she adjusted the dials and equipment.

"Everything ready?" he asked, raising an eyebrow.

Emma grinned. "Yep, all set. Got a little surprise for you and the listeners today."

Julian raised an eyebrow in curiosity. "Oh? What's the surprise?"

Emma's eyes sparkled. "I invited Ardi to join us for the broadcast. I think her story could be a good one for our listeners. She's got a perspective that will connect with people, especially after everything we've been through.

Julian's face softened, realizing what she meant. "Yeah, you're right. People need to know they're not alone, and hearing her story will help. Let's do it."

Before they could say anything else, there was a knock at the door. Julian opened it, finding Ardi standing on the other side, a little nervous but looking more confident than the last time they'd met. She smiled shyly.

"Hey," Julian greeted her warmly. "Ready to go?"

Ardi nodded. "Yeah, I think so."

"Alright," Julian said, stepping aside to let her in. "We're live in a second, but we'll need to get situated first."

Emma gave a small nod and reached for the equipment. "We'll be right with you. We're just going to do a quick intro, and then we'll dive in."

Ardi sat on the couch, still looking around the small apartment as if taking in the moment. She wasn't quite used to being in a place like this, but there was a comfort in the simplicity of it all.

The familiar sound of the station's intro music filled the air, signaling the beginning of the broadcast. Emma glanced at Julian, who gave her a quick nod. She pressed a button, and the mic went live.

"Good morning, everyone," Emma's voice flowed smoothly into the airwaves. "This is Emma and Julian, and we're back on air with something a little special today. We've got a guest with us—Ardi, who's going to share her story. Ardi's originally from Jakarta, and she's been living here in Australia for a while now. Ardi, welcome to the show."

Ardi smiled and waved into the microphone. "Thanks for having me. I'm a little nervous, but I'm glad to be here."

Julian grinned. "No need to be nervous. We're just having a conversation. So, tell us a bit about yourself—how did you end up here?"

Ardi breathed, her eyes drifting as she thought about how to start. "Well, I was studying at Torrens University before… everything changed. I came to Australia as an international student from Indonesia. Jakarta wasn't exactly a peaceful place before the EMP, to be honest. There were always struggles, always something happening. But when the EMP hit, it felt like the whole world just… stopped. But in a way, it wasn't too different from what we had back home."

Julian nodded thoughtfully, a small frown on his face. "Yeah, I remember hearing about Chemtech and how controversial they were before all of this. It's crazy how much control those tech companies had, and how little people knew about the full extent of it."

Ardi looked at him with a mix of agreement and sadness. "Exactly. I was actually an intern at Chemtech, working in their design department. It was a great opportunity at the time, but I knew about the controversy. The company was always in the spotlight for the wrong reasons. I saw it firsthand, the shady practices, the way they pushed for control, but I had to keep my head down and focus on my work. I always wanted to work at a design house somewhere—somewhere like the place you were at before everything fell apart. I used to listen to your podcast, Julian. It was always so informative, always felt like you were on top of things."

Julian blinked in surprise. "You listened to my podcast?"

Ardi nodded with a soft smile. "Yeah. You always had this way of making everything make sense. The tech world, the companies, everything was so chaotic, but your podcast helped me understand the bigger picture. It felt like you were doing more than just reporting. You were trying to make people think. I respected that."

Emma leaned forward, a curious look in her eyes. "That's pretty incredible. It's funny how, in this mess, we're all trying to hold on to something that made sense, you know?"

Ardi gave a small, sad laugh. "Yeah, exactly. But after the EMP… it was like the rug got pulled out from under us. Jakarta wasn't any better than it was before. I had a life there, a future, but when everything collapsed, I had to leave. And now, I'm just trying to find a way to survive like everyone else."

Emma leaned back, taking in Ardi's words. "It's wild how everyone's story intersects in ways we don't even realize. The collapse hit everyone differently, but at the same time, we're all facing the same problems. It's hard to wrap your mind around."

Ardi nodded. "It's like the whole world fell apart and people were left to pick up the pieces. In some ways, it's not so different from what I was used to. The resource wars in Asia, the control the tech companies had, all of it—it was just… pushed into the open. They couldn't hide it anymore, and then everything just stopped."

Julian shifted in his seat, a flicker of understanding crossing his face. "I know what you mean. The world changed so fast. Do you have any idea who might have been behind the EMP? Have you thought about it?"

Ardi looked down for a moment, considering her answer carefully. "Indonesia and Australia, we always had a rocky relationship, but it was stable. I don't think it came from us. I'd be surprised if it was America, honestly. They always seemed to be after more power. But my guess? It was a tech company. The resource wars were already spilling over in Asia. Companies were already fighting for control, and a lot of them were the ones behind the chaos. One of them probably triggered the EMP—maybe it was their way of resetting the world for themselves."

Emma looked at Ardi, a somber expression on her face. "That's a chilling thought. But it does make sense, doesn't it? The world was already so divided, and those companies had so much power. They could've been the ones to pull the trigger."

Ardi nodded. "I think that's the most likely explanation. Asia was hit the hardest, and the tech companies had the resources. It's a messed-up situation, but it's the reality we're facing."

Julian looked at Emma and then back at Ardi. "Thank you for sharing that. It's difficult to talk about, but people must understand the bigger picture. We're all just trying to survive, but maybe by talking about it, we can start to make sense of things."

Emma turned back to the mic, her tone brightening a little. "Well, that's all we have time for today, folks. A huge thanks to Ardi for joining us and sharing her perspective. We hope this helps you understand just a little more about the world we're all trying to navigate. Stay safe, everyone, and we'll be back soon."

As the broadcast ended, the room felt quieter, as if the weight of the conversation had lingered in the air. Julian couldn't shake the feeling that things were slowly shifting—that the world might be falling apart, but there were still stories to be shared and connections to be made.

Chapter 43:

The room was still vibrating with the buzz of the broadcast's energy. Julian sat back in his chair, his fingers idly tapping the edge of the desk as the outro music's last notes faded. Emma was adjusting the equipment, but her thoughts seemed distant. Ardi, quiet for a moment, took a deep breath as if returning to the present.

"That was…" Ardi started, but she wasn't sure how to finish the sentence. "I don't know. It felt different. Talking like that. I mean, I didn't expect to get into all of that."

Julian turned to her with a soft, understanding smile. "Yeah, it can be intense. But it's good to have those conversations. It's part of what we do now, right? Share what we've all been through."

Emma looked over at Ardi, offering a reassuring nod. "You did great. Honestly, your perspective is something people need to hear. They need to know they're not alone in this."

Before Ardi could respond, the sudden ring of the comms system cut through the air, followed by a familiar voice.

"Oi, you two. That was a good broadcast. I heard it." Flynn's voice crackled through the speakers, warm but with his usual edge. "But let me give you a bit of advice. Maybe don't go too deep into resource wars and who's behind the EMP. We don't know who's listening, and we don't know who we might need down the line."

Julian exchanged a glance with Emma, who gave a subtle nod. Flynn always had a point, especially when keeping things low-key.

"Understood," Julian replied into the mic. "We'll be more careful about that next time. But, I mean, it's hard not to talk about the things that shape our lives now. But yeah, we get it."

Flynn's voice was back a moment later, the crackling noise slightly louder. "Yeah, yeah, I get it. Just… you never know who's out there. You never know if the bureaucrats in Canberra are still alive, let alone if they're listening. I'd rather not be on anyone's bad side, you know?"

Ardi, still sitting in the room, visibly stiffened at the mention of Canberra. Flynn's casual way about the government's uncertainty made her uncomfortable. She shifted in her seat, trying not to let the unease show too much.

Flynn didn't seem to notice. "Anyway, I'll be in tomorrow morning. I've got something for you. A little rifle, some ammo. I'll drop by before sunrise. Stay safe, alright?"

Julian gave a small smile, leaning back in his chair. "Thanks, Flynn. We'll be ready."

Emma nodded, adding, "Good broadcast, Flynn. And thanks for the heads-up. We'll be careful."

There was a brief pause, and Flynn's voice softened slightly. "Yeah, you too. Keep your heads down. The world's a little wild right now, and it's hard to say who's really running the show anymore."

The comms cut off, and the room fell briefly silent. Julian looked over at Ardi, who was fidgeting in her seat. Her expression was pensive, eyes clouded with something that might have been a flash of doubt or worry.

"Ardi?" Emma asked gently, her voice softer than usual.

Ardi looked up, forcing a small smile. "Yeah, sorry. Just... I didn't expect him to say that. About Canberra and the bureaucrats. It's just, the way things are now, it's hard to know who's really in control of anything."

Julian leaned forward, sensing her discomfort. "It's unsettling, I know. But Flynn's right about one thing. We don't know who's listening, who's out there. So we have to tread carefully."

"I understand," Ardi said quietly. "I just never thought I'd be in a world like this. It feels like things are so out of our control. And then hearing Flynn mention the people we thought we could trust, the ones who were supposed to have all the answers… it's just…" She trailed off, the weight of her words hanging in the air.

Emma reached over and placed a reassuring hand on Ardi's shoulder. "Hey, you're not alone in this. We're all figuring it out. One day at a time."

Julian nodded. "Exactly. We do what we can. And sometimes, that means just getting by. If we make it through today, we've done alright."

The three of them sat silently for a moment, the reality of their situation pressing around them. The broadcast had been a success, but it was clear that the world outside was far from simple. Conversations like this—about the EMP, about survival, about the people still out there—were all they had to make sense of it.

Finally, Ardi spoke up again, her voice steady despite the tension. "I think we'll be alright. As long as we keep talking, keep helping each other."

Julian gave her a firm nod, a faint smile tugging at his lips. "That's the plan."

Once again, the room fell quiet. The only sound was the soft hum of the equipment in the corner, the steady pulse of their shared resolve.

Chapter 44:

As the door clicked softly behind Ardi, Julian and Emma were left in the stillness of the apartment, the weight of their conversation lingering in the air. Ardi had headed back to her apartment five stories up, leaving them alone to process the broadcast, Flynn's words, and everything that had unfolded in the past few hours.

Julian slouched in his chair, letting the silence stretch between them, his fingers drumming lightly against the armrest. Emma stood by the window momentarily, looking out over the desolate streets, her mind elsewhere. The world's weight had a way of creeping into quiet moments like this. It wasn't just the chaos of the outside world but the lingering uncertainty of everything—their families, the future, and who could be trusted anymore.

Finally, Emma broke the silence. Her voice was soft and thoughtful. "Shouldn't we really be thinking about our families? You know, if they're okay? We've been so busy worrying about all of this," she motioned vaguely around the room, "that I forgot to think for a moment. Am I selfish for not thinking of them sooner?"

Julian leaned back, his gaze falling to the floor as he considered her words. There was truth to what she said. They'd spent so much time on the broadcast, keeping the community informed and surviving that the people they loved seemed to slip through the cracks of their minds. His own family, far away and unreachable, was a shadow he tried not to dwell on. But he knew he wasn't the only one holding on to the fear of the unknown.

"Maybe," Julian admitted, his voice quieter than usual, "maybe we need to check in. If Flynn's going out tomorrow, he might be able to help. Maybe we could get a loop going on the radio, something to keep the signal alive for a few days, so people don't forget about us. Just... keep it going."

Emma nodded, looking lost in thought for a moment. She ran a hand through her hair, then sighed, her shoulders slumping. "It feels strange, you know? We've been living on the edge of everything falling apart for so long that we forgot the things that used to matter. The little things."

Julian nodded, his heart heavy with the weight of those words. The world felt so much smaller now, yet they were all alone. But even in the darkest moments, there was still a glimmer of connection.

"Yeah," he murmured, "I think we've all been caught up in the survival part of it. It's hard not to forget, sometimes."

Emma turned back to him, a small smile tugging at her lips, though it didn't quite reach her eyes. "I miss chocolate," she said softly, "and ice cream. The simple stuff."

Julian chuckled lightly, his tired eyes lifting to meet hers. "I'd kill for some custard. The kind my mom used to make."

The words hung between them, an unspoken understanding of how much they had lost and still longed for despite the chaos. For a brief moment, the weight of everything outside seemed to fade, and in the quiet of their apartment, it was just the two of them. The world could wait.

Julian sighed, his gaze softening as he stood up from the chair and walked over to Emma's seat on the couch. Without a word, he sat beside her, the quiet companionship of their shared space enough to say everything they needed.

Emma leaned against him, her head resting on his shoulder, and for a moment, the silence between them felt comforting rather than unsettling.

"Do you think we'll ever get back to normal?" Emma whispered after a while, her voice barely audible.

Julian didn't have an answer, but he squeezed her hand gently, offering what little reassurance he could.

"I don't know," he replied quietly. "But we'll get through it. One day at a time."

They sat there for a while longer, the world outside still and quiet, as they took comfort in the presence of the other. It wasn't much, but in a world that had turned upside down, it was all they needed to hold on to for now.

Chapter 45:

The apartment was quiet, a calm that felt almost unnatural after the whirlwind of the day. Julian sat by the makeshift desk, fingers hovering over the radio equipment. It was much later than usual for reaching out to Flynn, but something was gnawing at him—a feeling of unease, a lack of closure. It wasn't just the constant uncertainty about the state of the world; it was more personal, too. His thoughts circled back to their families, the world outside, and Max.

He tried to reach Flynn again, but there was no immediate response this time. The seconds ticked on longer than usual, and Julian grew restless.

Usually, Flynn answered quickly, but the silence stretched unanswered tonight.

He exhaled sharply, rubbing his eyes as he glanced over at Emma. She was on the couch, a book in her lap, the dim light from the radio illuminating her face. He couldn't shake the feeling that it had been a lifetime since everything was normal, since life made sense.

Just as he was about to try again, a crackling sound broke through the static, followed by a voice he didn't recognize.

"Uh, hey, this is Corporal Ashley. Who's this?" Her voice was warm, a bit amused.

Julian leaned forward, surprised. "Hey, this is Julian. I was trying to get in touch with Flynn."

"Ah, Flynn, yeah," Ashley replied casually. "He's out at the Glenbrook Cinema right now. I'm on comms tonight. If you can hang on a little longer, he should be back soon. You can talk to him yourself."

Julian nodded, relieved. "Thanks. Actually, there's something I wanted to run by him."

Ashley's voice took on a teasing edge. "Ooh, an idea, huh? I'm intrigued. What's up?"

Before Julian could respond, she added, "And by the way, I'm kind of a fan of the broadcast. You guys are doing good work out there. And, just so you know...

Emma? Yeah, she's got a sexy voice. Thought I'd let you know."

Julian chuckled, feeling his cheeks warm slightly. "Thanks, I'll let her know. But, about my idea—"

He was cut off as Ashley's tone shifted, becoming more serious. "Wait a sec. Are you talking about Mad Max? Is that who you mean?" Her voice held a note of hesitation.

Julian's heart skipped. "Yeah, Max. What's going on? Is he okay?"

There was a long pause, and when Ashley spoke again, her tone was quieter, more careful. "We locked him up in room 17. He's... been showing signs of addiction. We don't know exactly what happened, but he's not the same. He's... not friendly anymore."

Julian's stomach twisted at her words. He feared this, but hearing it out loud hit harder than expected. Max was always reckless, but this... this was something darker.

"Thanks for telling me," Julian said quietly, trying to keep his voice steady. "I just needed to know."

Ashley's voice softened. "Yeah, I get it. Anyway, Flynn should be back soon. If you stay up a little longer, you can talk to him yourself."

"Thanks," Julian replied. "We'll wait."

Emma, who had overheard part of the conversation, appeared beside him. "Who was that?"

"Corporal Ashley," Julian said, rubbing his face. "Flynn's out on a raid at the Glenbrook Cinema. We'll have to wait to talk to him."

Emma nodded thoughtfully. "I guess we'll just have to be patient. We'll wait together."

Julian managed a small smile. "Yeah. For now, it's just us."

They both sat in the quiet of the apartment, the faint hum of the radio filling the space between them. The weight of the conversation with Ashley still lingered, but they could do nothing about it now. So, they sat side by side, the night stretching on as they waited for Flynn.

Chapter 55: Waking Up

The lounge felt unusually comfortable after the long day, the radio buzzing softly in the background. Emma's head had found a spot on Julian's shoulder, and the exhaustion from the night's broadcast finally took its toll on them. They'd fallen asleep side by side, the low hum of static in the air.

The soft glow of the clock on the wall showed that it was well into the early morning hours when Julian was suddenly jolted awake. Flynn's familiar voice crackled through the radio, but this time, it was different—faint, tired, with a certain edge of urgency.

"Julian, Emma, are you two still awake?" Flynn's rough voice had an unmistakable authority, even through the static.

Julian blinked, groggy from the sleep he'd barely had. Emma stirred beside him, rubbing her eyes as they sat on the couch. "Flynn? You're up late," Julian muttered, trying to clear the fog from his mind.

Flynn's voice came through, this time with a soft crackle of pain mixed in. "Yeah, well... took out some nasty bush rangers at the Glenbrook Cinema. Got a bit of blood in my eye, but nothing serious. Just getting patched up by the medic now."

In the background, Julian could hear the unmistakable sounds of a medic's clipped and dry voice: "Hi, Julian. Hi, Emma. I've had children tougher than you."

The teasing remark broke the tension a little, and Julian could imagine the medic working on Flynn, patching him up after the raid. He and Emma exchanged glances, still dazed from their unexpected wake-up. But there was something important they needed to ask.

"Flynn," Emma began, her voice still thick with sleep. "We were thinking, could we put a loop on the radio for a bit? Just to keep the broadcast going while we go check on our families? Maybe tomorrow or the next day?"

There was a pause before Flynn responded, his voice rougher than usual. "I get it. Not something I usually do, but... yeah, we can do that. I'll check with the others, but it shouldn't be a problem. You guys are right to be worried. Where do you need to go?"

Julian sat up a little straighter, suddenly awake. "My family's out in Bradfield, near the airport, near Penrith," he said, feeling a knot in his stomach as he spoke about his family. "It's been a while since I've been able to check on them."

Flynn acknowledged the location with a grunt. "Yeah, I know that area. We'll figure out the best way to get there."

Emma spoke next, her voice quieter. "I'm from Blackheath."

Julian hadn't known that before. He glanced over at Emma, his curiosity piqued, but he didn't ask any more questions now. It wasn't the time.

Flynn's voice came through again, this time more matter-of-fact. "The Bells Line of Road's a mess right now, but there are other ways to get around. We'll find a route. Could be tomorrow, or the day after that."

Julian nodded, the gravity of their conversation sinking in. "Thanks, Flynn. We appreciate it."

"You got it," Flynn responded. "I'll be in touch about the loop. Stay safe out there, both of you."

The connection cut off, leaving only the soft static sound once again. Julian leaned back against the couch, rubbing his face with his hands. His thoughts returned to the families they needed to check on, the uncertainty of it all. Emma sat beside him, quiet as they considered the journey ahead.

The apartment fell silent again, the only sound the low hum of the radio as they sat together, waiting for the next step in this fractured world.

Chapter 46:

The morning light filtered through the dusty windows, casting long shadows across the room. The apartment was quiet, save for the soft hum of the radio and the distant sounds of the ruined world outside. Julian and Emma were still waking up, the previous night's exhaustion hanging over them like a thick fog. They hadn't quite made it out of their dreams when the knock came—a sharp, urgent tap on the door.

Emma stirred first, sitting up on the couch. Julian groaned, rubbing his face with his hands before standing up to answer. The door creaked open, and Flynn stood looking messier than usual. His uniform was dirtied, bloodstained in patches, with a few more bullet holes than before. He hadn't slept much; that much was clear. His eyes were bloodshot, and the exhaustion on his face was obvious.

Flynn gave them a tired nod, stepping in without waiting for an invitation. He was carrying a long, worn rifle slung over his shoulder, with a small pack of ammo hanging from his belt. He dropped the rifle and ammo onto the table in front of them with a soft thud.

"Got what you need," Flynn said, his voice low and rough. "Just remember, these aren't the fancy energy guns or the stuff you might've heard about from the old days. These are bolt-action, old-school service rifles. They have a kick to them, so don't get too comfy." He paused, glancing at the rifle on the table.

"You load one round at a time, aim well, and take your shot. Don't waste your ammo."

Emma nodded, taking in the advice. Julian was quiet, his eyes on the rifle, his mind racing with the reality of the situation. A real weapon—something he'd never imagined himself using. But now, in this world, it was a necessity.

Flynn straightened up, wiping a smear of blood from his forehead. "I'll let you know tonight about the expedition. Probably tomorrow or the next day. We'll see how the roads look. But you two should stay ready."

Emma hesitated for a moment before speaking up. "Flynn… go check on Ardi. She mentioned she's in the building still. If you can."

Flynn gave a tired half-smile. "Yeah, I'll swing by. Don't worry about it."

He gave them a final glance, then turned toward the door. "Take care of yourselves. I'll check in later. Happy broadcast, alright?"

The door shut behind him, and Julian and Emma were again left alone in the silence. The rifle sat there on the table, a stark reminder of the new world they now inhabited. Emma ran a hand over the cool metal, her face drawn with concern.

"Tomorrow," Julian said quietly. "We'll check on our families."

"Yeah," Emma replied, her voice soft. "Tomorrow."

It was a tentative agreement, a promise to face the uncertainty of the world together, no matter what came next. But for now, they sat there, letting the moment out between them, each lost in their thoughts about what was to come.

Chapter 47:

The soft hum of the radio filled the small apartment as Julian and Emma sat before the microphone, their words heavy in the air. They had decided to put the next few days on a loop—broadcasting a mix of old stories, some music, and the occasional sponsor mention. Emma had insisted on recording some extra content to keep the broadcast more than just static. The old world had been filled with so much noise and chatter— sometimes, it felt like they were trying to recreate a piece of that lost world with their small, humble station.

Emma adjusted the microphone, her fingers brushing over the dials. "Alright, everyone, we'll be putting the next few days on a loop," she said, her voice steady but tinged with an undercurrent of fatigue. "But don't worry. I'll be recording a few goodies to keep things interesting—so it won't be all music and sponsors. Sounds like the old world, doesn't it?" She smiled faintly, her eyes meeting Julian's as she spoke.

Julian leaned into his mic, his voice taking on a more serious tone. "We'll be back soon, but for now, we need to check on our families. It's been a while since we've done that, and well... we need to make sure they're alright."

Emma nodded, her expression softening. "Yeah, it's been too long. Time to get out there, see what's left of the world, and make sure the people we care about are still safe."

They shared a brief, meaningful look before Julian adjusted the controls, setting the loop to begin. As the first strains of a familiar song filled the room, the broadcast shifted into a quiet lull. The only sounds now were the soft hum of the equipment and the distant echo of life beyond the walls of their apartment.

Emma sat back in her chair, her fingers tapping absentmindedly on the desk. "I'll record a few more pieces. We'll make sure the airwaves stay active, even if we're not on them every moment."

Julian nodded, but his mind was already racing. The idea of heading out to check on his family, to see if anyone was still out there, was daunting. But it had to be done. They couldn't keep hiding in their little bubble forever.

"I'll help," Julian said after a moment, his voice quieter now. "We'll get through this. One step at a time."

Emma smiled faintly. "Yeah, one step at a time."

With that, the broadcast rolled on, leaving the pair in a quiet moment of anticipation for what the next few days might bring.

Chapter 48:

The radio station's hum filled the space between the broadcast's breaks. Outside, the world carried on—quiet, still, yet filled with an underlying tension. In the dim light of the station, Julian leaned back in his chair, the weight of the last few days pressing against his chest.

Emma had just finished another quick recording for the loop, her voice warm and steady as she transitioned back into the calm of the night. The music flowed in the background, familiar and comforting, but the silence between the songs lingered longer than usual. It was during one of these pauses that Julian broke the quiet.

"Hey, Emma," he said, his voice softer than usual. "Before all this... before the collapse, what was it like for you? I mean... school, university... life, I guess?"

Emma glanced up from her notes, her fingers still hovering over the dials. She hadn't expected the question, and for a moment, she was quiet, considering the words. Then, she leaned back in her chair, a small smile on her lips as she thought back.

"Well, I grew up in Blackheath," she began, her tone hinting nostalgia. "Even before everything changed, it was... a quiet place. Not as high-tech as the rest of the world. It was still beautiful, though. Lots of greenery, fresh air, the kind of place you'd get lost in the mountains for days. It's always been a bit of a retreat, even before the collapse. Not much of the tech craze ever touched it, so when I was growing up, it felt... peaceful."

Julian nodded slowly, absorbing the words. He had known her for a while now, but there were still layers to Emma's past that he hadn't peeled back.

"I never asked," he admitted. "But that sounds nice. Peaceful."

Emma shrugged lightly, her fingers drumming on the desk absentmindedly. "It was. But schooling there was tough. I hated school. I wasn't one for the structure or... I don't know, the whole system. But university, that was a different story."

Julian's curiosity piqued. "University? You liked that?"

"Yeah," Emma said, her eyes softening. "I went to UTS. The city was so different from the mountains. Chippendale was bustling, tech everywhere. It was a bit of a shock, honestly, going from the quiet mountains to the city's chaos. But I loved it. The freedom, the opportunity to really get into something I cared about. I studied communications, which felt like the right fit. It was hard, but in a good way. Worth it, though."

Julian leaned forward slightly, intrigued by her response. "Sounds like it was a big change, though. From one extreme to the other."

"Yeah, it was," Emma replied. "But I was ready for it. The city, the challenges. It pushed me, in a way. And I'm glad I made the choice."

Julian was quiet for a moment, reflecting on her words. "I went to Western Sydney University in Parramatta," he said suddenly, catching her off guard. "Same as my grandfather, actually. I never really thought about it until now, but... it's kind of funny. I guess I just followed the family tradition. Didn't really change much. But it was... solid, you know?"

Emma smiled at that, her eyes twinkling with a knowing look. "I can see that. It's funny, isn't it? How much we're shaped by those traditions, even if we don't realize it at first."

"Yeah." Julian's voice grew thoughtful. "I guess it's something I never really thought about until now. Life felt different then, before everything went to hell. The world felt... more sure, in a way."

Emma nodded, her gaze distant for a moment. "Yeah, sure. The world felt like it had some kind of direction. Like everything was moving forward. I miss that certainty sometimes."

Julian leaned back, the weight of her words settling in. "I guess we just have to figure out where we go from here, huh?"

Emma turned to him, her smile soft but genuine. "One step at a time, Julian. One step at a time."

The music picked up again, the soft notes filling the space between them. It was a quiet moment of understanding, of remembering the world before the collapse, before everything was turned upside down. The stillness was broken only by the soft hum of the radio equipment and the distant memories of a time that now felt like a dream.

Chapter 49:

———————>⚬◦⚬<———————

T he station was quiet again, save for the low hum of the equipment. The air felt thick with the weight of the world outside, but within the confines of the station, Julian and Emma had found a semblance of routine. They had their jobs, their broadcasts, and the brief moments of normalcy they could cling to.

Emma had already done her part—recording a series of quirky quips, reminders, and her signature charm to keep the loop fresh. Julian, however, was sitting at his desk, eyeing the setup. They needed the loop to run for the next few days, something to keep the station going while they checked on their families. It must be varied, interesting, and random enough to feel like a real broadcast.

"Alright," Julian muttered to himself, clicking through the interface. "If we're doing this right, I'll add a bit of variety like Emma did."

He worked quickly, figuring out how to get the songs to auto-play in shuffle mode. It wasn't too complicated—he'd dealt with radio tech before, back in the old days, but it felt different now. The old days were just that—old.

Once the music was set, he focused on the rest of the loop. They needed something with more substance than just songs, something that would make it feel like there was a connection to the world they were in.

"That's right," Julian thought aloud, remembering the interview with Trent, the Gameboy repair man. "I'll add a mention of Trent. People liked hearing that. It gives them a little something to hold onto."

He typed out a brief mention, reflecting on Trent's impact on their little community—a nod to the past and a touch of the present.

Then, he thought about the poems they had both thrown into the loop. Banjo Paterson was easy enough for Emma to recall. But Julian had one tucked away in his memory, one he hadn't thought about in years. He wasn't sure why, but it felt right.

With a deep breath, Julian typed out the words of a Shakespearean sonnet.

"Shall I compare thee to a summer's day?

Thou art more lovely and more temperate:

Rough winds do shake the darling buds of May,

And summer's lease hath all too short a date."

He paused after typing the last line, the words familiar but still strange in the context of everything happening now. Was it out of place? Maybe. But it was something they could hold onto—something to remind them of who they were before.

"Done," he muttered with a satisfied nod. He clicked the button to test the loop and sat back as the music began to play again, mixed with the random notes and quirks he'd just programmed in.

Emma, who had been busy adjusting her settings, turned to him. "What did you add?" she asked, her eyebrow raising slightly.

Julian grinned. "I figured I could throw in something for variety. A mention about the guy Trent mentioned, the gameboy guy, and... well, I added a Shakespeare sonnet."

Emma blinked. "Shakespeare? You know that off by heart?"

Julian chuckled. "I mean, not exactly. But I remembered enough of it from back in the day. Figured it's better than just throwing in random commercials."

Emma stared at him momentarily as if processing that Julian had entirely remembered a Shakespearean sonnet. "That's... impressive. I didn't expect that from you."

Julian shrugged, a bit embarrassed but still proud of himself. "I think I was just trying to hold onto a piece of the world that feels like it's slipping away."

Emma smiled softly. "I get that. It's a good addition, Julian. It feels... more connected, somehow. More real."

"I thought so, too." Julian leaned back in his chair, glancing over the broadcast loop again. The songs flowed smoothly, now with the extra randomness he'd added. Trent's mention, the Shakespeare lines, the quirky reminders—it felt like something they could live with, something that kept a connection to the old world alive.

Emma nodded her eyes on the screen, a thoughtful expression. "I'm impressed. You're more than just a tech guy, huh?"

Julian chuckled, rubbing the back of his neck. "Guess I've got a few surprises up my sleeve. Just need to keep things interesting."

The radio station continued to hum in the background, and for a brief moment, it felt like they were still living in the world they once knew—a world where Shakespeare was remembered, where a guy could fix an old Game Boy, and where music and stories could still be shared through the airwaves.

Chapter 50:

———— >⚜< ————

The last broadcast of the day was over, the loop was set to run for the next few days, and the silence in the room was oddly comforting. The soft hum of the equipment was the only sound, a familiar rhythm they had grown used to over the last few weeks. Julian clicked off the last control, his hands moving on autopilot as his mind wandered. He was exhausted, his body heavy with fatigue, but his thoughts were racing, an endless replay of everything that had happened in the weeks since the collapse.

He sank back into the couch, the weight of it all pulling at him. On the other hand, Emma seemed to settle easily next to him, her presence a comforting warmth. She nestled against his side, resting her head on his shoulder with a soft sigh. It had become a routine of sorts—after the broadcasts and chaos of the day, they found themselves here in this quiet moment.

The station had been busy. The days had blurred together, and now, in the stillness of the night, everything seemed louder in his mind.

Emma tilted her head, glancing up at him. "Hey, you okay?" she asked softly, her voice filled with concern.

Julian blinked, pulling himself from his thoughts. He hadn't realized how deep he had sunk in his mind. He managed a tired smile, but it didn't reach his eyes. "Yeah," he said, his voice quiet, "just thinking."

"About what?" Emma asked, her curiosity piqued as she adjusted herself, sitting up straighter but still leaning into him.

Julian hesitated, his eyes unfocused as he stared at the faint glow of the equipment. It was strange how everything had changed. The world they had known and the lives they had led felt so far away now. He thought about the people they used to be, the comfort of routine, of stability. All of it felt fragile now.

"I'm just thinking about everything that's happened," he finally said, his voice rough from exhaustion. "The collapse, the broadcasts, the fact that we're still here… I'm not sure how we got here. How we're still here. It's like we're living in a different world now, and I don't even know what to make of it anymore."

Emma's hand found his, her fingers curling gently around his as she listened intently. Her touch grounded him like a tether to something solid in all the uncertainty. "I know," she said, her voice quiet but steady. "I think about that too. How much has changed. How much we've changed. But..." She paused, looking up at him. "We're doing the best we can, right?"

Julian exhaled slowly, the weight of the world pressing on his chest. "I hope so. I just... I didn't expect any of this, you know? To be here, doing this, trying to hold things together. It's like we're all just trying to survive, and I can't help but wonder if we're really doing enough."

Emma squeezed his hand, a small but meaningful gesture. "We're doing more than enough. We're keeping the broadcast going, reaching people, giving them something to hold onto. And we're sticking together. That counts for something, Julian."

Julian turned his head, meeting her gaze, and for a brief moment, the weight of his worries seemed to lift just a little. He gave her a tired smile, his fingers gently brushing through her hair. "I guess you're right. We are doing something. Maybe that's all we can do."

They fell into a comfortable silence that didn't need words. Emma snuggled back against him, and Julian's exhaustion finally caught up with him. His thoughts slowed, and he allowed himself to close his eyes momentarily despite the uncertainty still hanging in the air.

Emma's soft voice broke the silence, her words playful but tender. "You're overthinking again, aren't you?"

Julian chuckled softly, the sound barely a breath as he nodded. "Yeah. I guess I am."

"Well," she said with a grin, her head resting against his shoulder again. You should stop thinking for a bit. Just be here with me."

He smiled, feeling the weight of his worries ease as she nestled into him. "I think I can do that."

They sat there in the quiet, the hum of the equipment providing a strange comfort as the night stretched on. Emma's presence was the only thing that felt certain and kept him tethered to the present moment.

As the exhaustion finally claimed him, Julian found himself drifting off, the sound of Emma's steady breathing beside him a lullaby in the room's stillness. For a brief moment, there was peace.

Chapter 51:

Julian's mind slipped from the quiet reality of the present into the realm of dreams. It was a sudden shift, almost like walking through a doorway into another time. The familiar weight of Emma beside him faded, replaced by the buzz of office lights, the soft murmur of voices, and the unmistakable scent of coffee wafting through the air. He was no longer in the broadcast station's small, dimly lit room. He was back at DisruptTech.

It was his first day on the job, a fresh start that felt more like a leap into the unknown than a confident step forward. The hum of the office was alive with activity, employees moving between desks, voices rising in discussion, and the soft clatter of keyboards filling the air. Julian was sitting at his new desk, his fingers fidgeting nervously with the edge of a coffee cup. He could hear the faint whir of a nearby air conditioning unit, the occasional ringing of a phone, and the low buzz of the breakroom fridge.

He remembered the pressure.

DisruptTech had been a major name in the tech industry, and when Julian first joined as an associate producer, he never could have imagined the intensity of the role. His first real task? Hosting a podcast. But it wasn't just any podcast—it was the podcast, the one that followed in the footsteps of the popular and well-established host who had left.

Julian had been given the opportunity, but with it came an immense weight.

His first guest was a well-known expert in e-medication—a dry, clinical topic that most people wouldn't dream of discussing on a podcast. But Julian had to make it work. He had to. It was his big break. He could still remember the feeling of his palms sweating as he prepared for the interview, the buzzing nerves that ran through him like electricity.

He wasn't ready for the pressure. The expert was sitting across from him in the studio, his face impassive, his eyes hidden behind thick glasses. The room felt small, the walls lined with recording equipment, microphones in front of them like silent, watchful sentinels.

Julian's heart raced as he turned on the mic. The recording light flashed on, and for a brief moment, everything in the room went silent. His voice, shaky and uncertain, cut through the stillness.

"Welcome to the DisruptTech podcast," Julian had said, trying to sound confident but feeling the words fall flat. "Today, we're diving into the topic of e-medication, and, uh… well, we have Dr. Hargrove here with us, an expert in the field. Dr. Hargrove, thank you for joining us."

The guest nodded, his voice deep and monotone as he began explaining the complexities of e-medication. Julian tried to focus on the words, but his mind kept racing ahead. Did I ask the right question? Should I ask more? Is this boring?

He had always been a perfectionist, and that day was no different. He kept pushing through the interview, trying to bring life to the conversation, even though it felt more like an interrogation. The pressure to perform weighed on him, making each question feel like a tightrope walk.

He'd tried to keep it conversational, as instructed, but it was hard. How could you make a discussion about digital prescriptions sound exciting?

"Now, Dr. Hargrove," Julian had said, his voice higher than usual. "I've read some studies suggesting that—uh—that e-medication could change the way we approach, um, healthcare in general. What do you think this means for the future of healthcare providers and patients?"

It was a weak attempt to keep the conversation going, but to his surprise, the expert had seemed to respond. Slowly, carefully, they'd started to find a rhythm. Gradually, Julian began to relax, though he could feel sweat sticking to the back of his neck.

But then, the interview ended, and Julian listened to the playback afterward, cringing at the awkward pauses and the uneven flow. He had tried hard to make it work but knew he hadn't nailed it. He'd taken over the podcast from a host their audience had beloved, and the fear of letting down the listeners felt suffocating.

The next few weeks were a blur of similar interviews—technical, dry topics—and Julian continued to work himself ragged, trying to prove he was capable. He made mental notes and tried to improve after every recording, and slowly, the nerves began to ease.

Emma had made him feel at ease during those early days. She was a producer on the show, her presence calm and confident. Julian had always admired her sharp wit and ability to stay grounded, even when things got chaotic.

He remembered the first time he talked to her after one of those long, late-night recordings. She had leaned over the desk with a smile, handing him a coffee and saying, "You did fine today. No one's perfect, but you're getting better. And that's what matters."

It was simple, but it meant everything to Julian.

Max, too, had been there. A bit of an enigma at the time, his sharp tongue and blunt honesty had sometimes put Julian on edge, but over time, they became a team. The three of them worked together on the podcast, bouncing ideas off one another and helping each other improve. It wasn't just about the technical aspects of the job—it was about finding their rhythm. It was about building something that could connect with people.

The flashback faded as the dream started to blur again, and Julian's mind drifted further into the past. Those early days at DisruptTech had been tough, but they had shaped him. He had been scared and unsure, but he had learned.

He had learned how to control his fear and become a part of something bigger, something meaningful.

As the memories faded into the haze of his dream, Julian felt a strange warmth—nostalgia mixed with a tinge of longing. For the first time in a while, he felt a sense of hope, the kind he hadn't felt in the wake of the collapse. Maybe they could do this. Maybe they could survive.

And as the dream shifted again, he found himself back in the present, Emma beside him, her presence a steady anchor.

He smiled softly in his sleep, feeling a small comfort in the chaos.

The dream deepened, and the passage of time stretched out. Julian found himself standing at the entrance of an apartment building, the doors sliding open as he stepped inside. The building smelled faintly of fresh paint and new wood—a scent that seemed to hang in the air, a reminder that it was all new.

It was his apartment. The one in Ultimo.

He could remember the first day he'd moved in, the excitement mixed with a deep sense of uncertainty. The city buzzed around him, but inside the apartment, it was quiet, almost eerily so. There hadn't been much to it at first—just the bare essentials—an old PlayStation he'd brought with him, the flat-screen TV that was more of a distraction than anything else, and a bed—a small bed, just big enough for one person.

The kitchen was minimalist—barely enough to cook, but that was fine; he wasn't much of a cook. The apartment felt empty and full, like a space that had yet to be claimed. It was his, but it didn't yet feel like home.

He remembered the commute after long days at DisruptTech, the bus ride through the city's heart as the skyline loomed in the distance, catching the last of the sunlight before it faded into the night. The city was always alive and always moving.

But it had always been the end of a long day for Julian. The way he'd step off the bus, tired but feeling a sense of purpose, knowing he was on the path to something, even if he wasn't entirely sure what it was.

As he stood in the hallway of the apartment building, he could hear the hum of the elevator as it arrived, the door sliding open to reveal the familiar space that had become his sanctuary after a day of work. He stepped inside, feeling the day's weight lift off his shoulders as he made his way to his apartment.

The apartment door clicked open, and he stepped inside, greeted by the soft glow of the lights, casting long shadows on the walls. The air felt cooler than it had outside, and for a moment, everything was still. With a soft thud, he dropped his bag on the floor and looked around at the space. It was quiet here, too—quiet in a welcoming way, a space just for him.

He sank onto the bed, the only piece of his furniture, and stared at the ceiling. The walls were bare, no pictures, no decorations. Just white. Plain. Simple. But it was his.

He picked up the old PlayStation controller on the floor beside the TV. It was well-worn, the buttons slightly faded from use. He flicked the power switch on the TV, and the familiar startup sound of the PlayStation filled the room. The screen flickered to life, and he scrolled through the games he'd downloaded, none of them sparking the excitement he once had for them. They were just things to fill the silence.

Julian lay back on the bed, his eyes still fixed on the screen, but his mind was elsewhere. He wasn't sure what he was looking for, but the city outside, the bustle, and the constant hum felt distant now. Like everything was slipping through his fingers, but at the same time, he was okay with it. He didn't need to have it all figured out. Not yet.

In that small apartment, alone but not entirely, he could breathe.

But he knew he would need to get up again to face the challenges ahead. The uncertainty of the future, the fear of making it on his own, and the constant weight of expectations would still be there when he woke up.

And then, the dream shifted.

Julian found himself sitting in a café—a different place entirely. It was a bustling little spot near the office, where the barista knew his name, and he would stop by every morning to grab his coffee before heading to work. He could smell the fresh ground coffee beans, hear the chatter of people around him, and feel the sun's warmth through the windows. It was the beginning of something.

Something exciting. Something full of possibility.

But just as quickly, the dream began to slip away again, its edges blurring like fading memories.

Before it faded completely, Julian's eyes fluttered open, and he felt the familiar warmth of Emma beside him. The echoes of the past lingered for a moment longer, and he realized that even though he was far from the city and from that time in his life, the lessons, the memories, and the people who had shaped him were still there.

Even now. Even in the aftermath of everything that had happened.

The quiet hum of the present filled the space around him, and Julian took a deep breath, still grounded in the here and now.

Chapter 52:

Julian's eyes fluttered open to the soft murmur of Emma's voice. The dim light from the street outside filtered in through the window, casting long shadows across the room. He blinked a few times, his mind sluggish from the remnants of sleep. For a moment, he couldn't quite place where he was, but as the haze of slumber lifted, the cozy, familiar surroundings of the lounge came into focus.

Emma was perched on the edge of the couch, watching him with a gentle smile. Her eyes were soft, but she spoke with a hint of concern.

"You looked so happy," she said quietly. "I didn't want to wake you."

Julian shifted slightly, rubbing his face with the back of his hand. His body was still heavy with sleep, his limbs uncooperative as he sat up. The couch was comfortable, but he'd drifted off deeper than he had realized. His brain was foggy, a little slow to catch up with the present moment.

"Guess I needed that," he mumbled, blinking a few more times to clear the sleep from his eyes. The tiredness that had settled deep in his bones wasn't entirely gone, but he felt better for having rested.

Emma chuckled softly, a quiet sound that made him smile. "Well, it's late," she said, glancing over at the clock on the wall. "It's about 1:30 AM, but maybe we should pack a bag for tomorrow. We'll need to be ready to head out. We can't forget about our families."

Julian nodded, the weight of that responsibility sinking back in. They'd been talking about doing it for days now—checking on their families—but time seemed to slip away, and the weight of the world around them had distracted them.

"Yeah," he agreed. "We've got time." He paused, then sighed, "And, uh, we never did eat dinner, did we?"

Emma's expression softened into a small, knowing smile. "Nope. Guess we got a little too wrapped up in everything else." She stood and stretched, moving toward their things. "I guess we'll survive without it for now. But if you want to grab something, we can make do."

Julian pushed himself off the couch, feeling the familiar ache in his muscles, a mix of fatigue and the day's weight. As he stood, he realized how much had happened in the past 24 hours—and how much still lay ahead. Tomorrow would be another big day that would change things even more.

"Let's just get the bags packed," Julian said, rubbing his eyes again. "We can figure out food later. But yeah, we need to be ready."

Emma smiled, nodding. "Alright, let's get started. We'll be out of here soon enough."

They began gathering their things, moving in quiet rhythm as they packed the essentials—clothes, a few supplies they'd need for their journey, and whatever else they could fit in the bags. Their sense of purpose was starting to settle in again. They didn't know what they'd find when they reached their families, but they knew they had to try.

Julian glanced at Emma as they worked, feeling a small pang of gratitude. Despite everything that had happened, despite the fear and uncertainty, they had each other. And for now, that was enough.

"Let's make it count tomorrow," he said softly.

Emma looked up from the bag she was organizing, meeting his gaze. "We will," she said with quiet confidence, even though the weight of the unknown hung heavily over them both.

They continued packing, the minutes slipping by as they prepared for whatever the morning would bring.

Chapter 53:

As the sound of zippers and the rustle of clothing filled the room, Emma paused momentarily, her hands resting on the edges of the bag she was packing. Her eyes flickered over to Julian, a mischievous smile tugging at the corners of her mouth.

"So," she began, her tone light, but there was an edge of curiosity. "I'm going to meet your father. What should I expect? Should I be scared?" She raised an eyebrow, clearly teasing, but there was a hint of genuine nervousness behind her playful words. "I can't say a guy has ever wanted to bring me home to meet the parents before. I usually intimidate them. The term I was often called was a 'ballbreaker.'"

Julian chuckled at that. The thought of Emma intimidating anyone amused him. He shook his head, setting down the t-shirt he was folding.

"You? Intimidating?" he said with a grin. "I don't believe that for a second." He paused, thinking for a moment before continuing. "But, if you really want to know, my dad—well, he's a bit of a different breed."

He glanced down for a moment, his expression softening. "He was an engineer at VeloDyne Industries, you know, the ones who made the friction engines. He's a practical guy, always about getting things done. But before that, he owned a workshop, back when things were a little more... steady. The rent was hard to pay, and when that shop went under, he didn't give up. He just kept going. Did an apprenticeship through university at some solar tech company—'SOLARPUNK,' I think it was called."

Julian looked over at Emma, a small smile tugging at his lips. "Dad's salt of the earth, really. Not the most talkative, but he'll get a sense of you. And he's a hard worker. You'll see."

Emma nodded, taking in the information with a soft look. She then shifted her gaze back to Julian, her voice quieter and more thoughtful.

"And your mum?" she asked gently. "What's she like?"

Julian smiled warmly at the thought of his mother. "Mum's a nurse. She's always been caring—always looking out for others. Kind, thoughtful. You'll probably get along with her just fine. Don't worry about that."

Emma bit her lip, nodding again. She could tell this subject meant something to him. She had never really been good at these kinds of moments, the ones that made her feel vulnerable, but she wanted to put Julian at ease. She knew he was nervous, too, in his way.

"I'm sure my mum will love you too," Emma said with a soft laugh, her eyes warm and teasing. "She's not exactly a ballbreaker, though. More of a... peacekeeper. You'll be fine."

Julian looked at her, a genuine smile spreading across his face. "Well, if I make it through your mum, you can definitely survive my parents." He chuckled, shaking his head, though his heart fluttered slightly at the thought of Emma meeting his family.

"I guess," he said, standing up and grabbing the last few items, "we'll just have to take it one step at a time, right?"

Emma gave him a wink. "Exactly. And hey, if all else fails, I'll just bring out the ballbreaker persona."

Julian laughed, the weight of the situation lightening for just a moment. "I think you're safe. They're going to love you, Emma. I know it."

Julian smirked. "Maybe there's one last thing I should warn you about my father." Emma's ears perked up, sensing there might be something to be wary of. "And that is?" she asked with a curious grin.

"My dad has this joke," Julian continued. "When he says he stopped drinking, but you can clearly see he's still drinking. If you call him out on it, he just replies, 'This is goat's milk.' Then, when you ask why it's brown, he says, 'It was an ugly goat.'"

It was a joke Julian's father had picked up from a video game, one that always made him laugh.

Emma chuckled. "Well, at least he has a sense of humour."

She smiled at him, the reassurance in his voice settling her nerves just a little. It was funny how much of this felt like a step into a new chapter—not just with the world, but with each other.

Chapter 54:

The sun had barely started to rise when the hum of the truck's engine echoed in the underground car park. Julian and Emma, still a little bleary-eyed from their rushed morning preparations, shuffled out of the apartment building. Flynn, looking even more disheveled than before, was waiting for them by the truck. Now patched with more than a few bloodstains, his uniform seemed to carry the weight of long nights and tough battles.

"You guys ready?" Flynn asked, his voice low but with an edge of readiness. "We've got a bit of a drive ahead."

Emma glanced at Julian, who was adjusting the strap on his bag. "Ready as we'll ever be," she said, her voice tinged with quiet excitement.

Julian nodded, his mind half on the road and half on the strange sense of unease that always came with the unknown. They hadn't traveled far since the world had fallen apart, but this was different. Today, they were stepping into new territory. Meeting Julian's family felt like the beginning of something.

Before leaving the apartment, they flicked the radio dial to the loop Julian had set up the night before. The sound of the broadcast clicked in, the soothing shuffle of songs and intermittent transmissions filling the truck's interior. Julian gave it a final check, ensuring the loop would run smoothly while they were on the road.

"Alright, we're set," he said, looking at Emma with a small grin. "It's on. I think we're good for the next few days."

Emma leaned back in her seat, nodding. "It feels... weirdly refreshing, doesn't it?" she said. "Hearing something familiar. It's strange, but in a good way."

Julian glanced out of the side window, his thoughts swirling. As the truck pulled out of the parking lot, the familiar sight of Ardi waving goodbye from afar caught his eye. Ardi's silhouette was small but unmistakable, standing by the front door, hands raised in a casual wave. It wasn't much, but it felt comforting in a world that had lost so much.

"Looks like Ardi's on guard duty for the day," Julian murmured, his voice tinged with warmth.

Flynn, already in gear, didn't say much, but there was a flicker of acknowledgment in his eyes as he steered the truck out of the car park and onto the road.

"Bradfield first," Flynn said as he adjusted the truck's speed, "56.9 km via M5. But we're not taking the usual route. Too many bush rangers around. You'll want to get comfy. We might be taking a detour or two."

The truck rumbled to life as they merged onto the main road. Julian and Emma settled into the worn seats, and the tension in the air seemed to ease for the first time in days. As the truck bounced over potholes and cracked asphalt, they tuned into the radio again.

A soft melody played in the background, followed by the familiar broadcast static. The voices came through, gentle at first but gradually becoming clearer. The random loop of stories, music, and transmissions from other survivors felt like a comforting thread between worlds—between the old world and the new, between what was lost and what still mattered.

"It's like we're not alone," Emma murmured, her voice almost inaudible over the hum of the truck. She turned to Julian, her eyes thoughtful. "We're still connected to all of that."

Julian nodded, his gaze fixed out the window. "Yeah... it's a reminder, isn't it? That there's something else out there. Something that's still going."

He paused momentarily, staring out as the scenery began to shift, the wild, untamed landscape giving way to the more familiar surroundings of suburban streets.

Flynn didn't speak much on the drive, but his presence in the cab was reassuring. He knew these roads, the risks, and what it took to survive out here. As the truck continued its journey toward Bradfield, Julian couldn't help but feel that strange sense of anticipation rising again. A mix of nerves, hope, and something else—a whisper of normality that seemed so far out of reach, yet so near.

The radio crackled again, the soft voice of a survivor cutting through the static with a story of their own. Emma smiled softly to herself, her thoughts briefly drifting as she listened.

"Maybe we're all just trying to find a way to hold on," she said, more to herself than anyone else.

Julian glanced over at her. "Yeah. I think that's all any of us can do right now. Hold on."

The journey ahead was uncertain, but for now, the steady rhythm of the truck and the voices from the radio kept them grounded in the only way they knew how: together, with whatever fragments of hope remained.

Chapter 55:

As the truck rumbled closer to Julian's parents' home, his heart began to race. The familiar sight of the neighborhood was mostly the same, but something about the scene ahead felt different. A solid, reinforced steel wall had replaced the once modest fence that lined the front yard. It looked like a fortress—no, more like a castle. Heavy metal gates stood proudly, taller than ever before, with a visible layer of rust that spoke of a long, hard struggle to maintain what little safety they could in this chaotic world.

Julian's breath caught in his chest as he took in the sight. This wasn't the place he remembered, the home he had left behind. It was something else now. Something… defensive.

Emma and Flynn exchanged glances, both on edge, sensing the tension in the air. They knew Julian's family must be tough—he'd mentioned them enough—but this? This was something else entirely.

Julian cleared his throat, and, with one last deep breath, he stepped out of the truck and walked toward the towering gates, a sense of urgency pulling him forward. He wasn't sure what to expect, but part of him hoped this was still the home he remembered.

He knocked on the heavy steel gate, reverberating through the silent air. The waiting was agonizing, and the minutes stretched, feeling like hours. Julian could feel the weight of their eyes on him, but his attention was fixed on the gate, willing it to open.

And then, a voice broke the silence—loud, brash, and unmistakably familiar.

"If you're a bush ranger, fuck off or I'll shoot you where you stand!"

Julian froze, his heart skipping a beat. The voice was rough but familiar. It belonged to Aunty Gwin, his aunt on his father's side. She'd always been a force to be reckoned with—a woman who didn't take shit from anyone. He hadn't heard her voice in what felt like forever, but it brought a flood of memories rushing back.

The gate slowly creaked open, and she stood in the entryway with a rifle slung over her shoulder, looking as formidable as he remembered.

She blinked a few times as she looked at Julian, her sharp eyes narrowing. Then, as recognition hit, her face broke into a wide grin.

"Jules! You cheeky bastard, is that you?" Aunty Gwin's voice softened, and her face lit up joyfully as she lowered the rifle.

Julian couldn't suppress the smile that spread across his face. It had been too long—too much had happened, too many changes. But seeing his aunt again felt like a small victory in this moment.

"It's me, Aunt Gwin," he said, stepping forward as she wrapped her arms around him in a fierce hug.

"Shit, it's good to see you! Come on in, get inside, quick! Don't just stand there like a shag on a rock…. Or was it a lemon." Her eyes flicked to Emma and Flynn. "You two better not be with the wrong crowd, or I'll have to put a bullet in each of ya."

Emma raised an eyebrow, but Julian could see the smile tugging at the corner of her lips. "We're friends," she said, offering a polite but slightly wary wave.

"Well, as long as you're not a damn bush ranger, you're fine with me." Aunty Gwin stepped aside, ushering them all inside the fortress-like compound. "You better believe we've got our own defenses now. Can't be too careful out here, especially after the way things've been going."

As they walked inside, Julian couldn't help but take in the strange new world his family had created for themselves. The house had been fortified beyond recognition. Steel shutters over the windows, reinforced doors, and the remnants of makeshift barricades gave the place the feel of a military stronghold. Yet, despite the fortress-like appearance, there was something undeniably comforting about being here. The smell of fresh food cooking in the kitchen and the faint laughter of someone in another room felt like family, even if everything else had changed.

"Aunty Gwin," Julian said, stepping back as he noticed the others were gathering near the kitchen. "Where's Dad? What happened to him?"

Aunty Gwin's face faltered for a split second, a flicker of something Julian couldn't quite read crossing her features. But just as quickly, she masked it with a forced smile.

"He's fine, don't worry. Just a little banged up," she said, her tone light, but Julian could tell she was trying to downplay it. "Lilith's patching him up as we speak. He'll be alright."

The words didn't reassure him, but Julian decided not to press further. Instead, he followed her into the living room, where his father, Enoch, was seated on a recliner, his face drawn with pain.

Enoch had always been a towering figure in Julian's life—his broad shoulders and rugged features constantly reminded him of strength and stability. But now, seeing him in a chair, wounded and weary, it was clear that the world had taken its toll on even the toughest.

"Dad?" Julian called, his voice soft but filled with concern.

Enoch looked up, his face softening at the sight of his son. His lips curled into a faint smile, though it didn't reach his eyes.

"Julian, son," Enoch said, his voice raspy. "Didn't think I'd see you again. It's good to have you home."

Julian's chest tightened. This wasn't the man he remembered, the unyielding figure who'd always been his rock. But he was still his father, and Julian wouldn't let him slip away without a fight.

"What happened?" Julian asked, his voice barely above a whisper.

Enoch's gaze shifted, and for a moment, Julian thought his father might say something else entirely. But instead, Enoch sighed heavily.

"Raiders… They came at night. Tried to take whatever we had left. We fought 'em off, but…" His voice trailed off, and he looked down at the bandages wrapped around his abdomen.

Julian felt the weight of those words hit him hard. His father—the man who had taught him everything he knew about strength and resilience—had been attacked. They had fought back, but the scars of those battles ran deeper than he'd imagined.

"Dad, we're going to get you back on your feet," Julian said, his voice cracking slightly. "You're not alone in this."

Enoch's lips twitched into a small smile. "I know, son. I know."

And for a fleeting moment, despite the damage done to his body and the world around him, Julian knew they would face whatever came next together. They were family, and that was all that mattered.

Chapter 56: Shadows in the Dark

Julian's stomach dropped at his father's next words.

"They took Mum."

For a moment, the world seemed to stop. The quiet hum of conversation and the distant clatter from the kitchen faded into the background as Julian Julian tried to process what he had just heard.

"The bushrangers kidnapped your mother."

Julian clenched his fists, his breath hitching. "What do you mean they took her? Who? When?" His voice was raw, edged with panic and anger.

Enoch winced as he shifted in his chair, his weathered face etched with exhaustion. "They came in the night. We fought them off, but one of them— he moved like a shadow. Slipped past the gates somehow. Your mother was gone before we could stop them."

Lilith, silently tending to Enoch's wound, finally spoke. "It wasn't a normal attack, Julian," she said, her voice measured but laced with unease. "Look at this."

She peeled back the bandages, revealing a deep wound just above Enoch's ribs. It was unmistakable—a bite mark. Human teeth.

Flynn, who had seen his fair share of injuries, stiffened slightly. He had witnessed gunshot wounds, stab wounds, even shrapnel injuries—but this? This was something else.

"That's… unsettling," Flynn muttered, trying to keep his expression neutral.

Emma, standing beside Julian, swallowed hard. The sight of the wound made her stomach turn. She had seen blood before, but this was deeply wrong.

Gwin leaned against the kitchen counter, arms crossed. "That bastard was fast," she said bitterly. "Got in and out before we could even put him down. Lil and I got a couple of shots off, but he vanished into the dark."

"They weren't just trying to kill him," Lilith added, her voice lower now, almost hesitant. "They were… drinking his blood."

Silence.

Emma exhaled sharply, a mix of disbelief and disgust crossing her face. "Like a… vampire?"

Gwin snorted. "Dunno about that, love. But whatever they are, they ain't normal."

Julian felt his head spinning. His mother was gone. His father was wounded. And now, there were people—or something worse—lurking in the night, preying on the wounded like scavengers.

He turned to Enoch. "We'll find her, Dad. I swear."

His father gave a tired but determined nod. "I know you will, son."

Gwin took a deep breath, her sharp eyes flicking to Emma. "But enough of the horror stories for now— where are my manners? You must be Emma."

Emma straightened slightly. "Yeah. We, uh… we've been picking up your radio transmissions."

Gwin grinned. "Clever pair, you two. Gotta say, your setup's impressive."

Enoch, still in his chair, gave a small chuckle. "The radio is brilliant, kiddo. Kept us going. Kept us sane."

Emma gave Julian a sideways glance, a small smile tugging at the corner of her lips. "Told you it was a good idea."

Meanwhile, Lilith remained quiet. Julian noticed her brother's furrowed brow and a distant look in her eyes. She was thinking deeply.

Gwin, however, had already moved on, her gaze shifting to Flynn. She smirked, tilting her head as she looked him up and down. "And who's this tall drink of water dressed like a digger?"

Flynn was caught completely off guard and stiffened. He was used to hostility, used to being questioned or challenged—but being flirted with by a 71-year-old woman who looked far younger than her years? That was a new one.

"I—uh—" Flynn cleared his throat, suddenly flustered. "I should probably, uh, get the truck in the compound. Y'know. Before—uh—anything else happens."

Gwin raised an eyebrow, clearly amused. "Need a hand with that?"

Flynn gave a quick, nervous nod, his face slightly red. "Yeah. That'd—uh—that'd be good."

Julian smirked, nudging Emma. "Think he just met his match."

Emma chuckled. "Yeah, I think so."

As Flynn and Gwin headed toward the truck, Julian let out a slow breath, his gaze shifting back to his father.

They had survived another day. But the real fight was beginning.

Chapter 57:

The next few hours passed in relative calm. The tension from earlier had settled, and Julian could breathe for the first time in what felt like days.

Lilith suddenly broke the silence as they sat in the living room with a blunt but warm remark.

"So, Jules—Emma your girlfriend?"

Emma, caught off guard, immediately blushed, looking at Julian. He met her gaze, hesitated for a second, and then nodded.

Lilith grinned. "Good. Welcome to the family, Emma."

Gwin, who had been preoccupied with being weirdly touchy with Flynn—something he was partially loving despite his attempts to act indifferent—finally tore herself away from him. Flynn coughed and muttered something about needing air, making a hasty retreat outside.

Julian and Emma exchanged amused glances before stepping out onto the deck and settling into the old, sun-worn chairs. The night air was cool, and the sky was blanketed with stars, untouched by the artificial glow of a world long gone.

Inside, Enoch had finally passed out after taking some morphine for the pain. His breathing was steady and reassuring, but Julian could still feel the weight of his father's earlier words pressing on his chest.

Gwin followed them outside, leaning against the railing with a relaxed smirk. "So, Emma, I hear you're quite the producer."

Emma nodded. "I worked as Julian's producer at DisruptTech."

Gwin whistled. "If I knew that, I would've poached you both."

Emma laughed lightly. "Not sure how much Julian told you about me."

Gwin grinned. "Not much, honestly. But I'm not surprised. He's never been great at talking about himself." She stretched her arms. "Speaking of which, you probably don't know much about me either."

Emma shook her head.

Gwin smirked. "I ran Sacred Group."

Emma's eyebrows furrowed. "Wait—Sacred? Like the company behind Sacred Games, Sacred Films, and Sacred Books?"

"The very same."

Emma sat up straight. "As in the studio behind New World Order, Radioactive, Eternal Testament, and—" she turned to Julian, eyes wide, "—The Magic Thorn?!"

Julian sighed, rubbing the back of his neck. "Yeah… I may have left out some details about my grandfather."

Emma gawked at him. "You told me he was a designer and concept artist! You never mentioned he was the visionary behind some of the greatest games and stories of all time!"

Gwin chuckled, a wistful glint in her eyes. "Our dad—Julian's grandfather—was a storyteller through and through. Sacred was his legacy, passed down to me. But looking at the world now, it almost feels like one of his stories. Like we're stuck inside one of his dystopian worlds."

Julian exhaled, feeling a familiar weight settle on his shoulders. "Yeah. Feels that way sometimes."

Lilith, who had been quiet, suddenly chimed in. "I took a different path. I was an athlete—swimming and archery. Made it to the 2060 Sapporo Olympic Games, actually." She smirked. "Two silvers for Australia."

Emma's eyes widened. "That's incredible!"

Lilith shrugged. "It was fun. But after that, I came back and became a paramedic. Loved it. Saving lives is a different kind of rush."

Emma smiled. "I admire that."

Gwin stretched. "Well, you asked about our names earlier—why they're so unique."

Emma nodded. "Yeah, if you don't mind me asking."

Julian sighed, leaning back in his chair. The conversation was lighthearted, but in the back of his mind, thoughts of his mother still gnawed at him.

Gwin smirked. "Our father—Julian's pop—was a storyteller. He named all of us after legends."

She gestured to herself. "I'm Gwinevere, after the Arthurian princess."

Lilith nodded. "I was named after Lilith—the fertility goddess and, supposedly, Adam's first wife."

Emma's eyes flicked to Julian's father. "And Enoch?"

Gwin's smile softened. "Named after the man who, according to the Book of Enoch, became the Archangel Metatron."

Emma exhaled, taking it all in. "Your family is full of history."

Julian chuckled. "Yeah. You could say that."

But as much as the conversation offered a brief escape, the reality of their situation loomed ever-present in Julian's mind. His mother was still out there, somewhere. And whatever had taken her—whatever they were—needed to be dealt with.

Tomorrow, they would start the search.

Chapter 58:

The conversation had lightened Julian's mood, but only briefly. His mind kept circling back to his mother. She was out there somewhere, and every second they sat around talking felt like wasted time.

He stood up suddenly, clenching his fists. "I can't just sit here. We need to look for her."

Gwin's expression darkened. "Jules—"

"No," Julian cut in, his voice shaking slightly. "What if we wait too long? What if she's—" He stopped himself, unable to finish the thought.

Gwin sighed, rubbing her temples. "Going out at night? That isn't wise."

Lilith leaned forward, arms crossed. "That thing that attacked us wasn't just some bandit bushranger, Jules. It was something else." She met his gaze, her usually calm demeanor tense. "I've treated plenty of wounds, but that thing… it didn't just attack. It fed."

Julian shuddered. The memory of his father's wound—the jagged, human bite marks—flashed in his mind.

Flynn, who had been silent, finally spoke. "I'll go with you."

Julian looked at him, surprised. Flynn shrugged. "I get it. If it were my family, I wouldn't sit around either."

Before Julian could respond, Gwin slammed her hand against the deck railing. "Absolutely not." Her voice was sharp, her expression fierce. "I didn't keep this place standing just to let you both run off and get yourselves killed."

Lilith's tone was equally firm. "She's right. You don't know what's out there. We barely got away, and that was in daylight."

Flynn squared his shoulders. "I can handle myself."

Gwin scoffed. "And what happens when handling yourself isn't enough? You think a gun is going to stop something that moves like a shadow?"

Julian's chest tightened. He had always looked up to his aunts—they were strong, resilient survivors. But hearing the fear in their voices shook him.

Emma reached for his hand. "Julian…" Her voice was softer than the others but no less urgent. "Maybe it is too dangerous. What if they're right? What if we have a better chance at first light?"

Julian swallowed hard. Every instinct screamed at him to leave now, to do something. But as he looked at the people around him—those who cared about him—he hesitated.

Gwin placed a hand on his shoulder. "Morning, Jules. We go at first light."

Lilith nodded. "We'll be ready. Together."

Flynn exhaled through his nose, reluctantly backing down. "Fine. First light."

Julian clenched his jaw, his hands still balled into fists. He hated waiting. But as much as he wanted to run off into the night, deep down, he knew they were right.

Chapter 59:

Julian jolted awake as a hand gently shook his shoulder. His fingers tightened around the rifle Flynn had given him, instinct kicking in before his brain caught up. His breathing was sharp, his heart pounding like a war drum.

"It's just me," Emma's voice broke through the haze. She knelt beside him, her face soft with concern. "It's morning."

Julian blinked, shaking off the fog of sleep. The sun had begun creeping over the horizon, casting a golden hue over the compound. His muscles were stiff, his grip still firm on the weapon.

Emma tilted her head, studying him. This wasn't a side of him she'd ever really seen before. He looked hardened, his body tense as if ready for battle. Something was raw about it—this quiet, protective nature that had surfaced.

She couldn't help but find it charming in a way.

Julian rubbed the exhaustion from his face. "Did you sleep?"

"On the couch," she admitted. "Better than you, I'd bet."

Julian sighed and stood up, stretching his sore limbs. The others were already up.

Gwin stood near the truck, fastening the straps of a leather harness around her torso. She was dressed for a fight, her movements sharp and methodical. Lilith stood beside her, adjusting a quiver of arrows slung over her back.

Flynn let out a low whistle as he approached. "You two look badass."

Gwin smirked. "We are badass."

Lilith nudged her playfully. "Come on, let's go see what we can find in town."

Julian nodded, gripping his rifle. "We'll check the old heritage estate."

Gwin gave him a firm look. "Be careful, Jules."

He nodded. "You too."

With a final glance toward his father's resting form inside, Julian turned to Emma and Flynn. "Let's move."

It was time to find his mother.

Chapter 60: Bradfield City Centre

T he morning air in Bradfield was thick with the smell of burnt wood and rusted metal. Once bustling with people and traffic, the city was now a patchwork of makeshift barricades and empty storefronts. The few survivors left barely acknowledged Gwin and Lilith as they passed, their faces gaunt and wary.

Lilith adjusted the quiver of arrows on her back and whispered, "This place feels like a ghost town."

"It is," Gwin muttered. "But ghosts still talk."

They approached an older man sitting by a fire pit in what used to be a small park. His beard was unkempt, his eyes sunken. A group of other survivors huddled nearby, listening to a battered radio whispering static-laced transmissions.

Gwin crouched beside him, pulling a ration bar from her pack and holding it out. "We're looking for information."

The man took the bar hesitantly, sniffing it before biting into it. "Depends what kind."

Lilith leaned in. "A bushranger. Moves like a shadow. Attacks from nowhere." She hesitated, then added, "A blood drinker."

The man's chewing slowed. He glanced at the others around him. A woman sitting by the radio visibly tensed.

"Blackcreek," the man finally said.

Gwin narrowed her eyes. "That a place or a group?"

"Both." He swallowed hard. "The Blackcreek gang. They're not like the others. Most bushrangers will rob you, maybe rough you up if they're desperate. These ones... they take people. Feed on them like animals."

Lilith clenched her jaw. "Where?"

The woman on the radio finally spoke, her voice barely above a whisper. "Old heritage estates. The church."

Gwin swore under her breath. "That's where Julian, Flynn, and Emma went."

Lilith stood abruptly. "We need to warn them. Now."

The Heritage Estates

Julian walked ahead of Flynn and Emma, rifle in hand, his senses on high alert. The further they went into the estate, the quieter it became. The air felt thick, charged with something unnatural.

Emma stopped, pointing at a tree. "Look."

Scrawled in dark, dried blood was a message: KEEP OUT. TURN BACK.

Flynn exhaled sharply. "Not ominous at all."

Julian stepped forward cautiously, scanning the path ahead. More signs followed, each written in the same dark crimson:

THIS IS BLACKCREEK LAND. YOU'VE BEEN WARNED.

The trail led to an old, abandoned church. The stained-glass windows were shattered, the wooden doors slightly ajar. The building loomed over them like a corpse, long forgotten by time.

Flynn tightened his grip on his shotgun. "This is a trap."

Emma looked at Julian. "What do we do?"

Julian took a deep breath, eyes locked on the shadowed entrance of the church. "We go in."

From somewhere in the distance, a figure moved. Too fast. Too silent.

They weren't alone.

Chapter 61:

The old colonial church loomed over them, its sandstone walls weathered by time and the elements. The wooden doors were slightly ajar, creaking on their rusted hinges as Julian, Emma, and Flynn stepped inside, rifles ready. Dust hung thick in the air, swirling in the dim light filtering through the stained-glass windows, casting fractured colors across the worn pews.

Their footsteps echoed against the stone floor as they advanced cautiously. The altar stood abandoned, its once-pristine white cloth now stained and tattered. Candles long melted down to wax puddles, hinting at past occupants. But now, the church was silent—too silent.

Flynn signaled for them to spread out, eyes scanning every shadow. Emma moved toward the side of the room, fingers tight around her rifle. Julian approached the pulpit, glancing around for any sign of movement.

Then, a floorboard creaked.

Before any of them could react, a figure emerged from the darkness. Cloaked in tattered black, it moved with unnatural speed, a motion blur. In an instant, Flynn and Emma were thrown backward, sent crashing into the pews with bone-jarring force. The wind was knocked from Emma's lungs as she hit the wood, her rifle clattering from her grasp. Flynn groaned, dazed by the impact.

Julian barely had time to raise his weapon before the figure was upon him. Cold fingers clamped around his throat like a vice, lifting him off the ground with impossible strength. His vision blurred, the edges darkening as oxygen fled his lungs. He struggled, gasping, kicking, but the grip remained unyielding.

The last thing he saw before consciousness slipped away was the glint of unnatural eyes staring into his own.

Julian awoke to the sensation of something warm trailing down his neck. His head pounded, his limbs felt weak, and his pulse thudded unevenly in his ears. The first thing he saw was a woman—draped in a tattered black dress, smudged eye shadow framing her gaunt cheekbones, and blood smeared around her lips.

"Julian Hayes? The sexy radio man?" Her voice was both playful and venomous.

Recognition hit like a hammer. Tessa. They had gone to high school together. Back then, she had been a quiet, strange girl with an unreciprocated crush. Now, she was something else entirely.

Before he could react, she leaned closer, her breath hot against his ear. "I've missed you, Julian. You used to talk to me every night... through the radio. Only for me. You didn't even know."

His body tensed as her lips brushed his skin, then— sharp pain. Fangs piercing flesh. His breath hitched, an involuntary shudder racking his frame. The pain was raw, primal. But worse was the way she murmured as she drank, whispering sweet nothings like a lover lost in the moment.

"You taste divine… I always knew you would. You were made for this. For me."

Summoning every ounce of strength he had left, Julian shoved her away. She staggered back, licking the blood from her lips. Emma and Flynn had recovered, rifles raised, ready to end her. But Julian lifted a hand, stopping them.

Instead, he fixed Tessa with a look that cut deeper than any blade. "If you ever come near me again, I will make you regret it."

Tessa laughed, tilting her head like a predator intrigued by its prey. "Oh, Julian… you'll miss me. You'll see."

She grinned, her teeth stained with blood, the twisted expression sending a chill down Julian's spine. "I love you, Julian," she said, her voice low and almost mocking.

Julian's hand tightened around the gun. Without warning, he aimed it and fired. The shot rang out, and the bullet hit the ground just inches from her feet, kicking up dirt and splinters.

"Does this look like the face of someone who's fucking around?" Julian screamed, his voice raw with frustration and fury. "I'm not here for your games. I'm here for my mother." His finger was still on the trigger, his eyes burning with intensity.

Tessa tilted her head slightly, unfazed. She blew him a kiss, a cruel smile playing on her lips. "You really think that will make me scared of you?"

Emma, standing beside Julian, glanced at her disgustedly. Her hand instinctively reached for her weapon but hesitated, knowing this wasn't her fight. "You're sick," she muttered, her eyes fixed on Tessa.

Tessa's gaze never left Julian. "You always were a bit of a mama's boy, huh?" she teased, her voice dripping with sarcasm. "Tell me, Julian, what will you do when you find her? What if she doesn't want saving?"

Julian's jaw tightened. "I'll make her see reason. I'll make you all see reason."

"Sure, you will," Tessa said with a laugh that echoed like a slap. "But you're running out of time, darling. The clock's ticking, and we both know you don't have the guts to pull that trigger on me."

Emma's disgust deepened, and she stepped forward, her voice cold. "You don't know him as well as you think you do."

Tessa's smirk never wavered. "Oh, I know him better than anyone," she said, her eyes gleaming. "He's just like the rest of you. Weak.....but delicious." Then, before anyone could act, she vanished into the darkness.

Julian's wound burned, his mind spiraling. Deep down, he knew this wasn't over.

Chapter 62:

Emma and Flynn pushed forward, adrenaline coursing through their veins as they rushed toward the rundown shack where Julian's mother was held. The storm had only grown fiercer, the wind howling, but their focus remained locked on the mission ahead.

They burst through the decrepit door, splintering the wood as it crashed open. Inside, the dim light revealed a horrifying sight: Julian's mother, bound to a chair, her legs marred with deep, vicious bite marks. Her skin was sickly pale, the sickly sheen of blood loss visible even in the weak light. Tessa had been feeding on her, leaving behind the unmistakable signs of her cruel, unrelenting thirst.

For a moment, everything felt suspended, the room heavy with the stench of blood and decay. But then, the woman's eyes—Julian's mother's—fluttered open, and despite the agonizing condition she was in, she managed a weak but relieved smile when she saw her son.

"Julian…" Her voice was barely a whisper, weak but undeniably warm, filled with the relief of seeing him again. "You came."

Julian's heart clenched. He couldn't hide the rush of emotions flooding through him. He rushed forward without a second thought, his hands shaking as he moved to untie the ropes around her wrists. Every second felt like an eternity, but the situation's urgency pushed him onward.

As he freed her, the moment she caught sight of him more clearly—the torn collar, the fresh bite mark on his neck—her expression shifted. Her brow furrowed, her smile faltering as concern overtook her relief. She reached up with trembling hands, her fingers brushing gently over his wound.

"You're hurt," she murmured, her voice soft but insistent, the maternal instinct kicking in immediately despite the pain she was enduring herself. "Let me see."

Julian swallowed, his throat tight, but he forced a smile, which felt brittle on his lips. "I'm fine, Mum. Let's get you out of here first."

But she was already reaching up, her hands moving with a practiced grace that spoke to her years as a nurse. Her fingers inspected the bite with an expertise that only a mother—and a healer—could have. "You're lucky she didn't hit an artery," she whispered, her voice laced with both concern and a quiet, underlying strength.

Flynn and Emma exchanged uneasy glances as they helped her carefully to her feet. The shack seemed to close in on them, the air thick with the sense of danger still lingering. But Julian's mother, despite everything, was already in full control.

"I can patch this up," she said, her voice surprisingly steady, even after everything she had been through. "Just get me back to the house."

There was no hesitation in her tone, no fear. She was still thinking about others even amid their chaotic, blood-soaked world. She is still thinking about her family.

Emma nodded, gritting her teeth against the overwhelming surge of emotions. Flynn looked to Julian, his expression serious. "We're with you, man. Let's get her home."

Despite the devastation, despite the horrors they had all endured, Julian's mother still had that undeniable air of strength—something only a mother could carry. Even in the face of unimaginable terror, she was still taking charge.

And Julian, with the weight of his wounds, would follow her lead—because, in the end, a mother's care never fades, not even when the world crumbles around them.

Chapter 77: And the Thunder Rolled

As the rain begins to fall, the heavy drops hammering down in rhythmic pulses, Lilith and Gwin emerge from the storm's embrace, their figures cutting through the sheets of rain with purposeful strides. The wind howls around them, but their determination keeps them moving forward, each step heavy with the knowledge of what's transpired.

In the dim light of the storm, Julian, Emma, Flynn, and his mother are going down the road. The mother leans on Julian for support, her steps slow but steady, the weight of her exhaustion evident. Though their pace is weary, the relief of their survival hangs in the air like a fragile thread. They move together, a quiet unity in the face of the chaos that has chased them this far.

As Lilith and Gwin draw closer, they slow their steps, the sight of the others filling them with a deep sense of relief. The tension of the night seems to settle in the space between them. They've arrived just in time, but the weight of the storm pressing down on them all makes the moment feel like a heavy pause before the next chapter begins.

Gwin speaks first, her voice barely audible over the storm's roar. "You're okay," she says, and though the words are simple, the relief in her tone is unmistakable, as if the storm itself had been holding its breath in anticipation.

Lilith steps forward, her gaze sweeping over the group. "Looks like the storm's rolling in fast. Let's keep moving," she advises, sharp but laced with distraction. Even she can't shake the feeling that the storm is something more—its violence mirroring the tension that still lingers in the air, thick with everything that has happened, everything yet to come.

The rain pelts the earth like a warning as they move forward, but then, in the distance, a faint crackle catches their attention. The sound of tuning radios, distorted and warped by the storm, begins to filter through the air. It's unsettling in its faintness, like an eerie whisper of something much larger than them. The noise becomes louder and sharper, and then the unmistakable notes of "Thunder Rolls" by Garth Brooks begin to play. The haunting melody rips through the storm like a thread of fate, wrapping around their hearts and pulling them into its rhythm.

The valley feels small in the face of the song, its lyrics echoing through the air with an almost ominous weight. The wind shifts as though it, too, is listening.

The group stops, a collective stillness settling in. Emma shivers, her gaze shifting toward the distant radio's source. "Lady Blackcreek must have forgotten her radio," she says, her voice low, breaking the quiet spell. She looks up at Julian, her expression a mixture of curiosity and concern, but Julian remains silent, lost in thought. His mind is still tangled in everything that has happened—his mother's rescue, the haunting figure of Tessa, and the storm that seems to mirror the chaos in his mind.

But it's Flynn who's the most visibly shaken. He's standing off the side, his eyes distant, locked on the swirling horizon. The storm around them seems to close in tighter, the music on the radio gnawing at his nerves. He mutters under his breath, his words barely above a whisper. "I've dealt with bushrangers before," he says, his voice low and strained, "but not like her." There's a haunted edge to his tone, a clear scar in his psyche that the others can see but are unsure how to address. Tessa had broken something in him—a side of Flynn rattled by Tessa's strength and the unnerving hold she had over Julian. It's not just the fear of the unknown that bothers him. It's the way she made him feel small, insignificant.

Emma glances over at him; brow furrowed in thought before she speaks. "You need to explain all of what she was when we get back." It's not a question—there's no hesitation, no softening of her tone. She doesn't need him to answer now, but the look she gives him is clear. She's already starting to piece together the broken pieces of their ordeal and wants to know the truth. She notices Flynn's unease but doesn't push him for more. He'll come to her when he's ready or broken enough to admit the weight he's carrying.

Meanwhile, just out of their sight, standing in the distance with the storm swirling around her, Tessa watches them—her figure barely visible against the heavy rain and swirling darkness. She is an ethereal shadow against the backdrop of nature's fury. Her expression is unreadable, her face obscured by the storm's grip, but the way she hums softly to the tune of "Thunder Rolls" reveals something far darker.

The song's haunting lyrics echo in her mind, each word, each note like a sinister promise. She stands in the shadows, listening to the melody as it reverberates through her, the music entwining with her obsession. It's as if the song itself is a marker of fate—a prophecy of the future.

Her gaze locks onto Julian from afar, a smirk slowly curling at the corners of her lips. She knows, deep down, that she will have him one day. He's already hers, caught in the gravity of her pull. The obsession that started as a dangerous infatuation is far from over. No—this is only the beginning. The storm has just begun to roll in, and she intends to be there when it all falls apart. The storm outside is nothing compared to the storm she plans to bring into Julian's life.

As Julian, Emma, Flynn, Lilith, Gwin, and Julian's mother, Isla, reach the house, the rain begins to hammer down in thick, heavy sheets, and the wind howls through the trees. The storm roars above them, deep and rolling, like some great beast stirring in the dark. The house stands before them, its warm glow spilling onto the porch—a sanctuary against the night's chaos.

Before they can even knock, the front door swings open.

Enoch steps onto the porch, his cane clutched tightly in one hand, his weathered face pale with shock. His breath catches the moment his eyes find Isla, and for a moment, the storm's fury seems to fade, drowned out by the sheer relief flooding his expression.

"Isla?" His voice cracks, thick with disbelief.

Despite the exhaustion dragging at her body, Isla manages a small, tired smile. "I'm here, love."

A sharp breath escapes Enoch as if he'd been holding it for years. He moves toward her as fast as his old bones allow, his steps uneven but determined. When he reaches her, his hands tremble as he cups her face, his thumb ghosting over the bruises on her cheek. His throat bobs as he tries to speak, but all that comes out is a shaky exhale before he pulls her into his arms.

"I thought—" He choked on the words. "I thought I'd lost you."

Isla leans into him, her strength fading now that she's finally safe. "I know," she murmurs. "I know."

Lilith, ever the pragmatist, clears her throat. "Alright, enough standing in the damn rain. Inside, now. Both of you need patching up, and I need to check on Flynn and Emma." Her voice is sharp but laced with quiet concern as she herds them inside.

When they step through the threshold, the house swallows them in warmth. The fire crackles in the hearth, its glow casting long shadows along the wooden walls. The scent of old books, dried herbs, and faint traces of antiseptic lingers. Despite the storm rattling the windows, the house feels like a world away from the madness outside.

Gwin moves quickly, gathering bandages and supplies from a worn wooden chest. "Julian, sit. Isla, you too." Her voice is firm but gentle, the weight of responsibility settling on her shoulders.

Julian slumps into a chair, his exhaustion finally catching up to him. His shirt collar is stained red from the bite wound on his neck, the torn fabric clinging to his skin. Isla, despite her injuries, instinctively reaches for him, her fingers brushing against the wound with a nurse's practiced touch.

"You're hurt." Her voice is thick with concern.

Julian exhales, forcing a half-hearted grin. "You should see the other guy."

Lilith rolls her eyes. "Oh, shut up."

She turns to Flynn, who still hasn't sat down. He stands near the doorway, his face pale, his fingers twitching at his sides. His eyes are unfocused, fixed on something that isn't there. Lilith narrows her gaze. "You look like you've seen a ghost," she says.

Flynn shakes his head, his voice hoarse. "Something worse."

Emma slouched on the couch beside him and rubbed her temples. "You're telling me."

Gwin dabs antiseptic onto Julian's wound, and he hisses through his teeth, wincing. "Could you maybe be a little less aggressive with that?"

"Could you maybe stop getting bitten by things?" she counters.

Julian smirks, but it fades quickly. He leans forward, his elbows resting on his knees, his voice quieter now, as if saying it aloud will make it real. "Are we gonna talk about what the hell she was?"

A silence settles over them, heavier than the storm outside.

Emma glances toward Flynn, her expression wary. "Yeah, I think we need to."

Flynn swallows, his jaw tightening. He drags a hand down his face before finally looking up. "I've dealt with bushrangers before," he says, his voice flat and distant. But not like her."

Julian exhales sharply. "She was… something else. She—" He hesitates, searching for the words, for an explanation that makes sense. But nothing does.

Emma crosses her arms. "She moved too fast. Knew too much. That wasn't just skill."

Flynn shakes his head, muttering under his breath, "No. It wasn't."

A fresh gust of wind rattles the windows, flickering the firelight. The rain pounds against the roof in a steady rhythm, a reminder of the storm still raging outside.

Then, from the corner of the room, the radio crackles.

It's faint at first, just static whispering through the quiet. Then, buried beneath the distortion, the melody returns—soft, distant, unmistakable.

"Thunder rolls…"

The words murmur through the speakers like a ghost of the past refusing to be forgotten.

Julian lifts his head slowly, his stomach twisting. Gwin turns toward the radio, frowning. "I thought that was off."

Emma rises from the couch, crossing the room in two strides. She twists the knob, trying to silence it. The static sputter, the melody fading—but something else filters through just before it cuts out completely. A voice.

Soft. Lyrical. Humming along to the song.

Emma's breath catches.

Flynn stiffens, his face going pale.

Julian grips the arms of his chair.

Because they know that voice.

Tessa is still out there somewhere, beyond the safety of the walls, beyond the storm and the rain.

And she's singing.

A slow, knowing smirk creeps across her lips as she hums to the radio's static-laced tune. The storm howls around her, but she stands unmoved, her gaze fixed on the distant house.

Julian was right.

This isn't over.

Not even close.

Chapter 63:

T he silence in the room was thick, pressing in from all sides. Outside, the rain had slowed to a dull patter, the storm retreating but leaving behind a sky heavy with clouds. The house, usually a place of warmth and safety, now felt like a waiting room between two inevitable disasters.

Julian hadn't moved since Enoch's last words. His gaze remained locked on the window, his jaw tight, his fingers twitching where they rested on his knee.

"You alright?" Emma's voice was quiet, careful.

Julian blinked, shaking himself back into the moment. "Yeah. Just… thinking."

Flynn scoffed. "That's dangerous."

"Shut up, Flynn," Gwen muttered, tossing a cloth at him before returning to her work on Julian's wound.

Lilith folded her arms. "Alright, let's lay this out plain. Tessa, Lady Blackcreek, whatever she calls herself now—she's got history with you, Julian. And from what we saw tonight, she's not just another lunatic with a grudge. She's something else. Something unnatural."

"Yeah, no kidding," Flynn muttered.

Julian exhaled through his nose. "I don't know what happened to her. The Tessa I knew was obsessive, yeah, but she was just… a girl. Smart, weird, way too intense, but not like this. Not…" He gestured vaguely toward the door, as if the words to describe her now didn't quite exist.

Emma leaned forward. "She was playing with us. Like she knew exactly how things would unfold. Like she was waiting for us to show up."

Lilith nodded. "Which means she either has eyes everywhere, or she has an agenda."

"Both," Enoch said darkly.

The old man pushed himself up from his chair with a quiet grunt, moving toward the fireplace. The flames flickered, casting long shadows across the room as he stared into them, his expression unreadable. When he spoke again, his voice was distant.

"I've seen things in my time. People who change. People who aren't what they were before." He turned slightly, his sharp gaze settling on Julian. "When she spoke to you, did you feel it?"

Julian frowned. "Feel what?"

"Like something crawling under your skin," Enoch said. "Like her voice didn't just reach your ears but wrapped itself around your thoughts."

Julian hesitated. His mind flicked back to the moment in the storm, to the way Tessa had smiled at him, the way her voice had curled around his name like it belonged to her.

Julian.

He shuddered involuntarily.

Enoch nodded as if that was all the confirmation he needed. "She's got power now. More than you understand. More than any of us understand."

A hush fell over the room. Even the fire seemed to dim, as if the shadows were listening.

Then, from the hall, the radio crackled again.

They all turned.

The device sat untouched on the wooden table, its dials unmoved. The static was low, humming like an idle breath. Then—

"Julian."

The voice slithered through the static, unmistakable. Soft. Playful.

Gwen shot to her feet. Flynn cursed under his breath.

Julian felt his chest tighten.

Emma was already moving, yanking the plug from the socket. The radio went silent instantly.

The room held its breath.

But this time, the knock that followed wasn't so slow, so deliberate. It was a soft tap—almost as if the air itself had moved against the wood.

Nobody moved.

The minutes stretched on, but the storm seemed far behind them now. The tension that had hung in the air earlier, like a thick mist, had dissipated. They were here, together, in the warmth of the house, the storm outside nothing but a fading memory.

Then, as the fire crackled gently in the hearth and the night grew quieter, Julian finally spoke.

"We're safe. For now."

It wasn't a question, but it felt like one. It was the unspoken hope they were all clinging to—that, for once, they could simply be still, and let the world outside pass them by.

Emma, sitting back, let out a deep breath. "Maybe that's all we can do right now."

Gwen glanced out the window, her gaze scanning the darkness beyond. "Yeah. And just hope she stays out there."

Enoch stepped back from the fire, his face softening. "We'll be alright. Just need time."

Flynn, still shaken, leaned back against the wall. "Time. Right." He exhaled slowly, letting the calm wash over him.

The quiet stretched on, peaceful now. The storm was gone, the night falling like a blanket over them. But somewhere, in the farthest reaches of the dark, Tessa lingered, a shadow that wasn't quite gone, not yet.

But for now… they were safe.

And for now, that would have to be enough.

Chapter 64: The Nightmare

— ✦ —

Julian drifted off to sleep, the comfort of Emma's warmth beside him a small solace against the world's chaos. But his dreams took him somewhere darker. Somewhere he didn't want to go.

The first thing he noticed was the sound. The familiar static of the radio crackling to life. It was faint at first, but then a voice broke through the distortion.

"Julian..."

He stirred in his dream, his brow furrowing. The voice was unmistakable—Max. But this wasn't the Max he remembered. His tone was darker, colder, almost malevolent.

"Julian... you left me. You abandoned me."

The voice echoed in his mind, growing louder and more accusing. He looked around, still in bed with Emma, the room bathed in an eerie half-light. He reached for her, shaking her gently.

"Emma... do you hear that?" he whispered.

Before she could respond, the door burst open with a deafening crash. Julian's heart jumped into his throat as Max stepped into the room, a gun in his hand, his eyes wild and unforgiving.

"Max, wait!" Julian shouted, holding up his hands. "Please, I'm sorry. I didn't mean to leave you alone."

Emma shot upright in bed, her eyes wide with panic. "Julian, what's happening—"

The gun fired.

Emma's body jerked, and she fell back against the bed, blood soaking into the sheets. Julian screamed, his hands shaking as he reached for her.

"Max! Stop!" he cried, tears streaming down his face. "I'm sorry! I'm sorry!"

Max stepped closer, his face twisted with fury. "Sorry doesn't matter now, Julian."

The gun was raised again, pointed directly at him. The trigger pulled, and the world shattered.

Julian fell—not into death, but into something else entirely.

He was in a room now, vast and empty, the walls stretching endlessly into the distance. It was cold and colorless, a space that felt both infinite and claustrophobic. He took a step forward, and the sound of his footfall echoed endlessly.

"Where am I?" he muttered, his voice trembling.

He turned his head and froze. Another version of himself was standing just a few feet away, staring at him with wide, unblinking eyes. The other Julian moved when he moved, mirroring him perfectly.

"Who... are you?" Julian asked, his voice barely above a whisper.

The other Julian didn't answer. Instead, a crack appeared in the floor beneath his feet, and Julian fell through, tumbling into darkness.

He landed back in bed, Emma beside him again, her breathing slow and steady as if nothing had happened. The room was warm and calm, but dread crawled up Julian's spine.

Was this real? Was he awake?

The dream shifted again.

He saw himself standing outside, Flynn handing him a rifle. The metal was cold in his hands, and he could feel its weight, its deadly potential.

"You'll need this," Flynn said, his face expressionless.

Julian stared at the weapon, his grip tightening. A strange, consuming feeling washed over him. Anger. Power. Madness. He saw flashes of himself, shouting, firing the gun, his face twisting into a mirror of Max's.

"No... no, that's not me," he whispered, trying to drop the rifle.

But it stuck to his hands, as if fused to his skin.

The madness grew, a cacophony of voices and chaos, until—

"Julian!"

He jolted awake, gasping for air, his body drenched in sweat. Emma was leaning over him, her face etched with concern.

"Julian, are you okay?" she asked, her voice soft but urgent. "You were having a nightmare. I've never seen you like that before."

Julian struggled to catch his breath, his hands shaking as he sat up. "It... it was horrible," he said, his voice hoarse.

Emma placed a comforting hand on his arm. "Tell me what happened."

Julian hesitated, the images still vivid in his mind. Slowly, he recounted the dream: Max's voice on the radio, the gunshot, Emma's fall, the endless room, the mirror image of himself, and the madness that followed when Flynn handed him the rifle.

When he finished, Emma looked at him, her expression a mix of sympathy and resolve.

"It was just a dream," she said gently. "A horrible one, but still a dream. None of that is real."

Julian nodded, but the weight of the dream lingered. "What if... what if it's a warning?" he asked quietly. "What if I end up like Max?"

Emma cupped his face, forcing him to meet her eyes. "You're not Max. You're Julian. You're the man who keeps me safe, who makes me laugh, who gives people hope with every broadcast. Don't let a nightmare make you doubt that."

Her words settled over him like a balm, and he exhaled deeply, the tension in his shoulders easing.

"Thanks, Emma," he said softly, leaning his forehead against hers.

"Always," she whispered back, her voice steady and reassuring.

They lay back down together, Emma holding him close as he tried to let go of the lingering fear. But even as sleep began to reclaim him, the dream's shadow refused to fully fade.

Chapter 65:

The house felt warmer now, the flickering fire in the hearth casting a soft glow on the walls. The storm had passed, leaving behind a damp, almost eerie calm. It was the kind of night where everything felt still, where the only sounds were the distant hum of insects and the occasional creak of the house settling. They had made it through the worst of the night, but that didn't mean it was over. There was still a sense of tension hanging in the air, but for now, the immediate threat had faded.

Gwen stood by the door, her bags in hand, her gaze scanning the room. "Flynn," she said, her voice soft but firm, "I'm staying in the guest room at the end of the hall. You can crash there, if you want."

Flynn hesitated, glancing toward Julian, then back at Gwen. "You sure?"

Gwen gave him a small, understanding smile. "Yeah. You've had a rough time. You don't have to stay by yourself tonight."

Flynn nodded, running a hand through his hair. "Thanks, Gwen." He lingered for a moment, his eyes lingering on the others, before following her down the hall.

Meanwhile, Julian had been looking around the living room, noting how everything was still exactly as it had been when he left. The smell of dust mixed with old books, the worn armchair near the fireplace—it was all so familiar. Yet, it was as though he had never left.

Isla appeared beside him, her hand resting on his shoulder. "Come on," she said softly. "Let me show you your room."

Emma followed them up the stairs, her eyes darting from one familiar corner to the next. Julian's childhood home was still the same. The creaky floorboards, the family portraits lining the hallway. It all felt so… nostalgic.

When they reached the door at the end of the hall, Isla turned the handle and pushed it open. Julian's room was exactly how he remembered it—his old bed pushed against the far wall, the desk cluttered with papers and books he hadn't touched in years. His old guitar still leaned against the corner, the strings slightly out of tune.

"It's like you never left," Isla murmured, as if reading his thoughts.

Julian smiled faintly, feeling the weight of the room settle on him. "Yeah, feels like it."

Emma looked around, taking in the soft, dim light from the desk lamp that still illuminated the space. "It's nice. Feels like home," she said with a small smile. She glanced at Julian, a question in her eyes. "You alright?"

Julian nodded, though his mind was still heavy with everything that had happened. "Yeah, just… weird, you know? Coming back here, like nothing's changed."

Isla stepped in, giving them both a reassuring glance. "Take your time. I'll make sure everyone's settled."

With that, Isla left them alone in the room, and Julian stood there for a moment, staring at the familiar surroundings. Emma broke the silence.

"You're thinking about her, aren't you?" she asked softly.

Julian turned to face her, a weary look in his eyes. "I can't help it. After everything... I'm just trying to figure out how it all fits together. What happened to Tessa? What is she now? And why the hell did she have to drag us into it?"

Emma stepped closer, her expression serious but gentle. "You don't have to have all the answers, Julian. Not right now. You've been through too much. We all have."

He exhaled slowly, feeling the tension ease slightly from his shoulders. "I know. I just wish I could've done something. You know, stopped her before it got this far."

Emma reached out, gently touching his arm. "You can't control everything. You did what you could. We all did. And we're still standing. That has to count for something, right?"

Julian offered a tired smile, then moved toward the bed, pulling back the covers. "Yeah. I guess it does."

Emma climbed in beside him, the mattress creaking softly under her weight. She settled in, her back turned toward him for a moment as she tucked herself under the covers. "We'll figure it out. Together."

Julian didn't say anything, just turned off the lamp beside the bed and closed his eyes. The quiet of the room enveloped them both, and for a moment, there was peace. The kind of peace that had been hard to come by lately.

Downstairs, the house was quiet. Lilith had claimed the couch, wrapping herself in an old blanket she'd found in the linen closet. Her eyes fluttered closed almost immediately, the exhaustion of the day catching up with her.

Enoch, too, had retired to his room, the old man moving with careful, deliberate steps. He closed the door behind him with a soft click, and the house was still once more.

Upstairs, Emma and Julian lay in the dim light, the silence stretching between them. Julian's mind was still racing, but the weight of the night seemed to lift just a little with Emma beside him. The steady rhythm of her breathing soothed him, and after a long while, he finally spoke.

"Thanks, Emma. For everything. I… I don't think I could've gotten through all this without you."

She turned toward him, her eyes soft in the dark. "You don't have to thank me. We're in this together, remember?"

Julian chuckled quietly, the sound low and warm. "Yeah, together."

Emma smiled, settling back into her pillow. "Sleep, Julian. We'll deal with everything tomorrow." He nodded,

She nuzzled her head into his chest, "I love you….. More then you could ever realise" She whispered.

Julian kissed her forehead and whispered back. "I love you too"

Closing his eyes, feeling the weight of sleep slowly creep in. And for the first time in what felt like ages, he allowed himself to relax, the quiet of the night wrapping around him like a blanket.

Tomorrow, they'd face whatever came next.

But for now, they could rest.

Chapter 66:

The first rays of dawn filtered through the curtains, casting a soft, golden glow over the room. The light seemed to breathe life into the stillness, gently waking Julian from his sleep. He shifted, his senses awakening to the quiet of the morning, the warmth of Emma beside him grounding him in the present. Her steady breathing, the rise and fall of her chest, was a comfort that calmed the swirling thoughts in his mind. He brushed a strand of hair from her face, fingers lingering on her skin for a brief moment, his heart swelling with a mix of love and unease.

They weren't supposed to stay long.

Emma stirred beside him, her eyelids fluttering open. A soft murmur escaped her lips, the grogginess of sleep still clinging to her voice. She blinked a few times, her gaze meeting Julian's with a sleepy but warm smile.

"Good morning," she whispered, her voice barely above a breath.

Julian hesitated. "Morning," he replied, though his voice carried an underlying weight. He could feel the clock ticking, the urgency creeping in. They had to leave—now.

Emma stretched, her arms reaching above her head before she settled back with a sigh. "We should go soon," she murmured, as if reading his mind. "We weren't meant to stay."

Julian nodded. The visit had been brief—just long enough to check in, to make sure everything was alright. They had promised themselves they wouldn't linger, wouldn't risk getting pulled back into something they couldn't afford to stay for.

Downstairs, the house was already stirring. Julian's family moved about, their movements filled with an unspoken tension. It wasn't just the morning; it was the weight of knowing this goodbye was happening too soon.

As they descended the stairs, Gwin stood in the doorway, arms crossed tightly, her expression unreadable. She wasn't one for grand farewells, but the way she lingered spoke volumes.

"You're really leaving already?" she asked, voice soft but tinged with something that almost sounded like hurt.

Flynn stepped forward, shifting uneasily under her gaze. "We just needed to make sure everything was okay," he said. "We didn't plan to stay long."

Gwin nodded slowly, as if she understood—but didn't accept it. "Right."

A pause stretched between them before, without warning, Gwin closed the distance between them and pressed a gentle kiss to Flynn's lips. It was brief, but the weight of it lingered in the air. "Don't forget me, sweetie," she whispered, her voice barely holding steady.

Flynn froze, his breath hitching. He wasn't good at this—wasn't good at quick goodbyes or unexpected gestures. "I won't," he promised, his voice thick with emotion.

Emma placed a hand on Julian's arm, sensing the moment stretching too long. "We should go," she said softly.

Julian's mother stepped forward, pulling him into a tight embrace. "You take care of each other," she murmured, her voice thick with unspoken worry.

"We will," Julian assured her, though he could hear the hesitation in his own voice. Leaving felt wrong. It always did.

His father clapped him on the back, the unspoken support clear in the gesture. "You know where we are if you need us."

Julian nodded. "I know."

Aunt Lilith's sharp eyes softened for once. "You're always welcome here. Remember that."

Emma turned to Julian's mother, her hands squeezing hers briefly. "Thank you for everything," she said sincerely.

Isla studied her, then nodded, her grip tightening for just a moment. "Take care of him. He needs someone who won't let him shoulder everything alone."

"I will," Emma promised, her voice steady.

Gwin was the last to step forward. She looked at Julian, then at Flynn, her usual wit absent. "You better come back soon," she said, and it wasn't a request.

Julian hesitated, then pressed a quick kiss to her cheek. "We'll try."

It was the only promise he could give.

As they climbed into the truck, the weight of their departure settled over them. Julian gripped the wheel, his fingers tightening. Emma glanced back at the house, watching as the figures of his family stood together, watching them go.

"We left too soon," she murmured.

Julian exhaled, eyes fixed on the road ahead. "We had to. The Radio only had a loop of a few days"

The engine rumbled to life, and as they pulled away, the town of their past faded into the distance. Whatever lay ahead, they would face it together. But the echoes of their goodbye lingered, heavy in the air, as if urging them to return before it was too late.

Chapter 67:

The engine of Flynn's vehicle rumbled to life, a low growl cutting through the eerie silence of Bradfield's abandoned streets. The once-bustling town lay in a state of quiet decay—storefronts empty, windows broken, and the occasional rustling of wind through shattered glass the only sign of movement.

Emma double-checked their supplies, methodically going through each bag. Julian sat in the vehicle in deep thought, thinking about the radio station he left on loop, hoping it stayed stable in His and Emma's absence. Hopefully nothing too drastic happened that needed instant reporting. Julian also had a thought that he would need to report on Lady

Blackcreek, Tessa when he returns. He notes it down. As his childhood town of Bradfield faded into the distance, he swallowed hard, feeling the weight of another chapter closing.

The highway ahead was mostly clear, though rusted-out cars remained as stubborn relics of a time before everything collapsed. Abandoned billboards loomed overhead, their faded ads for once-cutting-edge tech companies now meaningless in a world without electricity. The tendrils of nature crept in— grass and weeds were beginning to force their way through cracks in the asphalt, vines wrapping around bent street signs, birds nesting in the shells of wrecked vehicles. The road ahead stretched toward uncertainty, but turning back wasn't an option.

As they entered the Blue Mountains, the terrain shifted. Towering cliffs enclosed the winding road, fog clung to the surface like a ghostly veil, and the vast wilderness pressed in from both sides. The mountains had always been isolated, but now they felt like a fortress of the forgotten.

Julian, ever watchful, tensed as he spotted movement ahead. A small group of men wearing slouch hats—Diggers—were shifting rusted wrecks off the road, their rifles slung lazily over their shoulders. Whether they were clearing a path for trade or for something more ominous was unclear.

Flynn slowed the vehicle and rolled down the window. "You boys working hard?" he called out casually. The one that seemed to be the self-established foreman of the group turned and said

"Yep". Flynn Chuckles and replies, "Don't work too hard."

One of the Diggers, a bearded man with sharp eyes, turned and nodded. "Clearing a path. You heading west?"

Flynn gave a slight shrug. "Passing through, Headed to Blackheath."

The Digger eyed the vehicle, then Julian and Emma. After a brief pause, he jerked his head toward the open road. "Stay sharp. You're not the only ones moving out here."

Flynn nodded in understanding before rolling up the window and easing the vehicle forward. Emma's fingers remained tight around the rifle at her feet, her eyes never leaving the men outside.

As they passed, Julian locked eyes with the bearded Digger for a moment. A silent, unspoken warning passed between them before the man turned away, letting them go without another word.

The air inside the vehicle remained thick with tension long after the Diggers had disappeared from view.

The climb into the mountains grew treacherous. The road narrowed, snaking along steep cliffs, some sections barely intact. Small landslides had buried parts of the highway, forcing Flynn to weave carefully around the debris.

They rounded a bend and came upon a burned-out convoy. Blackened husks of vehicles lined the road, riddled with bullet holes. Scattered bones and old, tattered gear told a grim story. A battle had taken place here, long enough ago that only remnants remained, yet recent enough to remind them that danger was never far.

Julian shifted in his seat, scanning the wreckage. "What kind of people survived out here?" he murmured.

Flynn exhaled sharply, gripping the wheel. "This place used to be busy with tourists... now it's just ghosts."

A crackle of static broke the silence. The car's radio—if it could even be called that anymore—flickered to life, catching a faint, broken signal. The words were indecipherable, but the sound alone sent a shiver down Julian's spine.

Someone was still out there.

A wrecked sedan sat just off the road, half-buried in the undergrowth. Flynn pulled over, and they stepped out cautiously, weapons within reach.

Julian rifled through the glove compartment and found a torn-up notebook. The faded handwriting spoke of a desperate journey toward Katoomba, its last entry ominously unfinished.

Emma rummaged through the trunk and pulled out a few cans of food. "Lucky us," she said dryly, tossing one into the bag. "Bad luck for them."

A cold wind howled through the trees, making the branches sway like skeletal fingers. There was something about this place—an invisible weight pressing down on them. Julian pocketed the notebook and climbed back into the vehicle, eager to be anywhere else.

Blackheath came into view through the thinning mist. The town was eerily quiet. Street signs still stood, houses still lined the roads—but the windows were dark, the doors shut tight, and most buildings were boarded up.

Flynn turned off the engine, and the silence settled around them like a heavy blanket. For a moment, no one moved.

Julian finally spoke. "Looks empty."

Flynn glanced at the buildings, then at the road behind them. "Let's hope this place is still safe," he muttered before stepping out.

The others followed, weapons ready.

The town held its breath.

Chapter 68:

As they approach Emma's childhood home, the atmosphere shifts—still heavy with the quiet of the mountains but less tense than Bradfield. The familiar scent of pine and damp earth fills the air, yet it feels strangely foreign after being away for so long. The house stands before them, its exterior freshly painted, and the windows and roof look new. The renovations are apparent, but there's a sense that something essential has changed—like stepping into someone else's life, a life that has moved on without her.

Emma's heart clenches. The house is both different and familiar, revived yet still holding echoes of the past. The familiar contours of the walls and the porch where she once sat with her family are all there but with new layers.

Julian follows her, trying to stay calm, knowing this is important for her. Flynn, as always, remains quiet, trailing a few steps behind, his eyes scanning the surroundings, a hand resting on the truck door.

Then, they see him—Jake. A man lounging in an old chair on the porch, a beer in hand, his slouch hat casting a shadow over his face. Despite the casual pose, there's something about the way he carries himself that suggests a man who's seen and experienced too much. He doesn't look like someone Emma's mom would be with, yet here he is.

Flynn mutters something under his breath as they get closer, his tone heavy with something Julian can't quite place. It's like he's seen a ghost.

Emma freezes, her footsteps faltering. "What's wrong?"

"That's Jake," Flynn says, his voice tight. "He outranks me in the Diggers. Last person I expected to see here."

Emma looks at him, confused, but Julian, more focused on keeping his nerves in check, doesn't ask questions. He nods and follows her.

The awkwardness is palpable as Emma leads them up the steps, her heart pounding in her chest, but she forces herself to smile. The door creaks open, and she calls out cautiously, "Hey, Jake."

Jake's eyes snap open at the sound of her voice, squinting against the bright sunlight. When his gaze meets Emma's, his lips curl into a lazy grin. "Well, look who it is. Thought you were a goner, Em. Your mum's gonna love this."

Emma's face softens with a touch of relief. "Good to see you're still here," she says, her voice steady despite the emotions running through her.

Jake grunts as he rises from his chair, stretching his arms as if he hasn't moved in hours. His shirt clings to his brawny frame as he extends a hand to Julian, who hesitates only for a moment before shaking it. "You must be…" there's a slurred pause. Julian? From the radio?"

Julian forces a smile. "Nice to meet you."

Jake steps aside casually, waving them in. "Come on inside. We were just talking about you." He pauses, eyeing Flynn as he enters. "I hope you're not here to arrest me."

Flynn doesn't respond; he only gives a slight nod, his silence hanging in the air.

Inside, the tension is slightly lighter, but there's an unspoken unease. The living room is cosy, but it feels like it's been lived in by people who are still looking for a place. The mismatched furniture and faded walls tell stories of another time, but it's not the same place Emma left behind.

"I'll go get your mum," Jake says as he walks into the kitchen, leaving Emma and Julian alone for a moment.

"Sorry about the awkwardness," Emma says softly, looking at Julian. "Jake's… well, he's different now. The Diggers and all. But he's been good to my mum, so…"

"I get it," Julian responds, trying to ease her worries with a reassuring smile. "I'm just trying not to make things weird."

Emma lets out a quiet laugh, the sound comforting in its familiarity. "It's already weird," she admits.

Just then, a voice calls from the kitchen. "Who's making things weird?"

Emma spins around, surprised. "Mum?"

A woman steps into the room, her greying hair tied loosely at the back of her neck, wearing a well-worn apron. Her tired but warm smile lights up her face as she sees Emma, and for a moment, time seems to stand still. Her eyes shimmer with tears, and she pulls Emma into an embrace, her arms tightening around her daughter.

"Em! Oh my God, I can't believe it's really you," her mother exclaims, her voice trembling with emotion.

Emma presses her face against her mother's shoulder, overwhelmed. A tear slips down her cheek as she whispers, "I didn't know if I'd make it back, Mum. I didn't know if you were okay."

Her mother pulls back slightly but still holds her close. "I didn't know either, sweetheart. We thought… we thought it was all over until the Diggers got the radio working and heard your voice. That was the first time we knew you were alive."

"I'm here now," Emma replies quietly, wiping her face. "I'm here."

For a moment, Julian feels like a quiet observer, unsure of how to fit into this intimate moment. But he doesn't mind. He's content to watch the reunion unfold, knowing that it's not about him—he's just a part of it now.

But the mood shifts again, unexpectedly.

Jake leans back on the couch, cracking open another beer with a lazy grin. "You know, we've been hearing some weird stuff around the valley. Yowies. Big ones. Heard about them?"

Flynn scoffs from his spot near the window. "Yowies aren't real, mate. Just stories for the gullible."

Julian, intrigued, raises an eyebrow. "Wait... like Bigfoot?"

Jake's grin widens. "Exactly. Some folks say they're wandering around these parts. Makes the valley feel a little... off."

Julian glances at Flynn, who only glares back. "But... are they real?"

Flynn shrugs, his expression stern. "No. They're not real. Just myths."

Julian, fascinated despite himself, can't resist. "Huh. I always thought they were just… like those dark chocolate eggs they sell at the supermarket."

Flynn rolls his eyes, but Jake bursts into laughter.

"Yeah, most people think that. But trust me—there's something out there. Something not quite right." Jake's voice drops into a whisper as though the air itself is holding some deep secret.

Before the conversation could spiral further, Emma's mum called from the kitchen, drawing everyone's attention. "Alright, enough of that for now. You two must be starving. I'll get some food ready. Just so glad to have you home, Em."

In the kitchen, Emma's brother—a lanky teenager with a quiet demeanour—turns around when he hears her. His eyes widen, and for a moment, he freezes, unsure if he's dreaming.

"Emma?" he asks softly, his voice laced with disbelief.

Emma chuckles, her throat tight. "Yeah. It's me." She steps forward, wrapping her arms around him in an awkward but heartfelt hug. "It's been a while."

Her little brother pulls back, a smile tugging at his lips. "Good to have you back, Em."

A weight lifts from Emma's shoulders. For the first time in years, she's home—and it feels right.

Later that evening, the table is set, and everyone gathers for dinner. The atmosphere has lightened somewhat, though a subtle tension lingers. Emma's mother is a woman of few words, her gaze sharp but softened with the years. The conversation flows between casual updates and awkward silences, Emma's brother occasionally glancing at Julian with a curious but friendly expression.

Julian is sitting across from Emma, trying to navigate the fine line between being a part of the family again and respecting their space. Her brother seems to like him—offering shy smiles and a few nervous laughs when Julian says something mildly funny. He's quieter than Julian expected, though not unkind. Emma's mother, on the other hand, is more reserved. She asks questions but always in a manner that makes Julian feel like she's measuring him, assessing him more than simply talking.

"So," her mother says between bites of dinner, the clink of her fork against her plate louder than the conversation. "What exactly is it you two are doing now? Out there...in the city?"

Emma glances at Julian and then looks down at her plate, her expression turning more guarded. "We're...figuring things out," she answers carefully, her voice lacking its usual confidence.

Her mother studies her for a long moment before nodding, her lips pressed into a thin line. "I see."

Flynn, sitting silently next to Emma's mother, nods politely, keeping the conversation flowing when needed. He doesn't intrude, but there's a calm presence about him that steadies the awkwardness in the room. Julian, trying not to feel the weight of the silence, tries to follow Flynn's example, keeping his answers short.

The quiet is broken when Julian's eyes catch something outside the window—a flash of dark, glossy eyes peering through the glass, watching them from the edge of the porch. His heart skips a beat, his instincts on high alert. He leans in, trying not to draw attention, but the figure disappears before he can fully process what he's seen.

A sudden chill grips the room.

Emma's mother is still talking, but her voice fades as Julian's mind races. He shifts in his seat, trying to shake off the unease, but his curiosity outweighs his caution.

"Excuse me," Julian mutters, standing abruptly from the table.

Flynn looks up, a quiet question in his eyes, but Julian only nods toward the window and then heads outside without another word.

He steps onto the porch, scanning the yard. The night is quiet—too quiet. Then, he hears it. A loud rustling in the bushes, followed by a strange, heavy thud, like something—or someone—jumping over the fence.

Turning toward the sound, Julian's breath catches in his throat.

There, silhouetted against the moonlight, is a massive, hairy figure. It's as if the shadows themselves have taken form, thick, dark fur covering the creature's body as it leaps the fence with an almost animalistic agility. The figure lands in a crouch, glancing back toward the house for a moment before darting into the woods, disappearing as quickly as it appeared.

Julian shakes his head in disbelief. He's seen strange things in his life, but this is something entirely different.

"Flynn!" Julian calls out, his voice urgent as he jogs toward the door. "I think the yowies are real."

Flynn stands up from the table, his eyes narrowing as he gives Julian a quick look. He's not startled, not afraid, but the calmness in his expression cracks for just a moment. "You saw it too, huh?"

Emma's mother looks between the two men, her eyes sharp. "What's going on?"

"It's...nothing," Flynn says quickly, trying to brush it off, but there's a subtle shift in his voice—a note of uncertainty. "Just...a possem, maybe."

Julian shakes his head, his heart still racing. "No, this wasn't a possem. This was something else."

For a moment, there's a long silence in the room as Emma's mother assesses Julian. Her gaze is sharp, but her lips press together, unwilling to show fear, though it's clear something about this situation unsettles her.

Her brother looks at Julian with wide eyes. "You're not joking, are you?"

Julian shakes his head. "I wish I was."

Emma glances at her mother, but there's no hint of disbelief in her eyes—only an unspoken understanding, as though this is just another strange, unexplainable part of their life here. "Mum... Do you think it's real?"

Emma's mother hesitates for a long moment, then finally lets out a sigh. "You'd be surprised at what's out there. Some things are better left...unspoken."

Julian feels the tension shift in the room. It's as if everyone has accepted the weirdness of their world, even though the truth remains hidden beneath layers of silence and old stories.

The air feels thick now, charged with a strange new energy. Emma's mother doesn't press the matter further, but the look she gives Julian lingers in his mind. There's more going on here than he understands.

Flynn, always the quiet one, looks outside, then back at Julian, his expression unreadable. "You'll get used to it," he says, as though nothing unusual has happened.

But Julian's not so sure.

Chapter 69:

The night had fallen quietly around Emma's childhood home. The air was crisp and cool, and the sounds of the valley outside grew distant. Inside, the house was still, save for the faint hum of the fridge in the kitchen and the occasional creak of the wooden floorboards.

Emma lay beside Julian in her childhood bedroom, the two of them tucked under the old quilt. This return to the past felt strange. The room hadn't changed much—though the faded posters and childhood toys had been replaced with more adult touches, it still carried an echo of who she'd been before everything fell apart.

Julian stared at the ceiling, restless. His thoughts wandered back to the dinner table, where Emma's mother had barely spoken to him. Her sharp, discerning eyes had not let him off easily, and he couldn't shake the feeling that she didn't like him, or at least didn't trust him.

"You think she hates me, don't you?" Julian asked, his voice quiet but carrying the weight of the question.

Emma shifted slightly, propping herself up on one elbow to look at him. The soft glow of the moonlight filtered through the window, casting pale shadows across her face.

"No," she said with a small smile, her tone gentle but firm. "She's just... protective. She hasn't seen me in so long, and she's probably worried I've changed.

Plus, you're a stranger to her, and she's had to get used to a lot of new things since everything fell apart."

Julian let out a small sigh, turning his head to meet her gaze. "I don't know. It felt like she was sizing me up the entire time. Like I'm some kind of... outsider."

Emma softened. "You are," she said with a teasing smile, but then her expression turned more serious. "But not in a bad way. She's just worried, Julian. You're important to me, and she's protective of me, especially with everything that's happened. It's... a mother thing."

Julian nodded, processing her words. He hadn't realized how much she'd been carrying, how much of it had been about finding herself again after everything had fallen apart. And now, with the collapse of the world as they knew it, Emma's mother was in the midst of her struggle—balancing between the past she couldn't let go of and the new reality she had to face.

"I get it," Julian finally said, though he still felt the tension from earlier hanging between them like a thread.

Emma shifted again, her voice softening. "It's just been a lot for all of us. The last four years... it's hard for anyone to understand unless they've lived through it. But I promise you, Julian, she doesn't hate you."

There was a pause, and Emma's thoughts wandered, remembering how tense dinner had been. "The yowie, though..." she said with a chuckle. "That definitely broke the tension. It was so thick, you could cut it with a knife."

Julian couldn't help but laugh at that. He had been just as surprised by the sight of the creature as Emma had been, and for a brief moment, it had seemed to ease the unspoken weight in the room. "Yeah, I think the yowie was the only thing that could've cut through that kind of tension. It definitely made everyone stop talking about... well, me."

Emma grinned, her eyes sparkling with a mixture of amusement and exhaustion. "Exactly. For a second, I thought we were all going to be stuck in some awkward silence forever. But then, bam—big, fluffy creature hopping over the fence like it was fleeing from something. Suddenly, the awkwardness didn't seem so important."

Julian rolled onto his side, propping himself up on his elbow, his face illuminated by the faint moonlight. "Do you really think it's real? The yowie?" he asked, his voice tinged with curiosity.

Emma shrugged, a smile playing on her lips. "I don't know. I've heard stories, but who knows what's out there now, right? I thought we were done with the myths, but maybe they're just... waiting for the right time to show themselves."

Julian nodded thoughtfully, his mind still buzzing with the thought of a creature like that in their world. "Yeah, maybe they're just out there, living in the shadows."

They lay in silence for a few moments, both of them reliving the events of the evening. The quiet of the room seemed to settle over them, and though Julian was still uncertain about what tomorrow might bring—about his place in Emma's world—he felt a little lighter.

Emma yawned softly, her eyelids growing heavy. "Well, let's just hope it doesn't break into the house next."

Julian chuckled. "I think we're safe for tonight."

"Yeah," Emma murmured, her voice trailing off as sleep finally began to claim her. "Safe... for tonight."

Julian lay there, watching her for a moment, a sense of peace settling over him. For all the uncertainty that still lingered, one thing felt clear: this—this moment with Emma—was where he belonged. And, maybe, just maybe, he could find a way to belong here, in this strange new world they were all trying to navigate.

Chapter 70:

———— ⟶ ✵ ⟵ ————

The first light of morning crept through the curtains, casting a soft glow over Emma's room. The night had been long, filled with quiet conversations and distant thoughts, but now, the new day felt like a fresh start. Julian lay on his back, staring up at the ceiling, thinking about the oddness of the previous evening. It had felt like a mix of old and new—awkwardness, tension, and then that strange, almost magical moment with the yowie.

Emma was still asleep beside him, her breathing slow and steady, and for a brief moment, he allowed himself to enjoy the stillness. But soon, the hum of life outside broke through the quiet, and Julian knew that the day would come with its challenges.

Later That Morning

The house was bustling with the usual sounds of a family waking up. Emma's mother was in the kitchen, already preparing breakfast, and Emma's brother, who Julian hadn't yet gotten to know well, was up, too—shuffling around, looking for his shoes.

Julian joined Emma downstairs after a quick shower. Her mother gave him a polite nod, but the coolness from the night before lingered in the air. Julian tried to ignore the awkwardness, but it was hard not to feel like he was under a microscope.

"Good morning," Emma greeted her mother, leaning in to give her a quick kiss on the cheek. She smiled warmly, and it was clear the connection between them was more than just the surface-level tension that Julian had picked up on.

"Morning," Emma's mother responded shortly. Her gaze lingered on Julian for a beat longer than necessary, but she quickly turned her attention back to the stove, flipping a pancake with a practised motion.

Julian shifted uncomfortably, wondering what had caused the coldness. Was it his presence here? The conversation last night hadn't been enough to crack the entire wall between them.

"So," Emma's brother, who Julian now knew as Lachlan, said with a grin as he came into the room, his hair messy from sleep. "Did you see anything else last night? Yowies, aliens, bunyip?"

Julian couldn't help but chuckle at the playful jab. "Nah, I think that was the only surprise for the evening," he said, trying to play along.

"Good," Lachlan said, sitting down at the table. "I'm kind of hoping they just stay out there in the bush, you know? Wouldn't want one of them to wander in while we're having breakfast."

"Don't worry, we've got the house locked down," Emma teased, her voice light but affectionate. She shot a glance at her mother, who was stirring the pot on the stove, looking far too focused on her task to engage.

"Speaking of the bush," Julian said, wanting to break the silence that had settled between him and Emma's mother, "do you think we should head out today? Check out some of the trails around here?" He looked to Emma for approval, hoping the idea would lighten the mood a little.

Emma raised an eyebrow but smiled. "You want to go hike in the bush today?"

"Why not?" Julian replied with a shrug. "We could use some fresh air. Plus, if we see more yowies, maybe they'll be a bit more friendly."

Emma laughed, and even Emma's mother shot a brief smile his way, though it quickly disappeared.

"Sure, why not?" Emma said, standing up to grab a plate. "A little adventure might do us all some good."

Later That Day

After breakfast, the group set out, bundled up against the morning chill. The bush was quiet, the sound of rustling leaves and distant birds the only noise filling the air. The sunlight filtered through the trees, creating dappled patches of light on the forest floor. Julian couldn't help but feel a sense of calm here, away from the tension of the house.

Emma's mother had joined them for the walk, though she wasn't much for conversation. She seemed to be content just walking beside them, her eyes focused on the trail ahead.

"So," Julian began, walking beside Emma as they moved through the underbrush, "this place... it's peaceful."

"It used to be a lot busier around here," Emma said with a hint of nostalgia. "The town wasn't huge, but there was always something going on. Since everything's changed, though, it's like the world's gone quiet."

"You miss it?" Julian asked, his voice low.

"Yeah," Emma said quietly, glancing at him. "Sometimes I do. But then, sometimes I don't. I think that's the hardest part. Not knowing whether you miss something because you've lost it, or because you don't really need it anymore."

Julian absorbed her words, the weight of them sinking in. It was a strange feeling, this sense of trying to rebuild after everything had fallen apart. The world was no longer what it had been, and they had to figure out how to live in this quieter, more uncertain version of it.

Chapter 71:

As they walked deeper into the forest, Julian couldn't shake the feeling that they weren't entirely alone. It wasn't the usual sense of being watched, but something different. It felt like the very air had shifted, as though the land itself was aware of their presence.

Emma's mother stopped suddenly, her head snapping in the direction of a distant sound—a rustling, almost animalistic in tone.

"What is that?" Lachlan asked, his voice tense, his eyes scanning the trees.

"I think we might have some company," Emma said, a wry smile tugging at her lips.

Julian's heart raced, his eyes scanning the trees. Then, just ahead of them, a figure appeared—a large, furry shape moving between the trees, low to the ground. The air seemed to hold its breath.

Emma's mother stiffened beside them, her expression unreadable, but she didn't back away. Julian could feel his heart pounding as the creature, the yowie from last night, stepped into view.

It wasn't the monstrous creature of legend—this was a creature filled with curiosity, cautious and wild but not hostile. It stared at them for a moment, its large eyes glimmering with unspoken emotion, before it disappeared back into the forest, vanishing as quickly as it had come.

The group stood there, silent for a long moment, the only sound the rustle of the trees in the breeze.

"See?" Julian finally said, his voice filled with awe and a slight disbelief. "I told you they were real."

Emma smiled softly, her eyes reflecting the same wonder that he felt. "Maybe they're not so bad after all."

Chapter 72:

As Julian made his way through the dense underbrush, the forest seemed to press in on him. The air was thick with humidity, and each step felt like he was trudging through a world waiting for something—something unknown. He could hear the faint rustling of leaves, but beyond that, it was unnervingly quiet.

His mind wandered briefly to Emma, her mother, and Lachlan. They were back at the camp, somewhere behind him. Emma's mother still didn't seem to like him much, and though Julian had tried to win her over, it never seemed to stick. Maybe it was his quiet demeanour or his unpolished communication, but whatever it was, it seemed like she'd made up her mind. He didn't blame her; he wasn't exactly the easiest person to get to know.

But today, as he moved deeper into the forest, a new kind of unease settled in. The silence felt heavy, oppressive even. Something was off. The trees stretched endlessly, and the world felt distant, almost alien.

And then, it happened. A rustling—a deliberate, purposeful sound. It wasn't the usual shuffle of tiny creatures. No, this was something more significant. The hairs on the back of his neck stood up as he stopped, heart pounding.

A shadow shifted between the trees, tall and massive. It wasn't an animal. No, this was something else—something much more significant.

His breath caught in his throat as the creature emerged fully into view.

It was unlike anything Julian had ever seen before. A hulking figure covered in thick, shaggy fur. Its face was hidden beneath layers of hair, but its dark eyes—cautious, curious—met Julian's. He froze, unsure of what to do.

The creature grunted softly, and Julian's stomach churned. The sound felt ancient—old and foreign in a way he couldn't explain.

"Ngaya garlu, ngiyani ngudju."

Julian's heart skipped a beat. The words were strange—nothing like the language he knew. But the emotion behind them was unmistakable: fear and a plea for peace. The creature wasn't here to attack. It was just as unsure as Julian was.

Unable to find the right words, Julian raised his hand slowly, instinctively. He meant no harm—a gesture of peace.

The creature tilted its head, eyes narrowing, studying him. It didn't retreat or charge forward. It just stood still, waiting to see what Julian would do next.

Then, there was more movement from the trees. More figures, one after the other—yowies, emerged cautiously from the shadows. Each one observed him, their dark eyes filled with curiosity, but none of them moved aggressively.

The leader of the group made a soft hum—low and comforting like an animal trying to soothe another. Julian exhaled slowly. These creatures weren't the monsters he'd heard about in the stories. They weren't lurking in the shadows, waiting to strike. They were survivors, just like him.

For a moment, he stood there, taking in the presence of the yowies. The forest felt different now, lighter in a way, though the air was still charged. Something fragile yet real was present in the stillness between him and the creatures. A bond, however small, was forming.

And then, from behind him, he heard Emma's voice.

"Julian?" Her voice was cautious, but she was close, along with her mother and Lachlan. He hadn't expected them to come this far into the forest, but they had—drawn by the same tension, the same curiosity.

Julian glanced over his shoulder, and there they were. Emma, her mother, and Lachlan are standing just at the edge of the clearing, unsure whether to approach or retreat.

"Mum… Julian?" Emma's mother spoke, her tone softer than Julian had ever heard it. She wasn't hostile, just uncertain.

"I think… I think they're not here to hurt us," Julian said, his voice steady despite feeling the weight of the moment. He wasn't sure why he was the one explaining, but the words seemed to flow from him. They're just as lost as we are."

Emma's mother hesitated for a moment, then took a cautious step forward. Her gaze never left the leader of the yowies, but Julian could see something shifting in her eyes. She was listening. She was beginning to understand.

Lachlan, always the curious one, took a few steps forward, too, peering at the creatures with wide eyes, but Emma stayed close to her mother. Julian could feel the air change as Emma's mother made eye contact with him, the first real moment of recognition between them.

The leader of the yowies, sensing the shift, let out another low hum—this time softer, gentler, more reassuring. It was almost as if the creature understood the weight of the moment as well.

And then, Julian saw it. Emma's mother's expression softened. She wasn't entirely convinced, but there was a flicker of something there—perhaps respect. Maybe even a trace of gratitude. For the first time since they'd met, Julian felt a small crack form in the wall that had always stood between him and Emma's mother.

"Thank you," she said quietly, almost to herself. "For showing us this."

Julian's heart lifted. Maybe this moment was enough to bridge the gap between him and Emma's mother. It wasn't much, but it was something.

The leader of the yowies grunted again, its dark eyes never leaving them. The world still seemed broken and lost, but in this quiet, shared understanding, it felt like there was a flicker of hope.

That may be enough for now.

Chapter 73:

Julian stood still for a moment, watching the leader of the yowies, his mind racing with thoughts he couldn't fully grasp. He wasn't sure how to explain it to Emma's mother or even to himself. This wasn't just a meeting of creatures from another world; this was something more profound—an exchange, a moment of quiet understanding in the midst of the chaos.

As the leader hummed softly, Julian felt a pull, a need to speak. "I think we should leave. This is just a scout party. They're not here to harm us, but… it's better we don't overstay our welcome." He glanced at Emma, his voice softer now, unsure of how she'd react.

She met his gaze with a quiet understanding. "Yeah, I think you're right. But…" Her eyes flicked toward the yowies, who were still overseeing them. "Are they… like, Indigenous Australians? I mean, they seem so much like regular people—just, you know, different."

Julian nodded, his brow furrowed in thought. "I don't know. It's like they've been here longer than any of us, but they're just trying to survive. I can't explain it. But they remind me of the stories— stories of ancient people who lived alongside the land, knowing it like no one else did."

Before Emma could respond, something caught Julian's eye. A brown snake slithering through the grass, inches away from where Lachlan was standing. His heart leapt into his throat as he saw the snake's head poised, ready to strike. He started to shout, but before he could get the words out, one of the yowies lunged forward, grabbing the snake by its tail and lifting it into the air.

The creature sank its teeth into the snake's body without hesitation, its mouth working through the scales with an unsettling ease. The sound of crunching echoed in the air. Julian watched in a mix of horror and fascination as the yowie devoured the creature with surprising speed.

"Yum," Emma's mother said dryly, her tone laced with sarcasm as she glanced at Julian. Lachlan, oblivious to the danger he'd been in just moments ago, stood frozen, his wide eyes watching the scene in disbelief. Emma shook her head, her expression amused, but there was an unspoken gratitude for the creature's quick actions.

"Thanks," Julian called out to the leader, his voice filled with genuine thanks. The yowie didn't respond with words, but it gave a low hum, a sign of acknowledgement.

He turned to Emma and her mother. "Let's head back to the house. It's getting late."

They crept, making their way through the dense trees and back toward the path leading to the house. Julian's mind was still spinning. The forest, the creatures, and the strange connection he'd felt with them—it all seemed like something out of a dream, but it was real.

As they reached the clearing near the house, they were met by an unexpected sight—Flynn. He stood near the house, holding a hand radio to his ear, a look of urgency in his eyes. Julian had no idea Flynn even had a functional radio on him.

"Flynn?" Julian called out, stepping toward him. "What's going on?"

Flynn didn't answer right away, his eyes scanning the surroundings before meeting Julian's gaze. "We've been trying to reach you," he said, his voice tight with concern. "There's something you need to know. Something... unexpected is happening."

Emma and her mother came up behind Julian, and Flynn's eyes shifted to them before he spoke again. "It's not safe out here right now. You need to come inside."

Julian felt a knot form in his stomach. He had no idea what Flynn was talking about, but the urgency in his voice was enough to make his pulse race. Whatever was going on, it wasn't just about the yowies anymore.

"Come on," Flynn urged, motioning toward the house. "It's important."

The group moved inside, the weight of the unknown settling heavily over them. As Julian entered, he caught Emma's gaze. Whatever had just happened in the forest had been strange, and even more so now, with Flynn's unexpected warning. But one thing was clear: they were no longer alone in the world. Something was shifting, and the questions were piling up faster than they could answer them.

As the door shut behind them, Julian's mind was full of nothing but the unknown.

Chapter 74:

Max paced the small, dimly lit cell, his boots making soft taps against the concrete floor. Room 17—he'd lost track of how long he'd been confined here. Days? Weeks? Time had blurred, twisted into a haze of frustration and restless energy. The light from the narrow window high up in the wall barely filtered through, casting long shadows that seemed to mock him. But today, something inside him snapped. He could feel it—the urge to move, to escape, to find out what the hell was going on outside these walls.

He glanced at the cracked mirror hanging above the sink. The reflection staring back at him was a stranger: a man he didn't fully recognize. His beard had grown wild, tangled, and unkempt. His hair, once neatly trimmed, now hung in dark, unkempt strands around his face. A scar ran down the left side of his lip, a reminder of the fights, the brutality, and the silence that had followed him here.

Max clenched his jaw, the frustration mounting as he studied himself. He didn't care about how he looked, not really. What mattered now was breaking out. It didn't matter if it took every ounce of his energy, every ounce of cunning. He had to get out.

The door to the hallway creaked open just a fraction, and Max froze. He was too close to being discovered. He quickly stepped back into the shadows of the cell, waiting for the footsteps to fade. A guard passed by, oblivious to his presence, and Max held his breath. The guard moved down the hallway, and the sound of boots clicking against the floor grew distant.

This was his moment.

Max knew the layout of the base, every corner, every shadow, every place to hide. He'd spent weeks memorizing it, watching for opportunities, waiting for the right time. Quietly, he moved through the narrow halls of the Glenbrook RAAF base, slipping past guards, his heart pounding in his chest but his movements steady and sure. His mind was sharp—he couldn't afford a mistake.

He found the comms room without incident. The door was slightly ajar, and the low hum of equipment filled the space inside. He knew this was his best chance. He glanced at the clock: the digger crewing the station was about to take a break, which meant Max had a window of only a few minutes.

He slipped inside. The room was empty, save for a few pieces of equipment and a radio crackling with static. He didn't hesitate. He knew exactly what he needed. Moving quickly, he scanned the room and spotted the radio. A soft buzz in the air made his heart skip a beat—voices.

Emma and Julian.

Their voices echoed through the static, faint but unmistakable. They were alive. They were out there. The relief was brief but sharp, enough to spur him forward. He wasn't sure how, but he knew their location. They were basing themselves out of a radio station in an apartment somewhere along Mountain Street in Ultimo.

Max smiled grimly to himself. There wasn't much to go on, but it was enough.

Then his eyes flicked to the gun locker in the corner of the room. His fingers itched. He didn't need much—a small pistol would do. He wasn't here to fight, not yet anyway. He just needed to make it out alive.

He moved swiftly, disarming the lock with ease. The pistol was cold in his hand, but it felt familiar and comforting. He tucked it into the waistband of his jeans, making sure it was secure.

Max heard the bathroom door swing open and the sound of boots shuffling toward the comms room. He froze. One glance at the door told him it was too late to sneak out the way he came in. He wasn't taking any chances. He dropped to the floor and slid under the desk, his breath shallow, listening to the guard shuffle inside.

The man walked past him, oblivious, mumbling to himself. Max waited, every second stretching out like an eternity. As soon as the guard moved away, he slipped out from under the desk and out the door.

No alarms. No shouts. No pursuit.

He was in the clear, for now.

Max moved through the base with the same calculated precision, his body a ghost in the shadows. The air outside the base was more incredible than he expected, but the adrenaline coursing through his veins made him feel like he was on fire. He knew where he was going—he could see it in his mind's eye, the apartment block on Mountain Street.

It wasn't going to be easy. He was on foot, and the walk was going to be long, the path uncertain. But Max wasn't afraid of a long walk. Hell, after everything he'd been through, what was another bloody trek?

With a final glance over his shoulder, he set off, the pistol heavy in his waistband. The sound of the base grew fainter, replaced by the quiet hum of the outside world. Max wasn't sure what waited for him in the city, but he knew one thing for sure: he was going to find Emma and Julian.

And nothing—no one—was going to stop him.

Chapter 75:

———————⊱•⊰———————

The warmth from the hearth flickered, but it did little to erase the chill in the room. Julian leaned back against the wall, arms crossed, his brow furrowed with a mix of fear and confusion. Emma sat opposite him, her face pale but determined. Flynn stood by the door, his posture tense as he kept a close eye on the situation. Meanwhile, Emma's mother, Janice, paced the room nervously.

"You're sure about this?" Flynn's voice cut through the silence, carrying the weight of urgency. "Max has escaped?"

Flynn's grim confirmation hung in the air like a storm cloud. "Room 17—empty. Not even a trace of him."

Julian's stomach twisted. He exchanged a brief glance with Emma, the memory of Max's face flashing before his eyes. Max had once been their friend. The person they could count on. But that was before everything fell apart.

Janice looked at them, worry etched across her face. "Who is this man? Why is he after you?"

Julian let out a sharp breath, trying to steady his nerves. Emma was the first to speak, her voice low. "Max wasn't always like this. He was a good guy. A friend. He was one of the core team members at DisruptTech. He helped us build everything—our podcast, our platform. He was the producer. He made it all work."

Julian nodded, the memories flooding back. "Back when everything was still functioning, before the collapse. We were a team. Me, Emma, Max, the whole DisruptTech crew. But everything changed when things started to break down."

Emma's eyes darkened. "Max... he didn't handle it well. When the collapse happened, we all did what we had to, but Max spiraled. He wasn't the same after he found that gun." Her voice trembled slightly, but she steadied herself. "That's when everything shifted. He got paranoid, started believing the world was out to get him. We tried to keep the peace, but it was too much. He wasn't just afraid of the collapse anymore. He was afraid of being left alone."

"That's when we knew we couldn't stay," Julian added. "He started turning on us. We didn't recognize him anymore. He became jealous—of me, of Emma. It wasn't about her; it was about us getting closer. I think... I think he was afraid we'd leave him behind. He couldn't stand the thought of being alone."

Flynn's eyes narrowed. "And that's when you left?"

Emma nodded. "We couldn't stay in the studio with him like that. We packed up and went to Julian's apartment. We set up a radio station there to keep the signal going, but that was always a risk. Max was too dangerous to be around."

Janice shook her head, trying to wrap her mind around the situation. "So this Max... he's been after you both for all this time?"

Julian's voice dropped to a whisper. "We didn't know it at the time, but yeah. We thought he'd calm down, but he didn't. We thought we were safe— until now. But it's not just about him coming after us. We've been running from him for too long. Now, he's free. And we're back where we started."

Emma's mother stood still, the weight of the truth settling in. "You're telling me that this man who's been locked up... is someone you once trusted?"

Julian nodded. "We trusted him with everything. We didn't think he'd go down this path. But after everything, I'm afraid of what he'll do now. He's not the person we knew."

Flynn clenched his jaw. "Then we need to act fast. If he's targeting you, we can't afford to stay here. We have to get to Ultimo—make sure the station's secure and figure out our next move."

Janice's voice trembled, but her words were firm. "You two better be ready for this. You're not just running from him—you're running into something bigger. I don't know what Max is capable of now, but I do know he's dangerous."

Julian turned to look at Emma, the same unspoken thoughts passing between them. They had faced this before. They had hoped it would stay in the past, but it was back now. They didn't know if they were ready to face Max again. But there was no choice.

"We'll leave first thing in the morning," Julian said, his voice steady but full of resolve. "But we have to be ready for whatever comes next."

Chapter 76:

The early morning light stretched across the ridges of the valley, mist clinging to the gums like a stubborn memory. Julian tightened the straps of his pack, standing by the old four-wheel drive as Emma hugged her mother one last time.

Janice clung to her daughter for a moment longer than usual, her fingers curled into the fabric of Emma's jacket. "You'll be careful, won't you?"

Emma let out a soft chuckle, trying to lighten the mood. "I always am, Mum."

Janice pulled back, her eyes scanning Emma's face like she was trying to commit every detail to memory. "I mean it. You're walking into something you might not be able to walk out of."

Julian shifted uncomfortably beside them, adjusting the radio slung over his shoulder. He and Emma had both hoped this visit would be something different—something normal. But nothing was normal anymore.

Flynn, standing by the friction engine, gave the lever one last hard crank, the battery humming to life. "Alright, kids, say your goodbyes. We're burning daylight."

Emma's younger brother, Lachlan, stood a few feet away, arms crossed. "You'll come back, right?"

Emma ruffled his hair. "Of course, knucklehead."

He scrunched up his nose but didn't argue.

Julian hesitated before finally stepping forward, offering Janice a small nod. "Thanks for everything."

She met his gaze, then surprised him by pulling him into a brief but firm hug. "Look after her."

Julian blinked, caught off guard, before he nodded. "I will."

With that, they climbed into the vehicle, Flynn at the wheel, the hum of the charged battery steady beneath them. As they pulled out of the driveway, Emma leaned against the window, watching her family grow smaller in the rearview mirror.

They hit the road, the Great Western Highway stretching ahead of them. It should have been a simple trip—1 hour and 44 minutes, 111 kilometers back to Ultimo. But nothing was simple anymore.

They drove in silence for a while, the hum of the engine the only sound. The empty road ahead felt endless.

Then, the radio crackled to life.

A familiar voice, strong and rhythmic, filled the car.

"There was movement at the station, for the word had passed around..."

Julian's breath hitched. He turned to Emma, who was already looking at him with wide eyes.

It was her voice.

Their voices.

They had recorded The Man from Snowy River only a few days ago, setting it into the loop for the radio station. The static between the verses sent a chill down his spine.

Flynn, completely unaware of the eerie familiarity, grinned. "Love a bit of Banjo," he said, tapping his fingers against the wheel in time with the words.

Julian exhaled slowly, his grip tightening on his knee. The words continued, echoing back at them from a past life.

They had sent that recording out into the world. Now, it had found its way back to them.

And somewhere out there, Max was listening too.

Chapter 77:

―――――――――――――>✢<―――――――――――――

Julian gripped the steering wheel tightly as they drove deeper into Ultimo, the once-thriving heart of the city now reduced to a hollow shell of its former self. The static on the radio grew more erratic with each passing second, a rhythmic glitch in the transmission that unsettled him. It was a familiar sound, one that marked the beginning of a breakdown—a glitch in the system that was quickly spreading across everything they had known.

As the truck rumbled down the street, the streets stretched out before them like a graveyard. The remnants of a once-bustling city now lay in ruin. Rusted metal and charred remains littered the sidewalks, the air thick with the acrid scent of burnt plastic and the distant trace of smoke that refused to die. The ghosts of civilization lingered in the shadows of broken windows, and the soft, mournful creak of twisted steel was the only soundtrack to their approach.

When they reached Broadway, the full extent of the violence that had swept through the area became painfully clear. Burned-out cars were scattered across the street like discarded toys, their skeletal frames still smoking, abandoned in a frenzy of desperation. Windows were shattered, leaving jagged edges that seemed to mock the fractured remains of the world. The occasional scream echoed off the walls of nearby buildings, haunting and distant, as though the city itself was mourning the loss of its pulse.

Flynn, ever the cautious one, gripped the wheel tighter as they slowed near their apartment complex. He studied the road ahead with narrowed eyes, scanning for any signs of danger. His hand, almost instinctively, reached for the door handle, and his voice, low and tense, cut through the quiet.

"Lock the doors. Get what you need done. If things go south, Glenbrook is still an option. We'll have a safe refuge there."

Julian and Emma exchanged a glance, an unspoken agreement passing between them. The plan was simple: get in, get out, and stay alert. If the storm had truly reached Ultimo, there would be no room for hesitation.

They nodded in agreement, but the weight of the silence between them was unbearable. Julian felt it settle into his bones, the quiet dread that always accompanied these types of returns. Emma's hand brushed against his as they exited the truck, and for a brief moment, the touch was enough to ground him. But only for a moment.

The apartment building loomed ahead, dark and uninviting. The entrance, once a welcoming door, now looked like an ominous threshold. As they made their way up the stairs, the faintest sounds of scuffling reached their ears. It wasn't enough to alarm them—yet. But Julian couldn't shake the feeling that they were being watched.

They reached the door to their apartment, the familiarity of it both comforting and unsettling. Julian paused before he pushed it open, his hand lingering on the doorknob. A chill ran down his spine, the weight of the world pressing down on him.

Inside, the air was thick, heavy with the smell of dust and old memories. The silence was suffocating, but it was the absence of life that made it so oppressive. The familiar hum of the fridge, the sound of a neighbor's radio, even the distant chatter of street vendors—all of it had vanished. The apartment felt like a mausoleum, a final reminder of what they had lost.

Emma moved through the small space quickly, almost mechanically, her footsteps muted against the worn wooden floors. Julian lingered, looking around at the remnants of their former lives. A picture frame lay shattered on the floor, the glass reflecting a faint glimmer of light. He picked it up, staring at the cracked photograph—a family, smiling, unaware of the chaos that would soon engulf them. His heart twisted in his chest, but there was no time for sentimentality.

"Are we really doing this?" Emma's voice broke through his thoughts, soft and laced with uncertainty. She stood by the kitchen counter, a half-open drawer in her hand, filled with items that no longer mattered.

Julian looked at her, his face hardening with resolve. "We have no choice," he said quietly, as though speaking the truth aloud would make it real. "We do what we need to do. We survive."

But even as the words left his mouth, a nagging feeling twisted in the pit of his stomach. The silence outside had changed. It was no longer the quiet of abandonment—it had shifted into something else, something far more dangerous.

Emma closed the drawer with a soft thud, her eyes meeting his. "I just want to get out of here."

"Not yet," Julian said, his voice low and strained. "We need to be sure."

A sudden noise from outside—a sharp crack followed by a distant yell—shattered the tension, and they froze. Julian's heart pounded in his chest, the sound of the scream reverberating in the stillness of the apartment. He exchanged a glance with Emma, and without another word, they both moved toward the window.

Outside, the city had come alive again, but not in the way they had hoped. The remnants of a battle still lingered, and the storm had finally reached them. They were no longer safe here.

The question wasn't whether they could stay—it was whether they could escape.

Chapter 78:

The hours dragged on in the dim light of their apartment, a space that had once been a sanctuary but now felt more like a temporary shelter against the chaos outside. Julian worked tirelessly at the radio, his hands quick and precise as he traced the wires and adjusted the dials. The low hum of electricity filled the room, its constant presence both reassuring and unnerving. Every flicker of the overhead light was a harsh reminder of how fragile everything had become—of how easily the thin threads that connected them to the world could snap.

Julian's frustration mounted with each failed attempt to reestablish the signal. His brow furrowed, sweat beading on his forehead, but he didn't stop. He couldn't. The silence from the radio had become unbearable, each minute stretching into eternity as the world beyond their apartment seemed to fade further away.

Emma sat across the room, watching him silently. She had been quiet for hours, her thoughts her own, but her gaze never strayed far from Julian. The tension between them had only deepened in the wake of their return to Ultimo. Whatever they were trying to hold onto—their past, their memories—felt more distant with each passing hour.

Finally, with a triumphant click, the radio sputtered back to life. The static cleared, the transmission loop crackling, and Julian's breath caught in his throat as the familiar voice of the broadcaster came through, though it was strained and distant.

Julian leaned into the microphone, his voice unsteady but determined.

"This is Julian. If anyone's out there listening—I'm still here. We're still here. We made it back... barely. But we're alive."

His fingers tightened around the microphone, as if anchoring himself to the words.

"We rescued my mother from the Bushranger Lady Blackcreek, but that's not why I'm here. This is a warning. If you're in Blackheath and you see Yowies—don't shoot. They're not the enemy. They're allies."

He took a shaky breath before continuing.

"Lady Blackcreek is terrorizing the people of Bradfield. Some say she's a vampire. And after what we saw... she's close to it. But the truth is, she's just a nutcase. A violent, ruthless nutcase. And if you're cornered—she might eat you."

The air in the studio felt heavier. Emma jumped in, her voice cutting through the tension.

"The Bushranger known as Mad Max has escaped custody in Glenbrook. If you're on the road heading into the city, keep your wits about you. Stay safe, kiddies."

She flashed a cheeky grin, throwing in the Three Dog reference just to lift Julian's spirits—if only a little.

Julian hesitated, the weight of their message settling over him. Was anyone even listening? Did it matter?

He swallowed hard and pushed forward.

For those still out there. For the ones who had survived.

It was the only thing he could give them

The broadcast ended with a soft click, the room plunging back into silence. For a moment, Julian just stood there, staring at the radio as though waiting for it to speak again. Emma's voice broke through the quiet, her words soft but carrying the weight of the question that had been lingering in the air all evening.

That night, as the sun dipped below the horizon, Julian and Emma lay side by side in bed, the weight of exhaustion pressing down on them. Julian stared up at the ceiling, his thoughts drifting, while Emma turned toward the wall, her gaze fixated on a framed photo.

It was an old photo—one of Julian with his siblings, back when the world had still made sense. He could barely remember the last time they had all been together. He had tried to keep in touch, but as the world shifted, so too had the bonds between them. They had scattered, each taking their own path, as though the distance between them was a reflection of what had happened to the world.

Emma's voice was barely a whisper in the dark. "Your siblings... no one talks about them."

Julian exhaled sharply, his eyes closing as the question tugged at his chest. It was a subject they had never discussed in depth, the silence around it more painful than any answer could be. "My brother's in Germany, teaching," he said, his voice distant, detached. "My other brother's in the Territory, driving trucks. My sister's in New York, scoring big in the tech world. My cousins? No clue."

Emma shifted beside him, the concern in her voice evident. "Do you think we'll ever get to see them again?"

The question hung in the air between them, unspoken fears wrapped in the simple hope of reunion. Julian turned toward her, but his eyes were distant, lost in thoughts he couldn't express. His gaze softened, though, as he reached for her hand in the darkness.

"I don't know," he replied quietly, his voice almost a whisper. "Change is coming, Emma. It's all changing. I can feel it."

The room felt colder then, the air heavy with something unspoken. They both knew it, knew that whatever had been left behind in the past—the lives they had once known—might never return.

Change was coming, and with it, uncertainty.

Emma's fingers tightened around his hand, and for a moment, neither of them spoke. But in the silence, in the shared understanding between them, they both knew one thing: they had each other, and whatever the world threw at them, that was something worth holding onto.

Chapter 79:

The air inside the abandoned warehouse was thick with dust, the once-vibrant walls now crumbling and covered in graffiti. Shadows lingered in the corners, stretching long in the dim light that filtered through broken windows. It smelled of rust and decay, a fitting reflection of the world that had fallen apart. Max stood in the center of it all, the remnants of his old gang now gathered in front of him, their eyes narrowed with suspicion.

He hadn't been back in months—months that had felt like years. The Diggers had taken him, held him prisoner, and in that time, everything had changed. But now he was here, standing in front of them, and he could feel the weight of their doubt pressing in on him. There was no room for weakness now. Not with Moody in charge.

Moody. The new leader of the gang. Max had always known him as a slippery character, someone who thrived in the chaos of the streets but lacked the true vision to lead. Now, the man had taken the reins, and with it came the shift in power. The tension in the room was palpable, as thick as the smoke that once filled this warehouse when it was still in operation.

Moody's face was hard as stone, his dark eyes scanning Max with cold calculation. He leaned in closer, the silence in the room hanging like a weight, before he spoke. "You got captured by the Diggers,

Max. How do we know you didn't turn? How do we know you're not one of them now?" His voice was low, controlled, but there was an edge to it. A challenge.

Max didn't flinch. He wasn't going to show weakness, not now. He clenched his jaw, his fists at his sides, the old scars on his knuckles still visible in the dim light. "I didn't turn," he said through gritted teeth. "But I want Julian. You help me get him, and you can have everything inside the DisruptTech offices. Everything. All the riches, all the tech. It's yours."

A murmur ran through the gang, some faces lighting up with greed, others staying still, unsure. Max could feel it, the hunger in their eyes. DisruptTech. The name alone was enough to make their pulses race. Whoever controlled the tech inside those offices controlled the future, the power to rebuild or destroy whatever they wanted.

Moody's gaze never left him, the flicker of greed in his eyes betraying his otherwise stoic demeanor. Max could see it now—the man was calculating. Weighing the offer. He could almost hear the gears turning behind those sharp eyes.

He knew Moody wasn't just going to agree easily. Trust wasn't something that could be bought with words alone, especially not with Max's history of betrayal and escape. But the promise of wealth—of tech that could change everything—was hard to resist.

Finally, Moody spoke, his voice low but firm, laced with suspicion. "Fine. We'll go after Julian. But if you hesitate, if you pull anything funny, you're dead too." His eyes locked onto Max's, the threat clear. He wasn't going to let anyone cross him—not even Max.

Max met his gaze without blinking. He knew the rules. He understood the stakes. Hesitation was death in this world, but Max wasn't the same man who had left this gang months ago. He had learned what it meant to survive. And right now, survival meant getting Julian back—getting what he had promised—and making sure no one stood in his way.

"I won't hesitate," Max said, his voice steady, but the words felt like a promise, a vow.

Moody stepped back, signaling the others to gather around. The air seemed to tighten even further, the room now electric with the tension of what was to come. No one trusted him—not yet—but Max could feel the shift. This was a deal, an unspoken agreement that, for now, would hold.

Outside, the world raged on, a ruin of its former self, but inside this warehouse, Max was beginning to reclaim control. Not just of his old gang, but of the future. And Julian? Julian would be part of that future, one way or another.

Chapter 80:

T he soft hum of the transmitter was the only sound in the room as Julian and Emma prepared for their broadcast. Their usual routine had become a ritual in the chaos, a small thread of normalcy in an otherwise fractured world. The studio was quiet, save for the faint crackling of static and the intermittent notes of a song they'd been looping in an effort to maintain some semblance of normalcy.

Emma was focused, adjusting the settings on the soundboard while Julian checked the feeds. Outside, the air was still, but the silence felt wrong—unnatural. Their hearts were already on edge, and the tension grew thicker with each passing second.

Then, the door slammed open, and Ardi burst into the room, breathless, her face pale with alarm.

"I saw someone trying to break in," she panted, eyes wide with urgency. "A group."

Julian's stomach dropped. It was happening again—people, raiders, desperate for supplies, for control. They had been preparing for something like this, but the reality of it always felt sharper, more immediate, when it finally arrived. Emma stiffened beside him, her hand instinctively reaching for her rifle.

The music on air played on, its eerie melodies an odd contrast to the rising panic in the apartment.

The rhythm seemed too calm, almost mocking, as if the world outside was untouched by the violence that loomed over them.

"Lock the door behind you," Julian whispered to Ardi, his voice low, as if saying it aloud would somehow make it worse.

Ardi nodded quickly and disappeared into the shadows of the hall, her footsteps silent but hurried. Julian and Emma exchanged a glance—no words were needed. They knew what had to be done.

Grabbing their rifles, they settled into their positions. Julian's heart pounded in his chest, but he forced himself to breathe. Focus. He couldn't afford to let fear cloud his mind.

They continued the broadcast, voices steady despite the adrenaline coursing through their veins. Julian kept talking, the words flowing as naturally as they could, but his mind was somewhere else, tracking every sound, every movement. The music on air seemed to mock him, each note bouncing around the room like an echo of everything they had to lose.

Then came the noise. A sharp bang followed by a clattering rustle—someone, or something, moving downstairs. A chill ran through Julian's spine, the sound familiar yet somehow more menacing.

Emma's face hardened, and without saying a word, she moved. She kissed him quickly, fiercely—her lips a brief, desperate touch. "Just in case," she murmured, her voice trembling but firm.

Julian nodded, his throat dry, but he didn't have time to reply. He ducked into the bedroom, leaving Emma near the hall, her eyes trained on the door.

Ardi was already on the balcony, her figure barely visible in the shadows. In her hand, she gripped a wok, her only weapon, but her stance was calm, steady. Ardi had always been resourceful—she would make do with whatever was at hand.

The apartment seemed to hold its breath. The seconds stretched into hours.

Suddenly, the door to the apartment burst open. Max stormed in, rage burning in his eyes. He was followed by Moody and the gang, each member scanning the space with hungry, predatory eyes. Max's expression was twisted with fury, his hands clenched into fists at his sides.

"Where is it?" he snarled.

His voice echoed through the empty apartment as Moody and the others spread out, looting, tearing apart the place in their quest for something—anything—that would be useful to them. But it wasn't the food or supplies that Max was after. No, he was after something far more precious.

Julian, hiding in the bedroom, could hear the gang ransacking the apartment, the sound of drawers being pulled open and contents spilling onto the floor. His grip on the rifle tightened. He needed to stay hidden. He couldn't risk making a sound.

Then, Julian heard it—the unmistakable sound of Max's footsteps growing closer, his voice raised in frustration. He could feel it, the tension in the air thickening. Max was close. And then, there it was—the unmistakable clatter of the transmitter being disturbed.

Max, in a fit of anger, found the transmitter. His eyes widened with recognition, and something inside him snapped. The noise was deafening as his fist collided with the fragile equipment, smashing it to pieces.

The music, which had been the only sound in the apartment, cut off abruptly. The silence that followed was suffocating. The hum of the transmitter, the familiar melodies that had kept them grounded, were gone. The void that followed felt like a death sentence.

Julian's heart raced. The silence was worse than any noise. In that moment, they were exposed. Max knew they were here. He could feel the weight of the danger closing in, but he couldn't risk making a move—not yet.

The apartment had fallen into a tense quiet, broken only by the distant sounds of the gang rummaging through their things. And in that silence, Julian knew that everything had changed.

Chapter 81:

The silence in the apartment was suffocating. Every footstep, every breath, felt amplified as Julian emerged from the bedroom, rifle in hand but lowered—his eyes fixed on Max. He had known this moment was coming, but nothing could prepare him for the weight of the confrontation. Max was standing there, his hand gripping a pistol with white knuckles, his face a mask of anger and betrayal.

Julian's voice broke the tension, steady despite the storm raging inside him. "You're not the same man I knew."

Max's jaw clenched, his eyes flicking over Julian before he spoke, the words sharp and cold. "You left. You abandoned me."

Julian swallowed hard. It wasn't just the words—it was the years of silence, the absence of Max in his life, that stung. The old wounds were fresh again. He could feel the pull of anger, of the shared history they once had, but he had to stay calm. He had to make him understand.

"We didn't leave because we hated you," Julian said, his voice firm, but with an undercurrent of pain. "You scared us away."

There it was—the truth that had never been spoken, the reason for their falling out. Julian had always hoped things would change, that the old Max would return. But the man in front of him, this stranger, had become a shadow of the person he once trusted.

For a moment, a flicker of something crossed Max's face. The old Max—the friend Julian had fought beside—was there, just for a second. The familiar, softer look of someone who understood him, who had been there. But it disappeared as quickly as it came, replaced by the hard edge of someone who had been through too much to ever go back.

Max's gaze hardened, and without warning, he raised his pistol again. Julian braced himself, but Max's hand didn't aim at him. Instead, it aimed at the transmitter—the very thing that had kept their connection to the outside world alive.

A deafening crack split the air as Max fired. Sparks flew, and the radio—their lifeline—was reduced to nothing but a smoldering hunk of metal. The silence that followed was deafening. No more music. No more broadcasts. Just the echo of a broken connection.

Max's voice was low, resigned. "Take Emma and go. Now."

The words hit Julian like a punch to the gut. He had never wanted things to end like this. But there was no more room for hesitation, no more time for words. The gravity of the situation settled in, and Julian's thoughts shifted to Emma. He had to protect her—he had to make sure they survived.

Shaken, but determined, Julian turned on his heel, rushing to find her. He found her in the hall, her eyes wide with fear but resolute. "We have to go," he said, his voice rough, the weight of Max's betrayal hanging heavy between them.

"What about Ardi?" Emma asked, a flicker of concern in her voice.

Julian paused, but only for a moment. "She's smart. She'll find her way."

The two of them moved toward the foyer, their footsteps quick and deliberate. But as they reached the door, they found it blocked. Moody stood in the entrance, a smug grin plastered across his face, his pistol aimed directly at them.

"Isn't this the guy you wanted to kill, Max?" Moody taunted, his eyes flicking between Julian and Max, as if savoring the tension. "You've gone soft." His voice was dripping with mockery.

Before Julian could respond, before he could even think, Moody pulled the trigger.

The shot rang out, sharp and cold.

Max moved faster than Julian could react. A blur of motion, a desperate act of protection. He stepped in front of the bullet, taking it full force.

Julian froze, his heart pounding in his ears. Time seemed to slow as Max collapsed.

The shot rang out, its echo reverberating through the apartment like a death knell. Max's body jerked violently, the impact sending him crashing to the floor, his face contorted in agony. Blood blossomed from the wound, pooling beneath him in a growing puddle. The world seemed to pause as the sight of his fall hit Julian like a hammer. Max was crumpled on the ground, gasping for air, each breath a struggle.

Without thinking, Julian's instincts kicked in. His rifle was already raised, his finger pulling the trigger before his mind even caught up with the chaos. Moody's smug expression turned to shock as the bullet tore through his neck. His hand instinctively grasped at the wound, but the blood flowed too quickly. The gang members behind him faltered, their eyes wide with disbelief as their leader choked, his hands desperately trying to stem the bleeding.

Moody crumpled to the ground, his final breath escaping in a choked gurgle. The remaining gang members, terrified, scattered in all directions, leaving their so-called leader to die in a pool of his own blood. The apartment was eerily silent except for the fading sounds of their retreating footsteps.

Julian didn't hesitate. His gaze snapped back to Max, who was still lying on the floor, struggling to speak despite the blood choking him. The man who had once been his closest friend, the one who had shared in the madness of the world's collapse, was fading fast.

"I was afraid," Max gasped, his voice hoarse, blood staining his lips. "Afraid of being alone." His eyes, once fierce and filled with ambition, were now clouded with regret. Julian could see the flicker of something deep within him—vulnerability, fear, and sorrow.

Julian knelt beside him, his hands trembling as he gripped Max's shoulder, trying to offer some form of comfort. "Then why do this?" Julian's voice cracked, his heart aching with the weight of it all. The betrayal. The violence. The man who had been a brother to him was slipping away.

Max's breath came in shallow bursts, each one more labored than the last. He coughed again, blood spattering across his chest. "I thought power was everything… but it wasn't," he whispered, his words barely audible. The regret in his voice was palpable, a sharp contrast to the arrogance that had defined him for so long.

Max's eyes closed, his body slackening. His final breath was drawn in a long, shuddering exhale. And then, just like that, the man Julian had once trusted was gone. His pulse had stopped, his body growing cold in Julian's arms. The finality of it was crushing, the weight of their fractured friendship sinking deep into Julian's chest.

For a long moment, Julian simply stared at Max's still form, his mind reeling. There were so many things left unsaid, so many unanswered questions. But now, there was no time. Emma's voice broke through the fog in his mind.

"Julian, we have to go."

He nodded, blinking as he shook himself from his stupor. A tear ran down Julian's cheek, and his voice trembled. "We can't leave him."

Emma paused, her heart aching for him. She stepped closer, wrapping her arms around him, steadying him as he broke down. His sobs were muffled against her shoulder, his grief raw and uncontained. Emma, too, cried softly, but she remained strong for him, holding him through the storm of emotions.

The city of Sydney was eerily quiet, save for the faint hum of distant electricity, a ghostly reminder of what had once been. The radio that had been their lifeline was now silent. The world was changing, and Julian could feel it deep in his bones. This wasn't just the end of Max—it was the end of something bigger. Something irreversible. The fight—whatever it was—was far from over.

Without another word, Emma gently pulled Julian to his feet, her grip tight on his arm, as though unwilling to let him fall. Together, they walked to the car park below. Their footsteps echoed against the concrete, a quiet rhythm of determination as they disappeared into the shadows.

As they began loading the truck, the sudden, familiar sound of footsteps reached their ears. Ardi appeared, as she always did, moving silently but purposefully. She didn't need to speak to convey her presence—she was just there. And with her, a quiet goodbye.

Emma gestured to her, her voice soft but insistent. "Come with us. It's no longer safe here."

Ardi hesitated for a moment, her eyes flickering with something unreadable, as if she were weighing a decision, deciding whether to follow or stay behind. Then, after a long pause, a broken smile touched her lips—a quiet acceptance, a shift in her resolve.

"Ya," she said in her thick Indonesian accent, her voice barely above a whisper, but the strength in it was unmistakable.

Julian, his mind still reeling from everything that had happened, couldn't shake the feeling that they were on the cusp of something far worse. The world around them was shifting in ways they couldn't fully understand, and there was no telling where it would take them.

But one thing was clear: they had to survive. They had to keep fighting. And they couldn't do it alone.

Epilogue.

The truck rolled steadily through the night, the engine's low growl barely breaking the silence of a city that had become a stranger to them. Sydney, once a vibrant metropolis, now felt like an abandoned ghost town—its streets empty, its lights dimmed, its heart seemingly ceased. Max's lifeless body, wrapped in an old, torn bedsheet, lay in the back of the truck. He was gone, but the weight of his loss hung in the air like a dense fog. The bed sheet had become his shroud, a strange and awkward farewell to the man Julian had once called a friend. The body was an empty vessel now, his power stripped away, the last vestige of a life that had been consumed by ambition, violence, and betrayal. It felt like the end of an era, but Julian wasn't sure if it was the end of this world—or if the real end had yet to come.

The city passed by in fragments—familiar landmarks that now seemed more like remnants of a forgotten time. They made their way slowly, a quiet procession of sorts, as if they were paying their respects to a city that had crumbled under the weight of its own greed and corruption. They first drove to the bookshop, the small corner store that had once been their refuge, a quiet place to get lost in the comfort of old pages. But now, the bookshop was silent. The windows were clouded with dust, and the door hung ajar, as though abandoned in a rush.

The truck's tires scraped against the cracked asphalt as Julian and Emma stepped out. They exchanged a silent glance, a shared understanding passing between them. They had once come here for answers, for something to anchor them to a world that felt increasingly unrecognizable. Now, it felt like a ghostly memory.

Emma walked up to the door first, her footsteps slow, hesitant. She could feel the weight of the silence pressing down on her. Inside, the air was thick with the scent of paper and dust, the same as it had always been. But everything was different now. The shelves stood, still laden with books, but the place was deserted—no clerk, no life. Just rows and rows of stories that had no audience.

Her eyes swept across the aisles, searching, until something caught her attention. A note, pinned to the counter. The familiar handwriting of Lucille, the shopkeeper, who had disappeared without a trace weeks ago. Emma's heart skipped a beat. She picked it up, and her fingers trembled slightly as she read aloud:

"Books are power. I took as many as I could, but I couldn't stay. To the lovely man and woman on the radio, if you find this, I left a pile of books for you. They're useful, and they're yours if you return. I'm leaving for Glenbrook. I hope I make it there. The hobbits did simply walk into Mordor. Maybe I can, too."

Lucille's words were simple, yet they carried a weight that settled deep in Emma's chest. Lucille had been a dreamer, a hopeful soul who had believed that there was something more to this world than just survival. The reference to The Lord of the Rings wasn't lost on Emma. Lucille had hoped, as they all did, that somehow they could make it through this—one step at a time.

Emma looked up at Julian, her eyes reflecting the understanding that had formed between them.

Lucille had left a message, a final piece of herself. It was a message to them.

Julian gave a quiet nod, acknowledging what they both knew. The books—they were the key. Knowledge had become power. The survival of their future rested not just on the food, the weapons, or the shelter they could find, but on the wisdom of the past.

They walked over to the pile of books Lucille had left behind. There were technical manuals—guides on building radios, setting up communications, surviving in a fractured world. There were novels, too—Matthew Reilly's Mr. Einstein's Secretary, a book of Banjo Paterson's poems, the collected Sonnets of Shakespeare, Emily Dickinson's verse, Robert Graves' writings, Tolkien's The Lord of the Rings, and even a book about rifles. But there was one more book that stood out—a text about corporate giants of the old world. Emma's eyes lingered on it for a moment longer than the others. It felt like a hidden message—one that spoke to what they had lost.

Without another word, Julian began loading the books into the back of the truck. The weight of each book felt like a small but significant victory in a world that had lost its narrative. Each one held the potential for knowledge, for survival, for understanding what had happened to bring the world to its knees.

Their journey wasn't over, not by a long shot. They still had to make their way to Glenbrook. But for the first time in a while, there was a glimmer of hope. They weren't alone in this. Lucille had left a message, and the books were a beacon.

Their next stop was DisruptTech—Julian's old workplace, the tech company where they had spent countless hours brainstorming, editing videos, and dreaming up ideas for a different world. But the building they arrived at was unrecognizable. It wasn't the place of hustle and energy it had once been. Now, it was quiet, still, but untouched, as if the world had simply frozen the moment they had left.

Emma was the first to step inside, her boots tapping on the floor as she glanced around. There was something unsettling about it all—the silence that had replaced the once-bustling office environment. The walls, still adorned with creative posters, looked faded, like a memory clinging to life.

Ardi, ever the curious one, walked in with wide eyes. She admired the space, though it was clear she was viewing it with a kind of reverence that was almost out of place in the new world they had entered. "It's beautiful," she murmured, her voice a soft echo in the stillness.

Julian moved toward his old desk, almost as if he were returning to a different life. He reached out to touch the smooth surface of the desk, and for a brief moment, the memories flooded back. Editing podcasts, sending emails, chatting with Emma and Max over coffee. It was hard to reconcile that version of himself with the person he was now—the person who had witnessed so much destruction and loss.

Emma, meanwhile, was at her desk, unclipping an old microphone she had used in the past for recording. As she cleaned up her space, she noticed something odd—a faint glow coming from the CEO's office, a light seeping through the closed blinds. It was a strange, inexplicable thing. She moved toward it, unable to shake the feeling that something wasn't right.

Julian, still at his desk, pulled open the drawer and found something that made his heart skip a beat—a crumpled note from Max. The handwriting was unmistakable, but the words were disjointed, chaotic. The spiraling message was an apology, a confession of sorts, but it grew darker as it continued. The tone shifted, turning from regret into resentment. Max's handwriting became more erratic, his words increasingly bitter as if he had been spiraling into hatred for Julian.

Julian's heart twisted with pity as he read the note, but he couldn't bring himself to feel anger. It was too late for that. The man Max had become was someone they could no longer save.

"Hey, Julian…" Emma's voice broke through his thoughts, and he turned to find her standing in the CEO's office. Her face was pale, her eyes wide with disbelief.

"I found something," she said, holding up the old computer from the CEO's desk. It was still running—how, they couldn't know. The EMP had wiped out most electronics, but this one had survived.

Emma quickly sat at the desk and began to search through the files. She found a notebook with passwords, and using it, she accessed the computer.

The screen flickered to life, and what she found next sent a chill down her spine. There was an email chain—dated just days before the EMP struck. It was from an operative at Voltum, the electric battery company.

"Get out of Sydney. Go to the coast, go underground. I can't give you the full details, but something's happening. You need to leave now."

Emma's voice faltered as she read aloud. The CEO had known. They had all been lied to.

"Julian," she said, turning to him with wide, horrified eyes. "The CEO knew. They knew something was coming, and they didn't tell us. They lied to us."

Julian's mind was reeling, his thoughts tumbling in a chaotic spiral. The betrayal was deep, too deep to comprehend fully in the moment. Their whole reality had been a lie.

Emma's voice was steady, but there was a fire in her eyes. "We have to take this computer. We have to tell the world the truth."

Julian nodded grimly, knowing there was no turning back now. He helped Emma load the computer into the truck, the weight of the decision sinking in. The road ahead was long, and they weren't sure what they would find in Glenbrook, but they had to try.

As they drove away, the city faded behind them, and the world ahead was uncertain. But Julian, Emma, and Ardi knew one thing for sure: this was not the end. It was the beginning of something else—a fight for survival, for truth, for a world that could rise again.

8 Months Later - New Year's Eve

The air was cool in the small house they had made their home, nestled in the Glenbrook RAAF base settlement. Outside, the stars twinkled brightly against the backdrop of the dark sky, the first clear night in weeks. Inside, the hum of a more stable and advanced recording setup filled the room, a far cry from the makeshift gear they'd once used. A small but comforting warmth radiated from the space, a reflection of the life they'd slowly rebuilt since the world had changed.

Julian leaned back, his face a bit rough with scruff, a reminder of the passage of time. His eyes sparkled with a mix of exhaustion and contentment, the kind that only came after surviving the storm. He strummed his guitar, the soft plucking of the strings resonating in the quiet room as Emma sat beside him, her voice warm and steady as she spoke into the microphone.

"Well, folks, it's been quite a ride, hasn't it?" Emma's voice flowed, and the familiar tones that once carried with so much uncertainty now felt grounded. She looked over at Julian with a smile, as if they were both trying to process just how far they'd come. "Eight months ago, we didn't even know if we'd make it through the next month, let alone be sitting here together, playing music for you all on New Year's Eve." She paused, the weight of the past year settling between them.

Julian gave a chuckle, his voice deep but filled with warmth. "No kidding, Em. This time last year, we were all gearing up for the Sydney fireworks, weren't we? Grapes in hand, ready to pop some bubbles, counting down to a year full of promises and resolutions. Who knew we'd all end up where we are now, huh?"

"EMP attacks, a new world, survival," Emma continued. "No one could have predicted the changes. The Bells Line of Road is finally clear, though, which means the path is opening again, one step at a time. And the Diggers? They stormed the trenches of the bushrangers and sent them packing. It's not much, but it's something."

The two of them fell quiet for a moment, taking in the weight of the year. They thought about the people who had made it, and those who hadn't, the ones who had fought, loved, and died. They both knew there would never be a way to truly honor everyone who had been lost, but it didn't stop them from trying.

Emma lowered her gaze for a second, then glanced back up at the mic. "But before we continue with the tunes, we want to take a moment to remember those who didn't make it through this year—the ones who kept us going, even when we couldn't see the way forward. They're with us, in the stories we tell, in the songs we play, in the memories we hold." She paused, as if gathering her thoughts.

Julian nodded, his usual confident demeanor softened in this moment of reflection. "To all those we've lost... you won't be forgotten." He spoke quietly, letting the words hang in the air for a moment, before the sounds of their music filled the gap. The gentle strumming of the guitar, the soft melody, became a tribute—a mournful yet hopeful remembrance, both for those who had passed and for the life they had to continue living.

After the song finished, Emma leaned back, looking at Julian with a glint of mischief in her eyes. "Now," she said, clearing her throat. "I've got a bit of a special announcement I want to make."

Julian, ever the curious one, raised an eyebrow. "Oh? What is it, Em?" He grinned, his voice teasing but filled with affection.

Emma laughed softly, her fingers tapping the mic stand as she steadied herself. "Well, to all you fine folks out there, and especially to you, Julian," she said, a playful glimmer in her tone, "I've got something we've been working on. Something that, I think, might just change things around here. And trust me when I say, it's big."

Julian leaned forward, clearly intrigued. "You're killing me with suspense, Em. What is it?"

Emma grinned, her eyes lighting up. "We've decided to take our little setup here—our station, our station that's kept us going for so long—and make it... well, official. We're starting a new broadcast. A proper one. Not just for us, but for everyone out there who's trying to make sense of this new world. Information, music, stories, and more... We're going to broadcast live, and we want you all to be part of it. It's a new chapter. A new beginning."

Julian's eyes widened in surprise, his jaw dropping slightly. "Wait. Wait. Are you saying—?"

"Yes," Emma cut him off, a laugh escaping her.

Emma gazed at Julian, a mischievous glint in her eye. "I've got something to tell you, Julian." Her voice was soft but firm, as though the moment had finally arrived.

Julian gave her a curious look. "What's that, Em?"

She leaned in close, her lips curling into a smile. "I'm pregnant. Two weeks."

The words hung in the air for a moment, but Julian, ever the resilient one, froze in disbelief. His eyes widened, and his jaw slightly dropped as he took in what she'd just said. "Wait, what?" His voice cracked a bit, the weight of her words sinking in. "Are you serious?"

Emma nodded slowly, the glow of her pregnancy already radiating in the quiet room. "I went to the medic last week. It's real. And I wanted to keep it a surprise."

The silence between them was heavy, both of them processing the unexpected news. Then, as the reality set in, Julian grinned, an almost nervous laugh escaping him. "Well, I guess we're gonna have to make the future a hell of a lot more interesting, huh?"

Emma chuckled softly, relieved by his response. "Definitely. But let's not think about that just yet. For now, let's usher in the new year the best way we know how."

"Yeah," Julian said, his voice low and filled with affection. "Let's."

He reached over and adjusted the mic, pulling it closer to his mouth. "Alright, folks. We'll be back at midnight. But first, let's get this year started the right way. This is for all of you out there, all of us, and for the world we're going to rebuild. Let's do it in style." He smirked, raising a hand to the air. "Enjoy the music, first up—'Animals' by Architects, because... well, you're all animals."

With that, Julian hit the play button, and the aggressive, driving riffs of the song filled the room. Emma leaned back, listening to the music for a moment, as the energy in the space shifted— everything felt like it was moving forward, toward something new.

When the song reached its peak, Julian turned to Emma, his face softening. He reached for her, pulling her close. Without a word, he cupped her face and kissed her passionately, a kiss that spoke of everything they had fought for and everything they still had to look forward to.

But as the kiss lingered, something caught Emma's attention. Her eyes flicked toward the window, where the faintest sound of a horse echoed in the distance. She paused, breaking the kiss. "Julian... do you hear that?"

Julian pulled back, furrowing his brow as he listened. "I don't hear anything, Em. What are you—"

Then, just as he finished his sentence, there was a sharp knock on the door.

Julian groaned, clearly irritated. "No more guests on the station until tomorrow. We're on a break!"

But as he opened the door, his words faltered. Standing in front of him was a man, tall and imposing, with tired eyes that spoke of long travels and too many nights on the road. He wore a dark acubra hat and an armoured jacket, his scruffy beard giving him a rugged, worn appearance. He had clearly seen better days.

Behind him, a woman stood with a torn skirt and a leather jacket, her smudged eye shadow and curly brunette hair a contrast to the worn-out look of her companion. She was gently stroking a horse that was tied to the fence post.

The man stepped forward, his tone diplomatic yet firm. "You must be Julian." His voice carried the unmistakable cadence of someone who once held a higher station in the world, before everything changed.

Julian's immediate reaction was one of defense, his body tense as he sized the man up. But then, something shifted. No one made it this far into the base without passing some sort of screening. Julian relaxed, easing his grip on the doorframe.

The man continued, his voice steady. "I know in this world we can't trust many people, but I have a story I need to tell. And so does my partner."

The woman walked up beside him with a soft, kind "hi," her expression warm but weary.

The man gave a small nod before continuing. "We came from Canberra. We followed your signal all the way here."

Emma looked over at Julian, her heart skipping a beat. They both knew this wasn't just a random visit. This was something significant. Someone was seeking them out—on purpose. The sense of foreboding in the air was almost tangible.

Julian's eyes narrowed, and he exchanged a quick look with Emma. "Canberra?" he repeated, his voice laced with skepticism. "That's a long way. And I didn't think anyone else knew about the signal. What do you want with us?"

The man's gaze was steady, his face calm, but there was a certain weight to his words that hinted at something far bigger than a simple visit. The air grew thick with uncertainty.

But before Julian could speak again, the woman stroked her horse one last time and gently whispered to it, a soft, unsettling sound in the quiet night.

And then, the man spoke again, but his words were cut off by something much louder—a distant rumble, a murmur that made Emma's blood run cold.

Something wasn't right.

And just as the man took a breath to speak, the door creaked in a way that made the hairs on the back of Julian's neck stand up.

What was it they had come for? Was this just the beginning of something else?

The world outside had been quiet for too long.

And that's when everything shifted.

The future wasn't just waiting. It was here.

When it rains, it fucking pours.

www.ingramcontent.com/pod-product-compliance
Lightning Source LLC
Chambersburg PA
CBHW020604040726
47498CB00003B/625